A PULITZER PRIZE WINNER

...THIS AIN'T!

But how many laughs are there in Pulitzer Prize winners? How many funny drawings? How many clever jokes? How many silly sayings? How many stupid ideas? How many pages of pure, unadulterated garbage? How many ... er ... how many times do we forget to quit when we're ahead?*@#*%*@!!!

**HURRY, HURRY, HURRY!
BUY THESE BOOKS!**

6

Only 12,256,677 copies of these treasured classics left in stock.

- ☐ Al Jaffee Gags (#E9546—$1.75)
- ☐ AL Jaffee Gags Again (#E9583—$1.75)
- ☐ Al Jaffee Blows His Mind (#AE1190—$2.25)
- ☐ More Mad's Snappy Answers to Stupid Questions by Al Jaffee. (#Y6740—$1.25)
- ☐ The Mad Book of Magic by Al Jaffee. (#Y6743—$1.25)
- ☐ Al Jaffee's Next Book (#W9260—$1.50)
- ☐ Rotten Rhymes and Other Crimes by Nick Meglin. Illustrated by Al Jaffee. (#Y7891—$1.25)
- ☐ Al Jaffee Bombs Again (#W9273—$1.50)
- ☐ Al Jaffee Draws A Crowd (#W9275—$1.50)
- ☐ Al Jaffee Sinks to A New Low (#E9757—$1.75)
- ☐ Al Jaffee Meets His End (#W8858—$1.50)*
- ☐ Al Jaffee Goes Bananas (#AJ1285—$1.95)
- ☐ Al Jaffee Meets Willie Weirdie (#AJ1088—$1.95)*
- ☐ Al Jaffee Blows A Fuse (#E9549—$1.75)
- ☐ Al Jaffee Gets His Just Desserts (#W9312—$1.50)
- ☐ Al Jaffee Hogs the Show (#J9908—$1.95)*
- ☐ Al Jaffee: Dead or Alive (#E9494—$1.75)*
- ☐ Al Jaffee Fowls His Nest (#J9741—$1.95)*
- ☐ The Ghoulish Book of Weird Records by Al Jaffee. (#W8614—$1.50)*

*Price slightly higher in Canada

Buy them at your local bookstore or use this convenient coupon for ordering.
THE NEW AMERICAN LIBRARY, INC.,
P.O. Box 999, Bergenfield, New Jersey 07621
Please send me the books I have checked above. I am enclosing $_____
(please add $1.00 to this order to cover postage and handling). Send check or money order—no cash or C.O.D.'s. Prices and numbers are subject to change without notice.
Name_____

Address_____

City _____ State _____ Zip Code _____
Allow 4-6 weeks for delivery.
This offer is subject to withdrawal without notice.

Al Jaffee
SHOOTS HIS MOUTH OFF

by
Al Jaffee

A SIGNET BOOK
NEW AMERICAN LIBRARY
TIMES MIRROR

NAL BOOKS ARE AVAILABLE AT QUANTITY DISCOUNTS WHEN USED TO PROMOTE PRODUCTS OR SERVICES. FOR INFORMATION PLEASE WRITE TO PREMIUM MARKETING DIVISION, THE NEW AMERICAN LIBRARY, INC., 1633 BROADWAY, NEW YORK, NEW YORK 10019.

© 1959, 1960, 1962, 1963, 1964, 1965, 1966 New York Herald Tribune Inc.

Copyright © 1982 by Al Jaffee

All rights reserved

Signet, Signet Classics, Mentor, Plume, Meridian and NAL Books are published by The New American Library, Inc., 1633 Broadway, New York, New York 10019

First Printing, June, 1982

1 2 3 4 5 6 7 8 9

PRINTED IN THE UNITED STATES OF AMERICA

An Introduction to
Al Jaffee Shoots His Mouth Off
by Willie Weirdie

The first thing I want to say is, I hate writing this introduction. But Al Jaffee insisted. He said I was spending too much time doing weird things and that I ought to do something useful for a change. Hah! Call *this* useful? Who reads introductions anyway? Oh, man! If you don't know why you bought this book in the first place, no introduction is going to explain it to you. Anyway, I tried to beg off, but Jaffee wouldn't let me. Would you believe——he even threatened me. I mean, he really *did*. He said he'd send my favorite pets "back to Transylvania where they belonged" if I didn't give in. Well, that did it. I mean, what's a clean-cut, 100 percent American kid going to do without his pet vampire bats and man-eating crocs? So here I am. But please bear with me. I'll try to make this whole miserable thing as short as possible.

The first thing I have to say about this book is that it is very funny. Of course, the expression "very funny" means different things to different people. Now, take *my* book, for example: *Al Jaffee Meets Willie Weirdie*. Would I call that "very funny"? No! I'd call that "hysterically funny"! Man, there are things in it that would crack an iceberg up. I mean, if it's laughter that counts, then that book has it with a capital HA!

I sure wish I could have written the introduction to *that* one. I'd never run out of good things to say about it. Not like what's happening to me now. So you'll have to excuse me if I run along. There's my next hysterically funny WILLIE WEIRDIE book to get out. Also, my Venus's-fly trap needs feeding and my black widow spider's getting married again.

So long till we meet again in *my* books.

Cartoon Folio Number One

SHHHHHHH . . . We're hiding in here so we don't have to read the next chapter in this book.

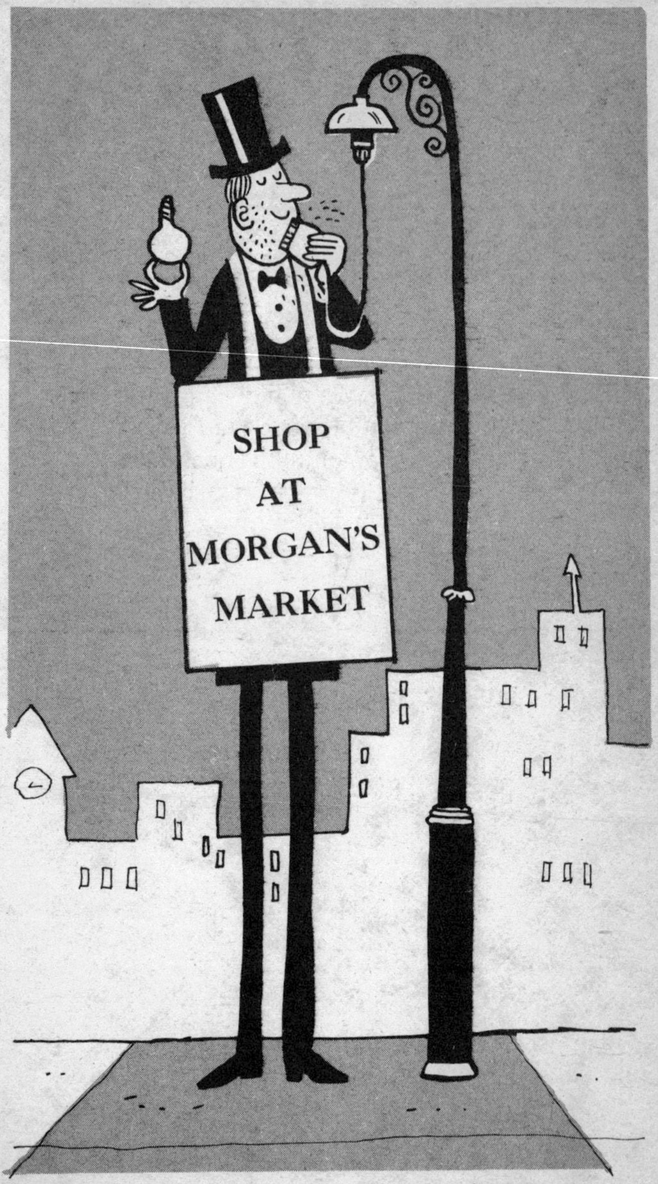
SHOP
AT
MORGAN'S
MARKET

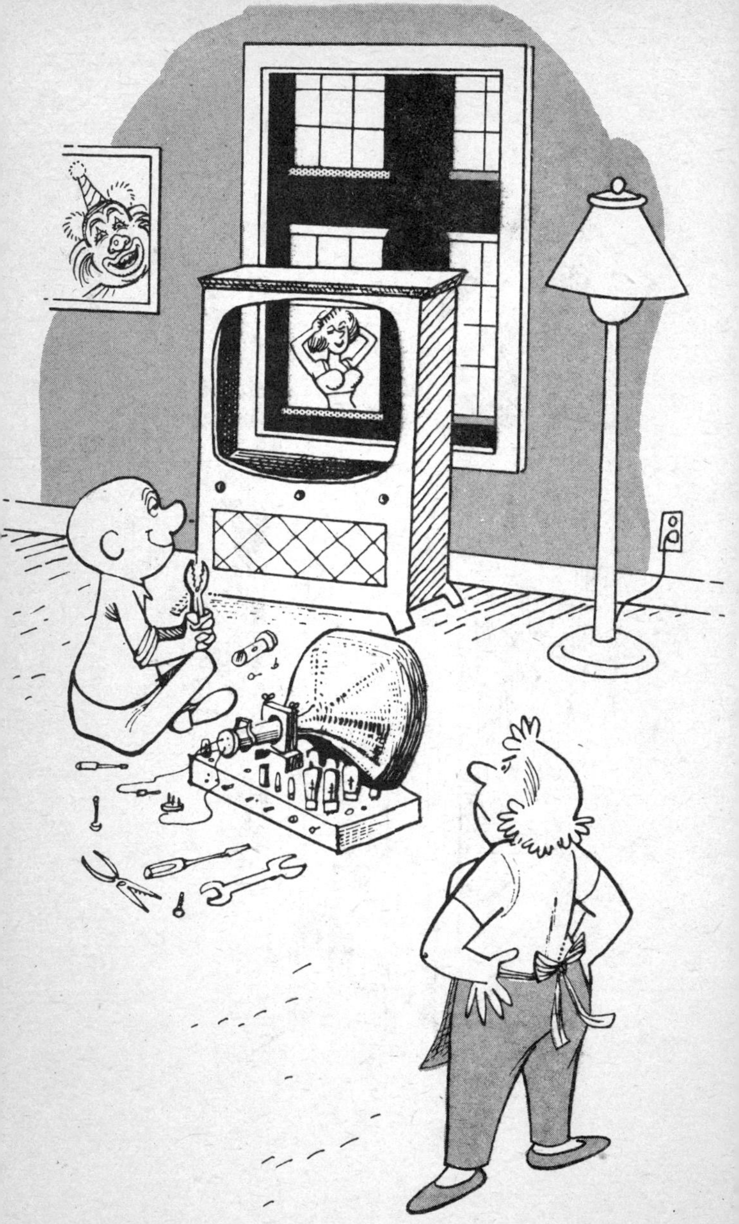

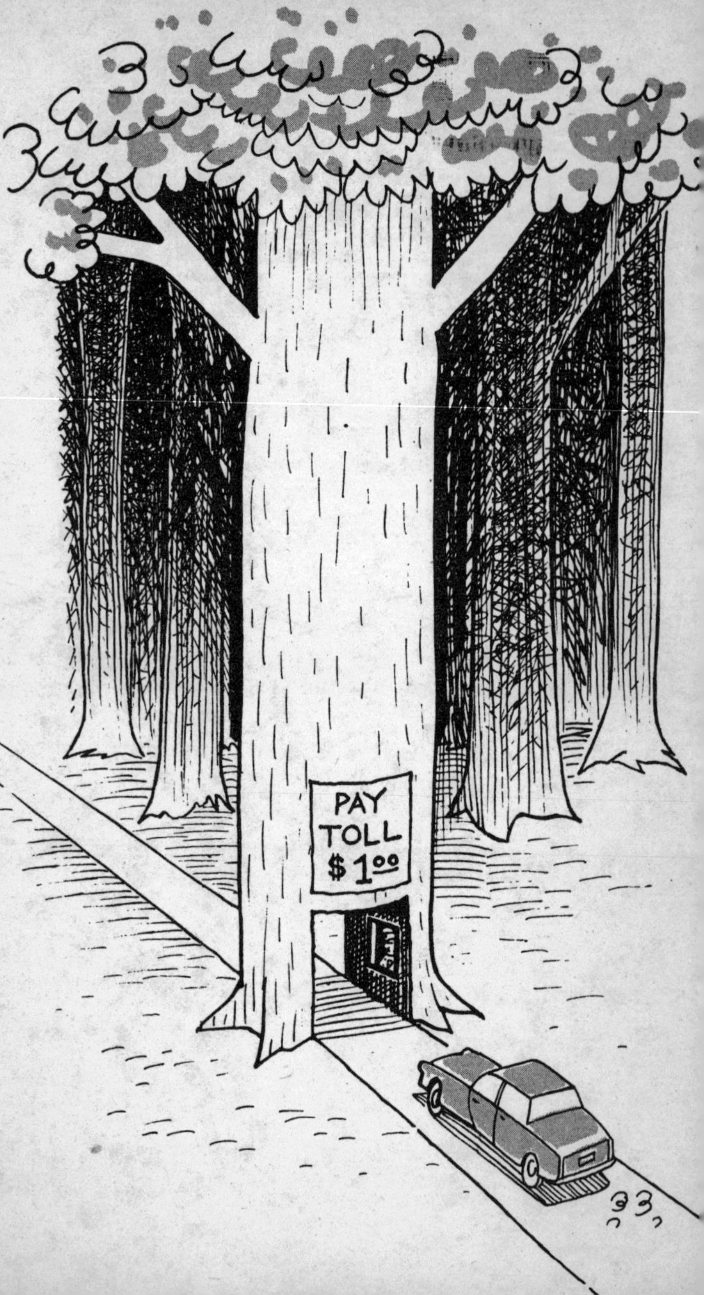
PAY
TOLL
$ 1.00

HONEYMOON HOTEL

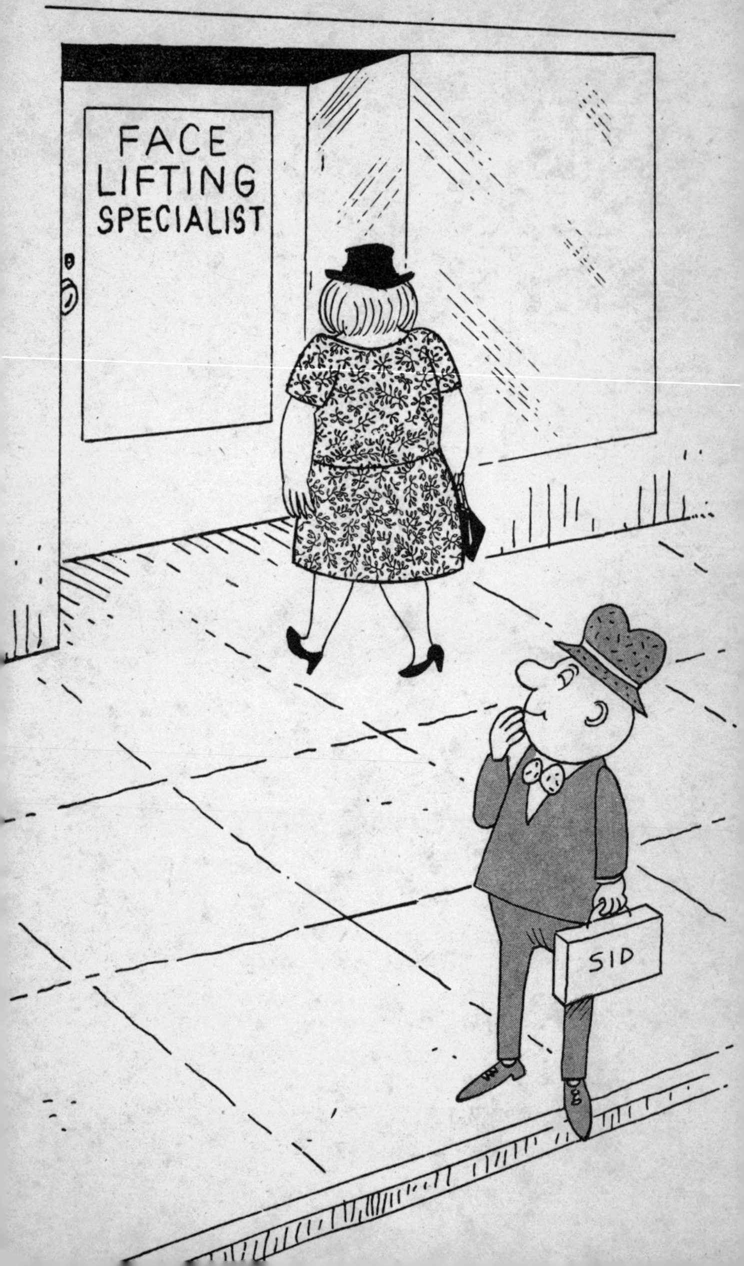
FACE
LIFTING
SPECIALIST
SID

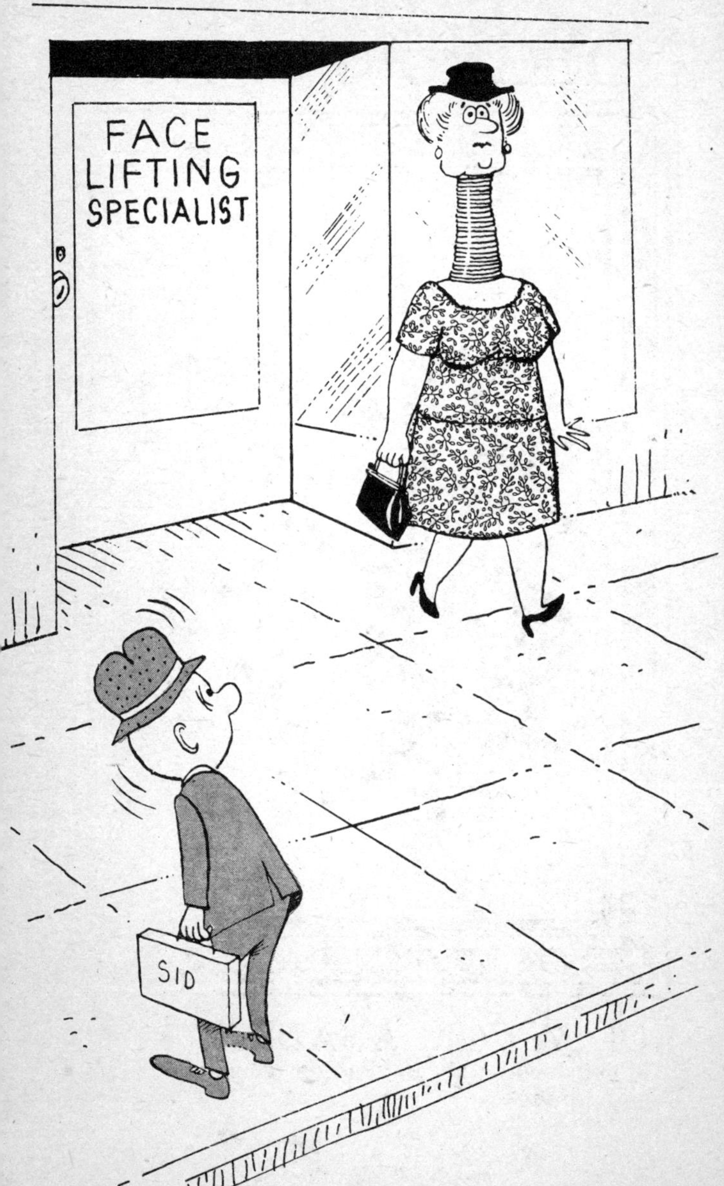
FACE
LIFTING
SPECIALIST
SID

A GALLERY OF INFAMOUS JAFFEES

OLGA VOLGA JAFFEE
Thin-blooded Arctic dweller, designer of first practical earmuffs set.

A PLAYPEN SITUATION THAT'S FILLED WITH FRUSTRATION

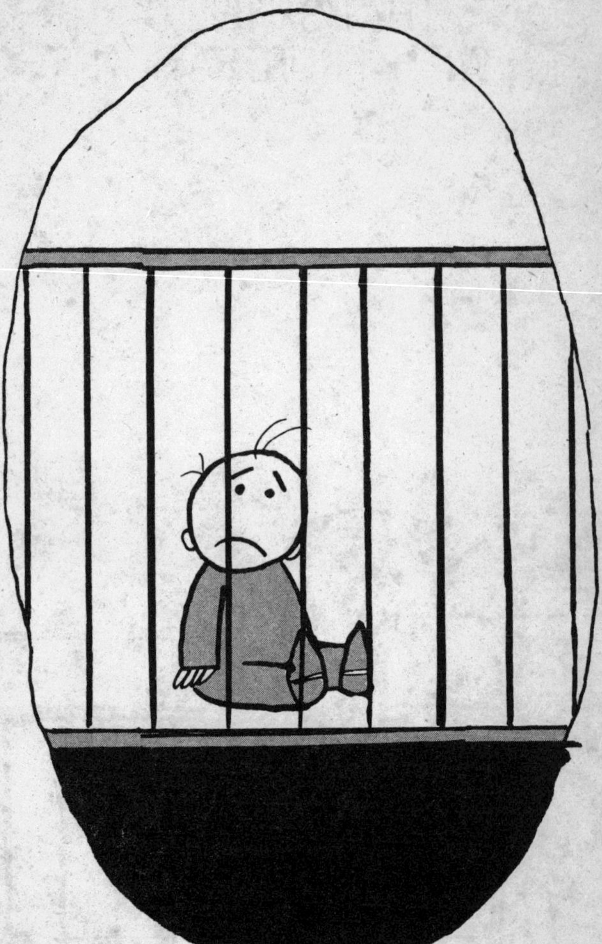

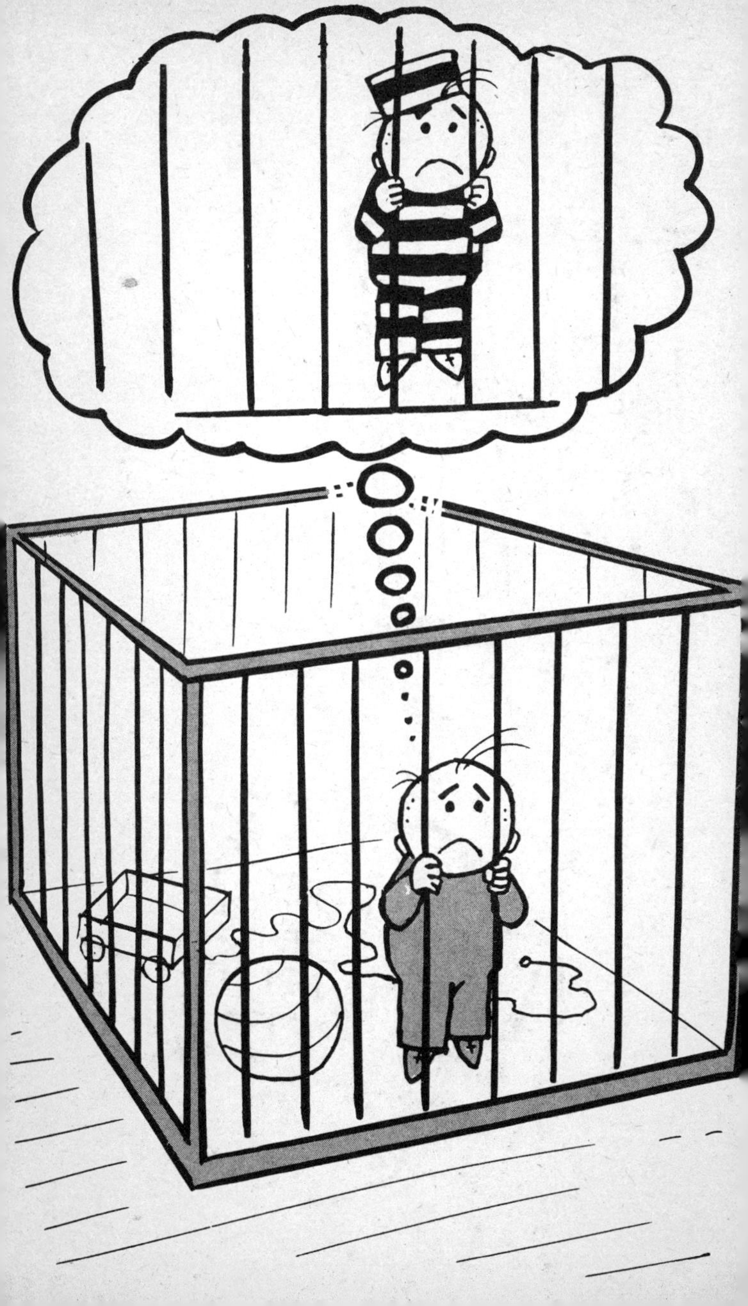

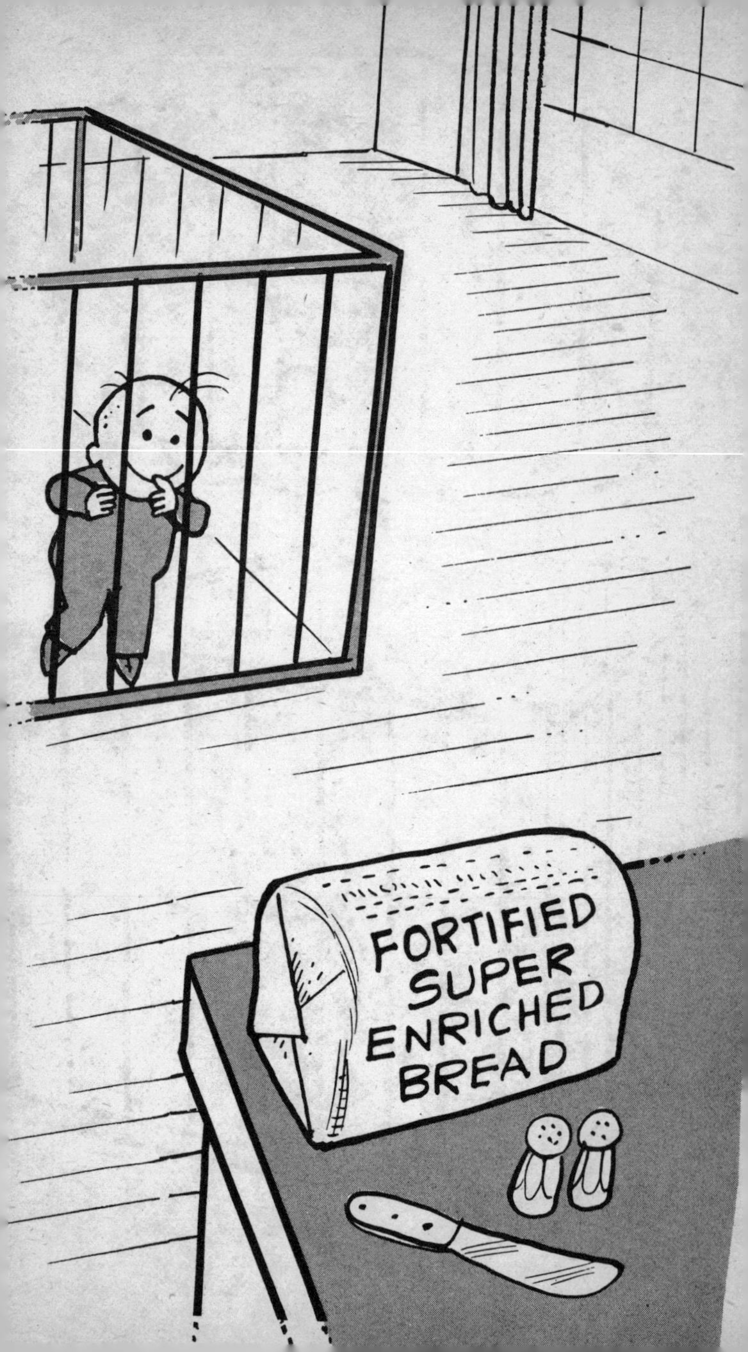
FORTIFIED
SUPER
ENRICHED
BREAD

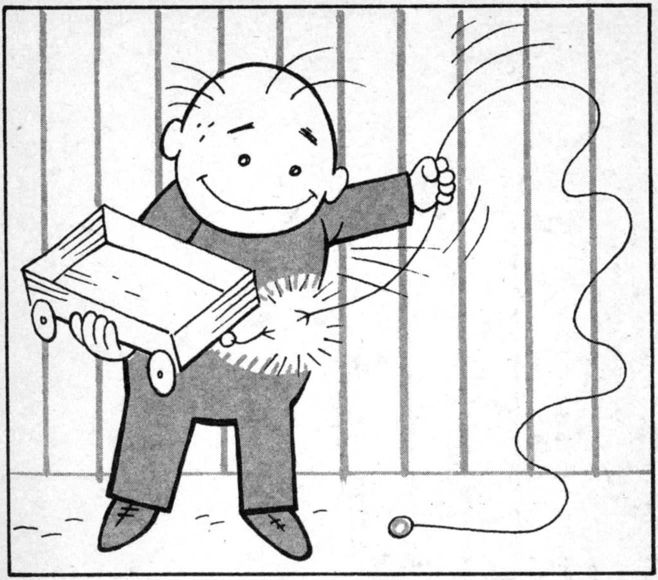
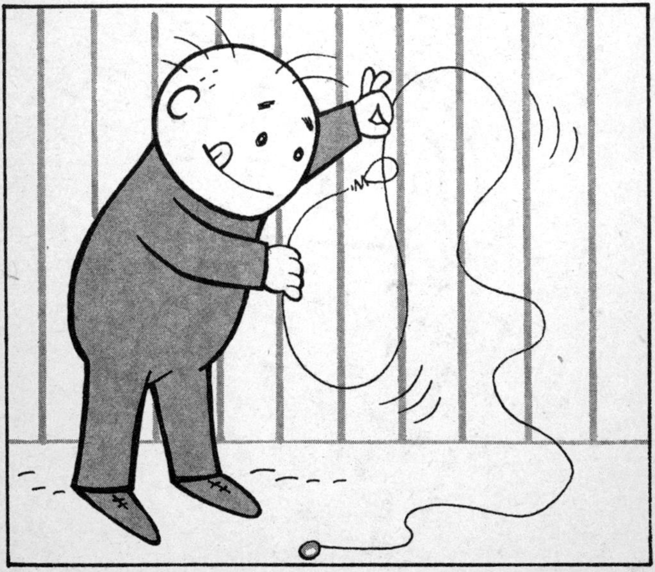

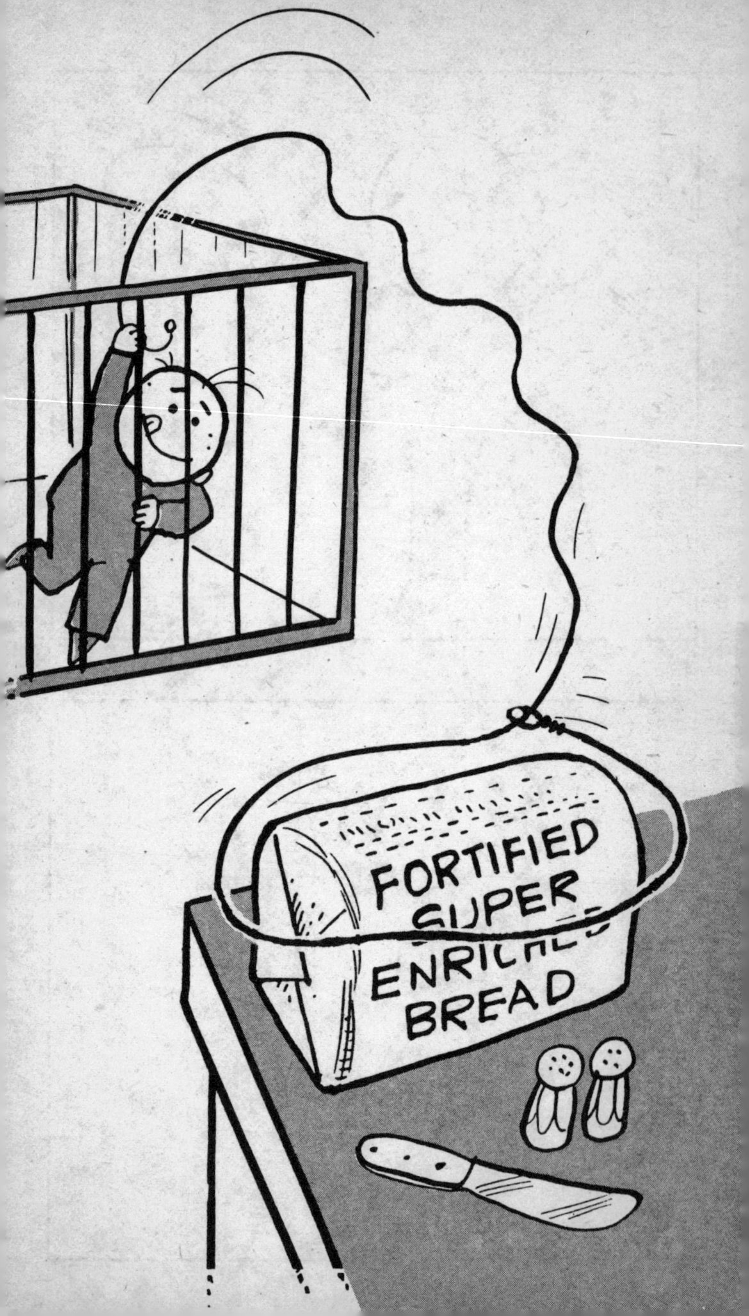
FORTIFIED
SUPER
ENRICHED
BREAD

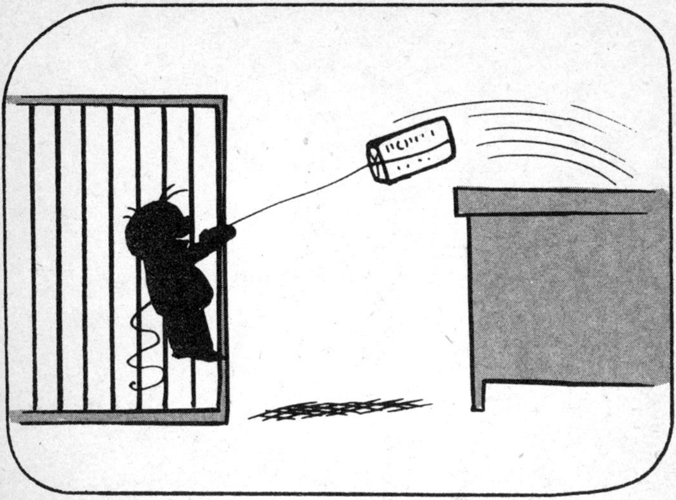

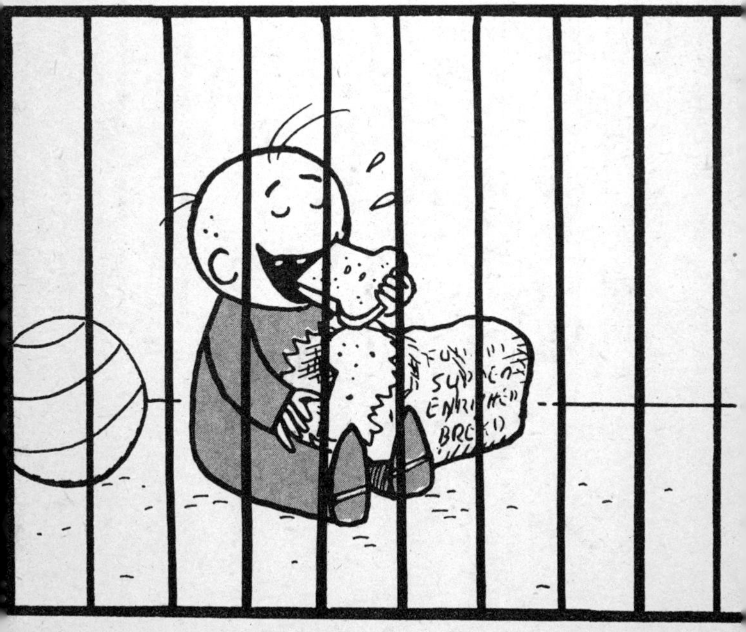

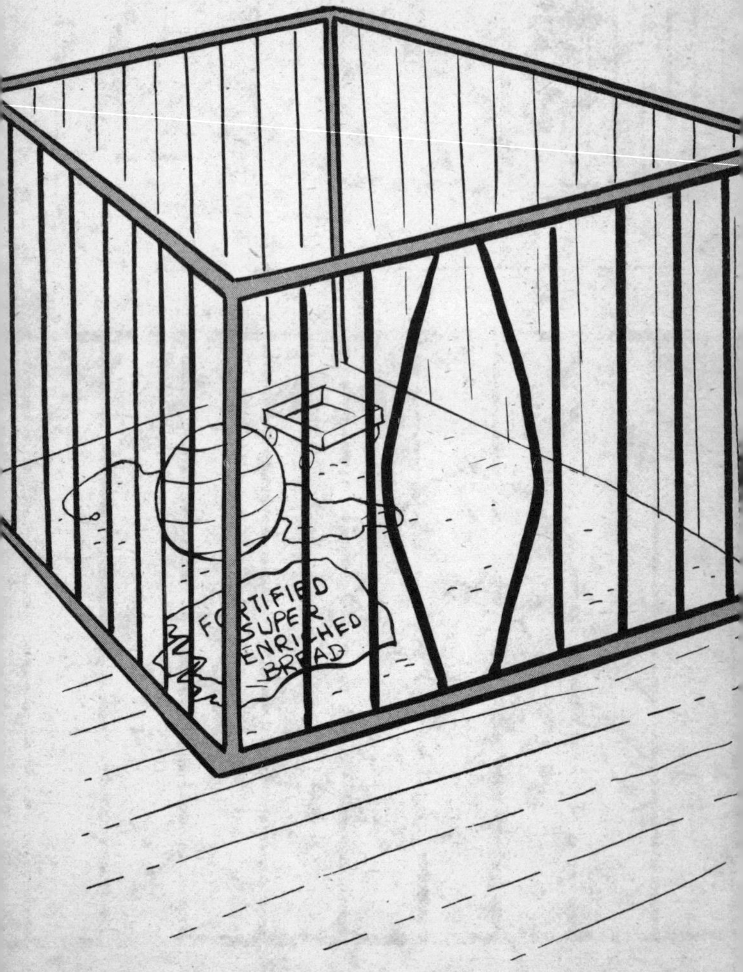
FORTIFIED
SUPER
ENRICHED
BREAD

Cartoon Folio Number Two

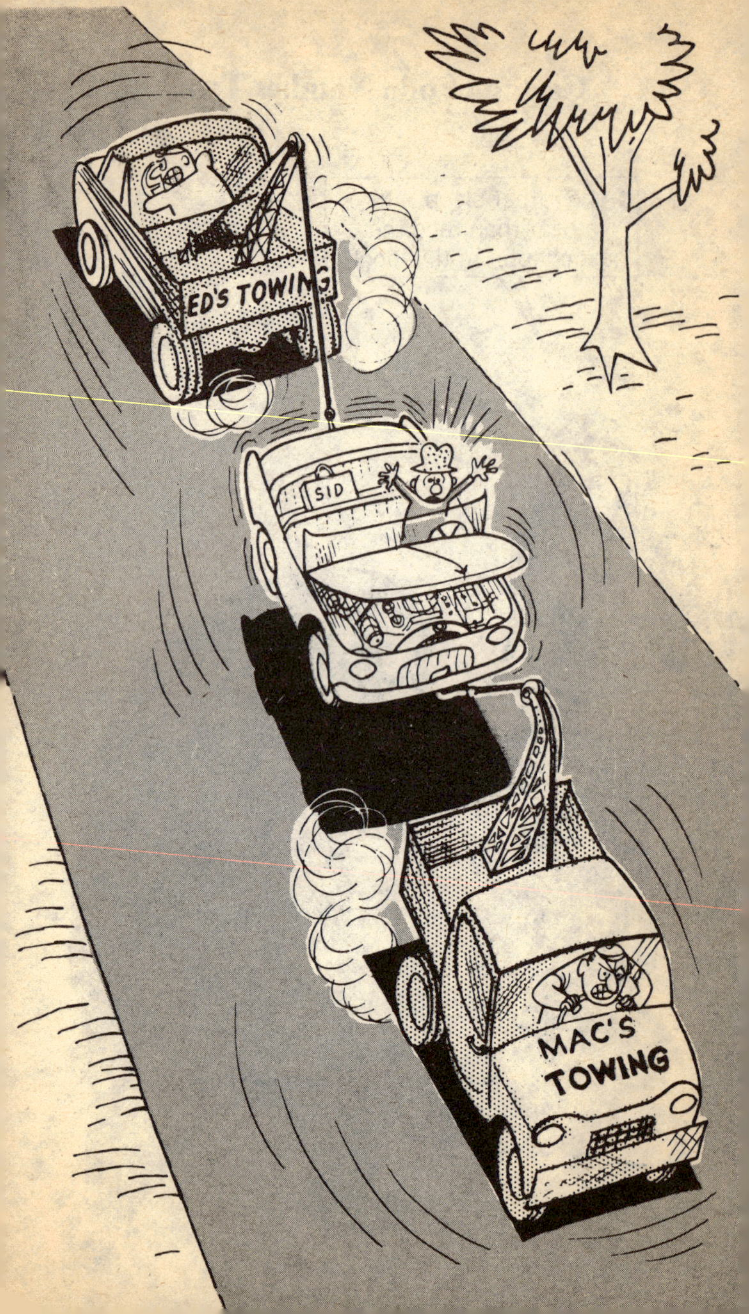

ED'S TOWING
SID
MAC'S TOWING

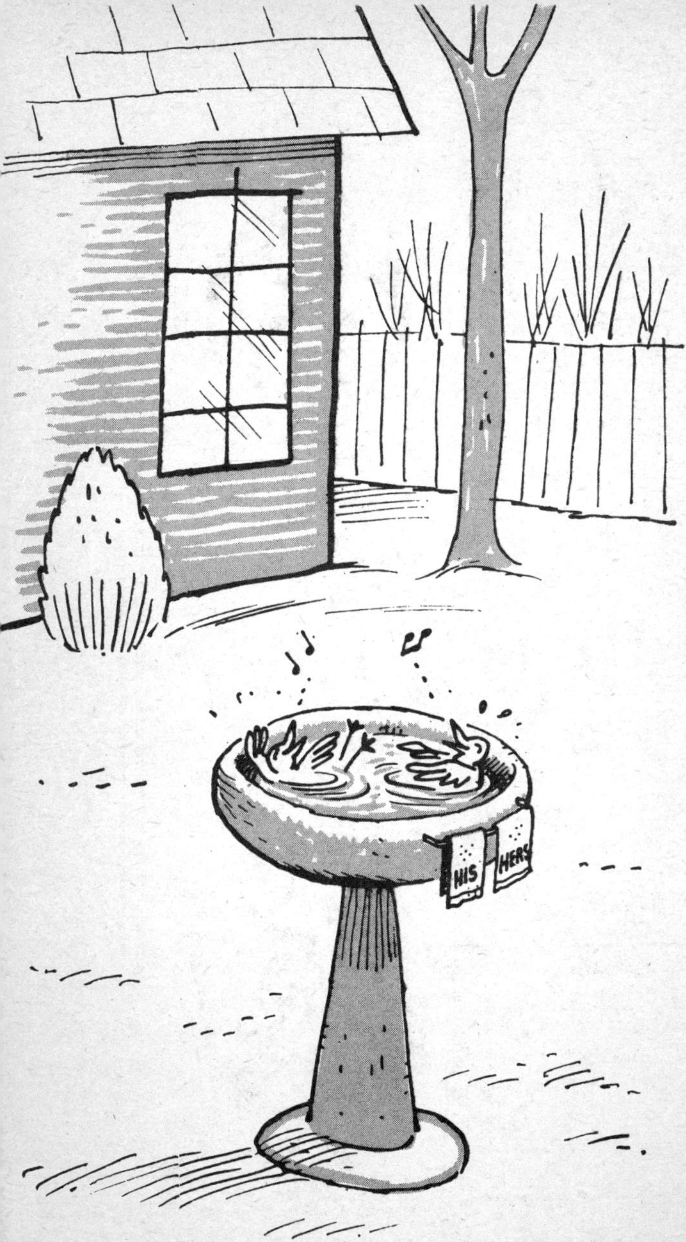
HIS
HERS

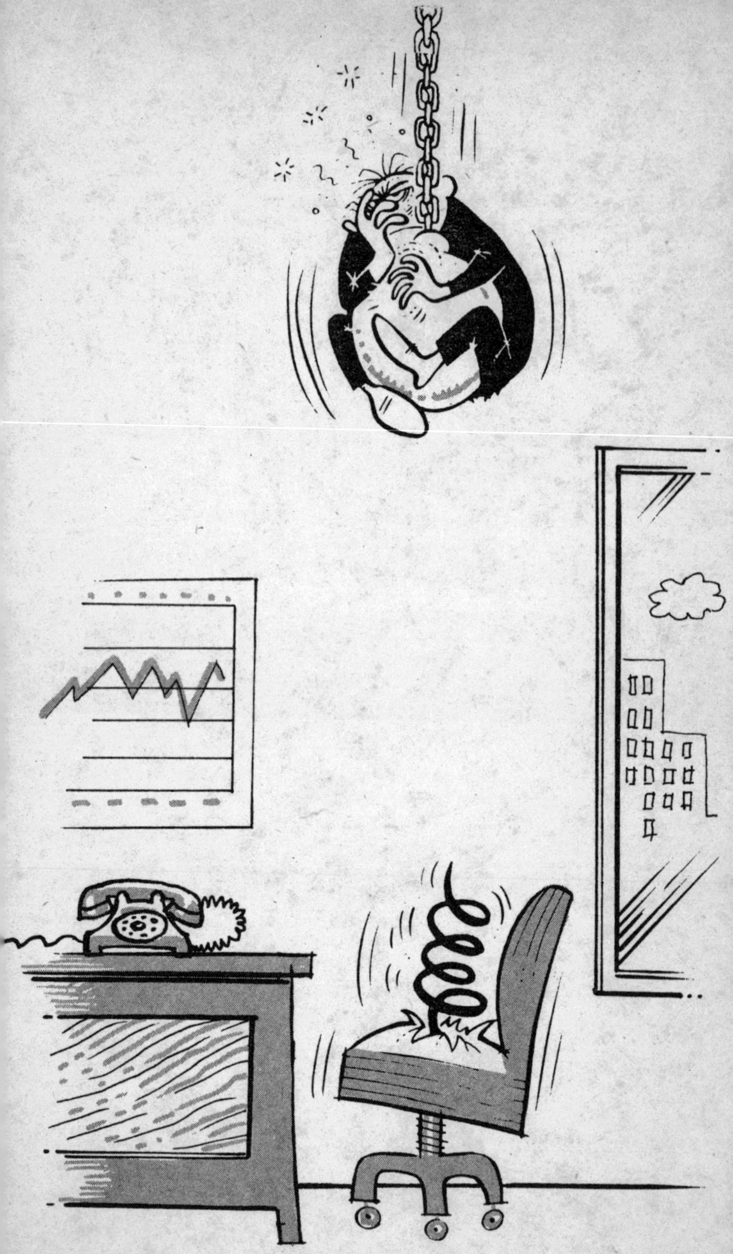

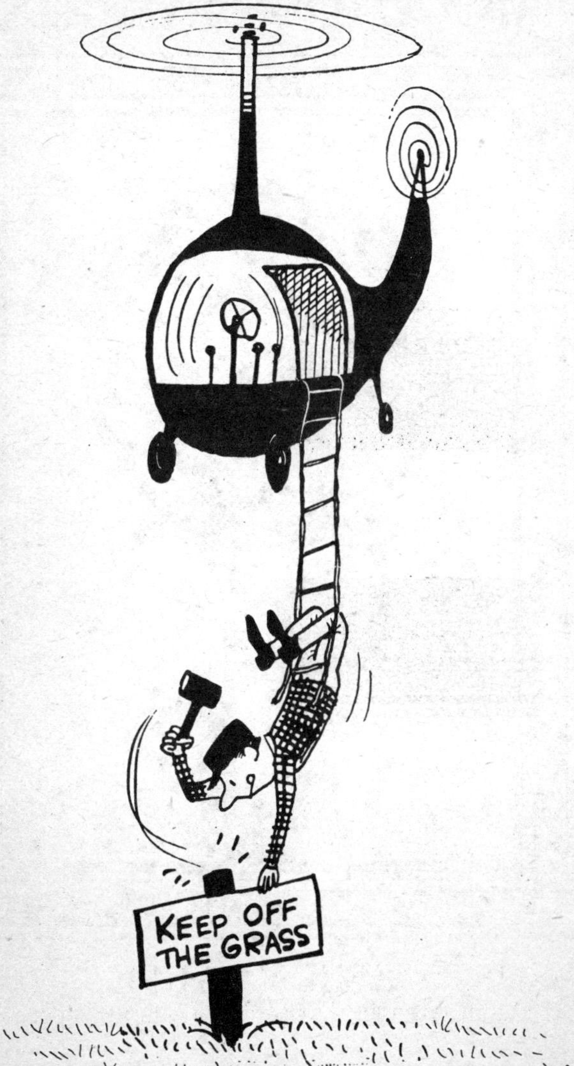
KEEP OFF
THE GRASS

A GALLERY OF INFAMOUS JAFFEES

BURPY SEEDY JAFFEE
Agricultural engineer. Grew world's largest gooseberry.

AN OLD STATUE STORY THAT'S NOT FILLED WITH GLORY

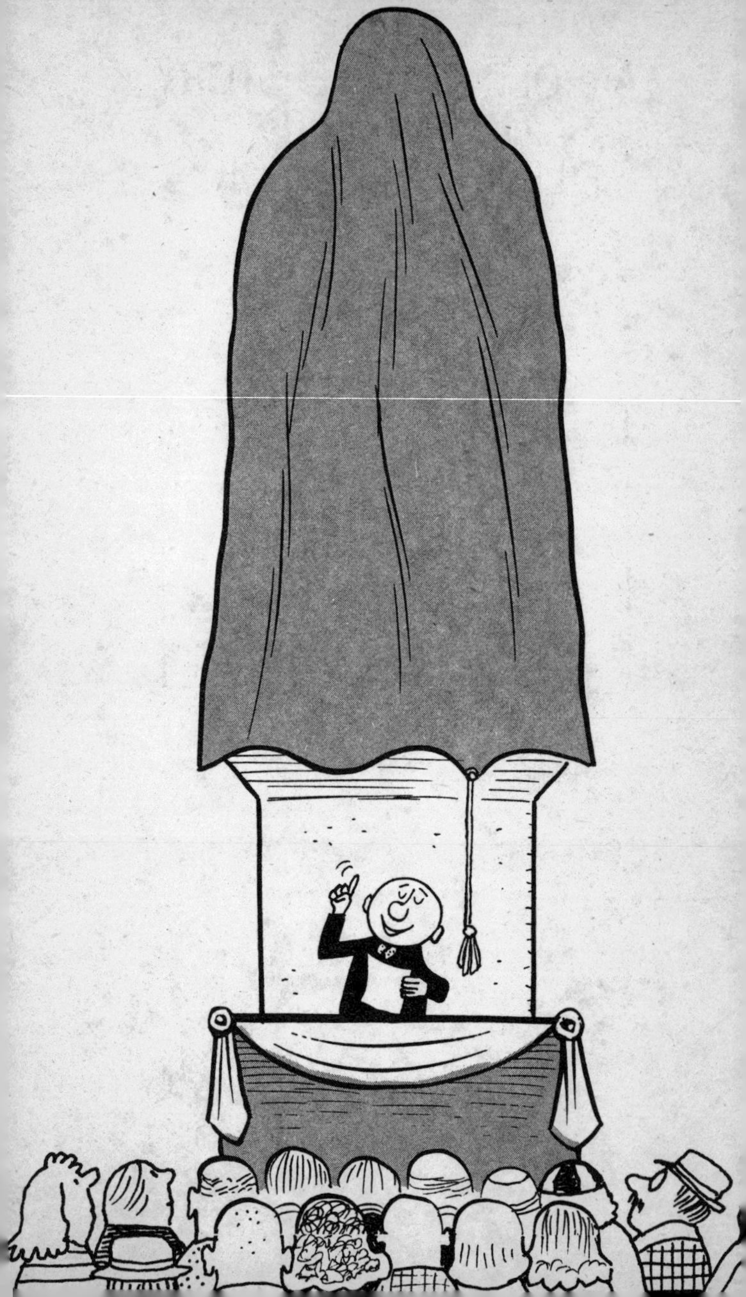

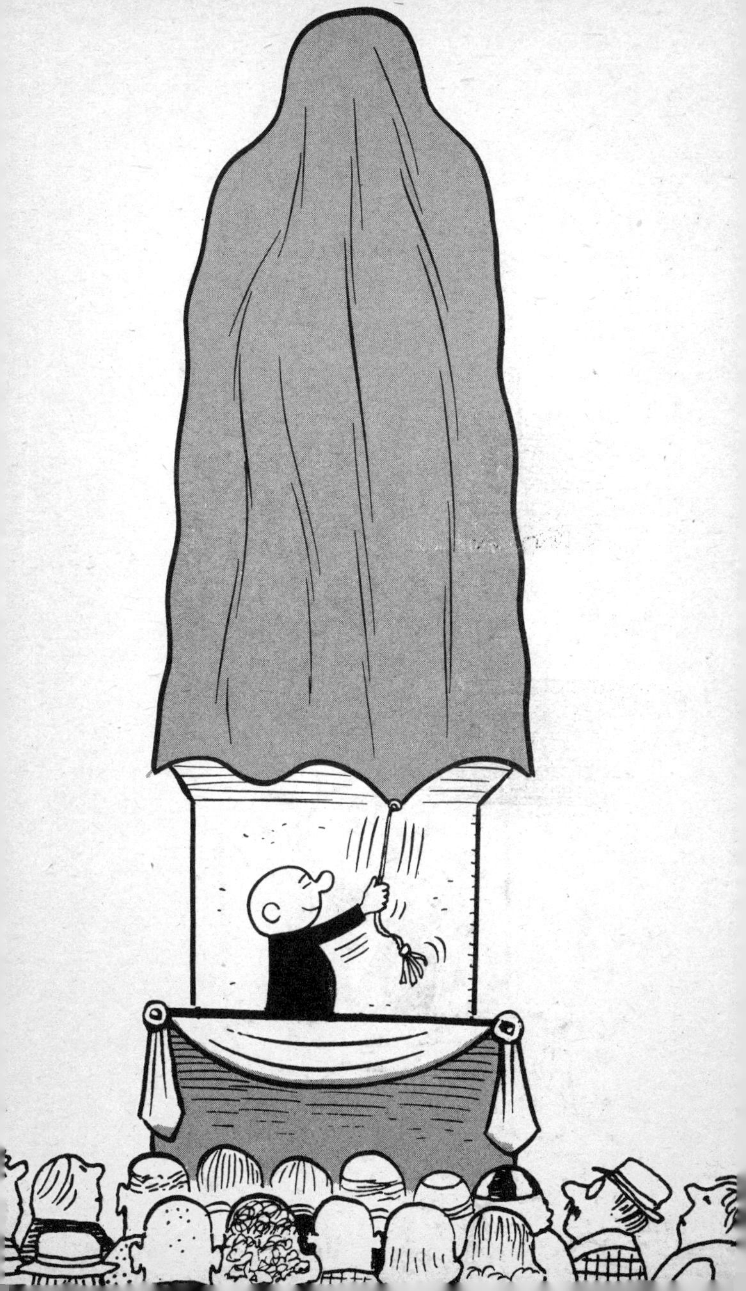

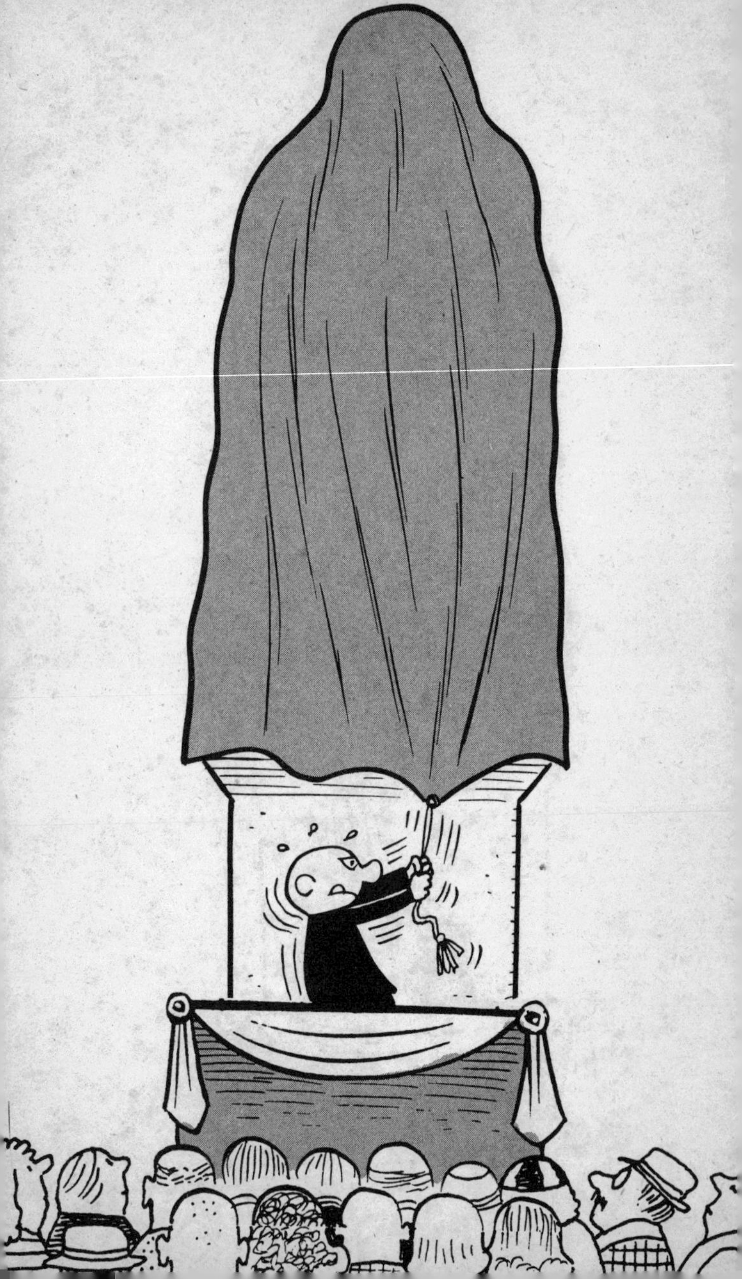

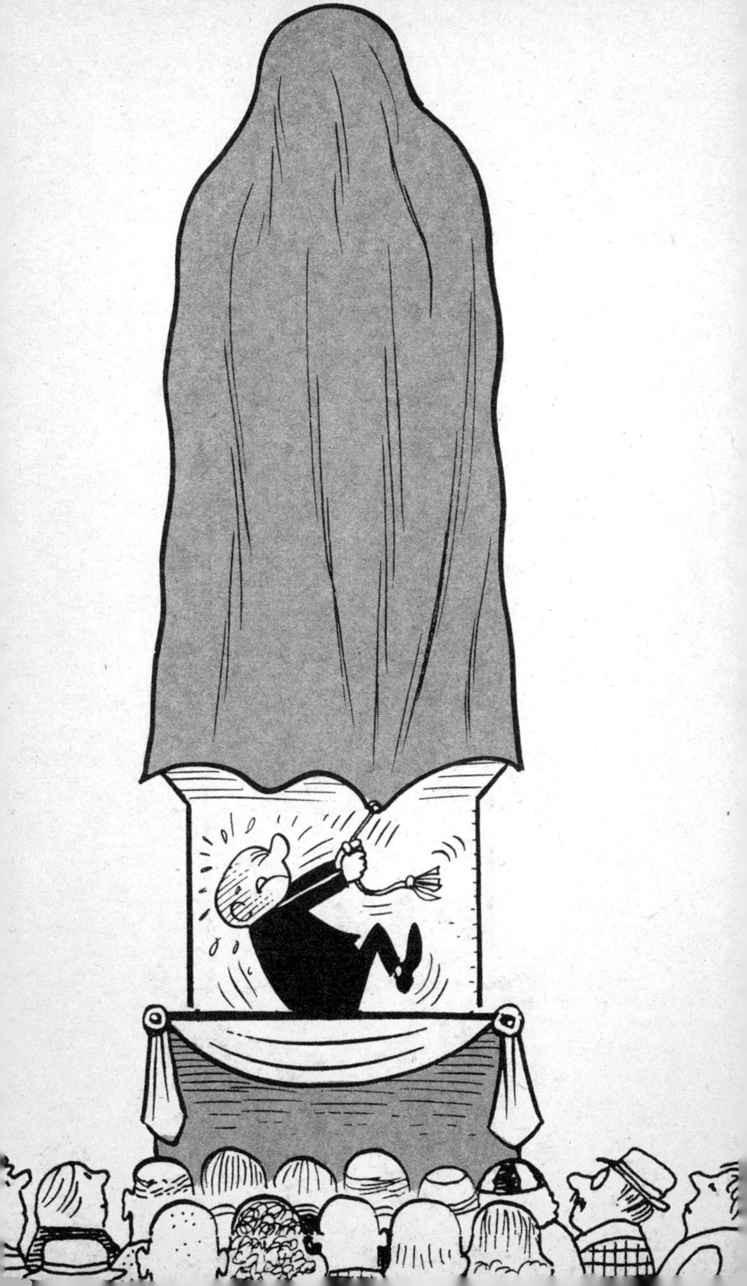

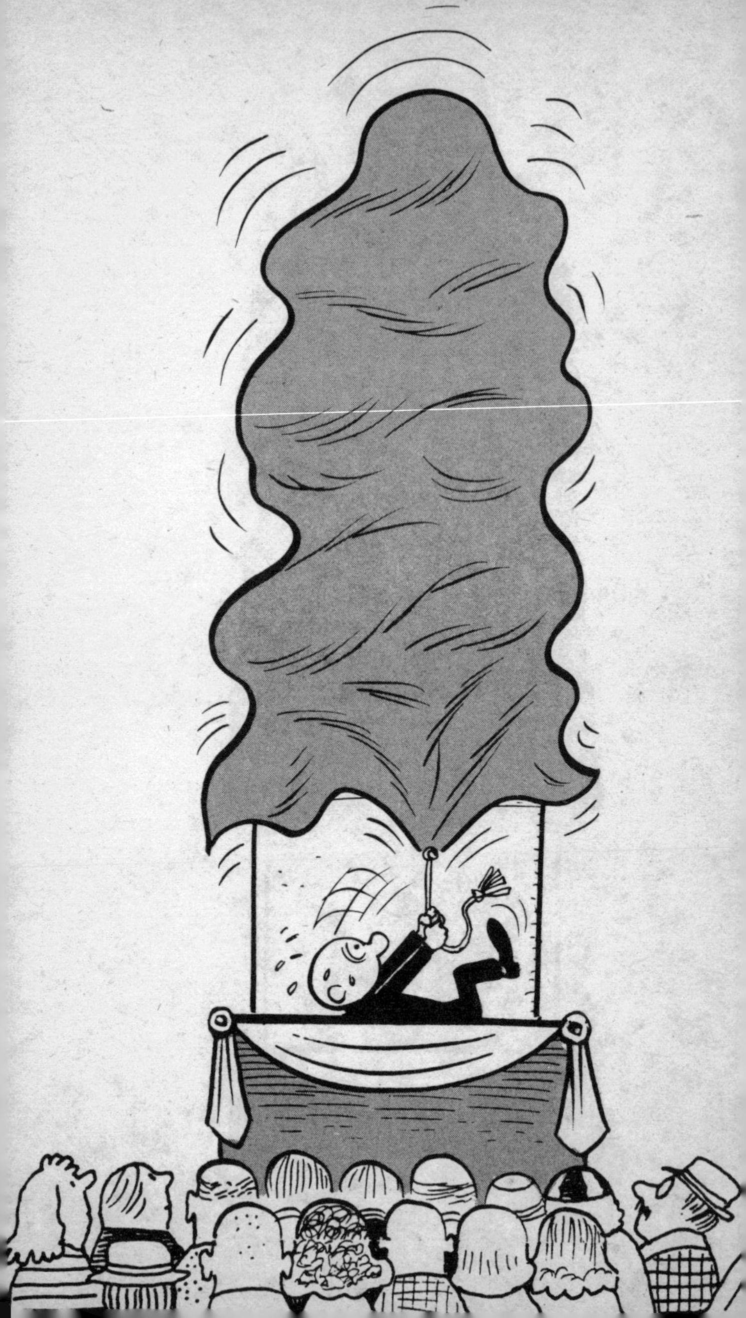

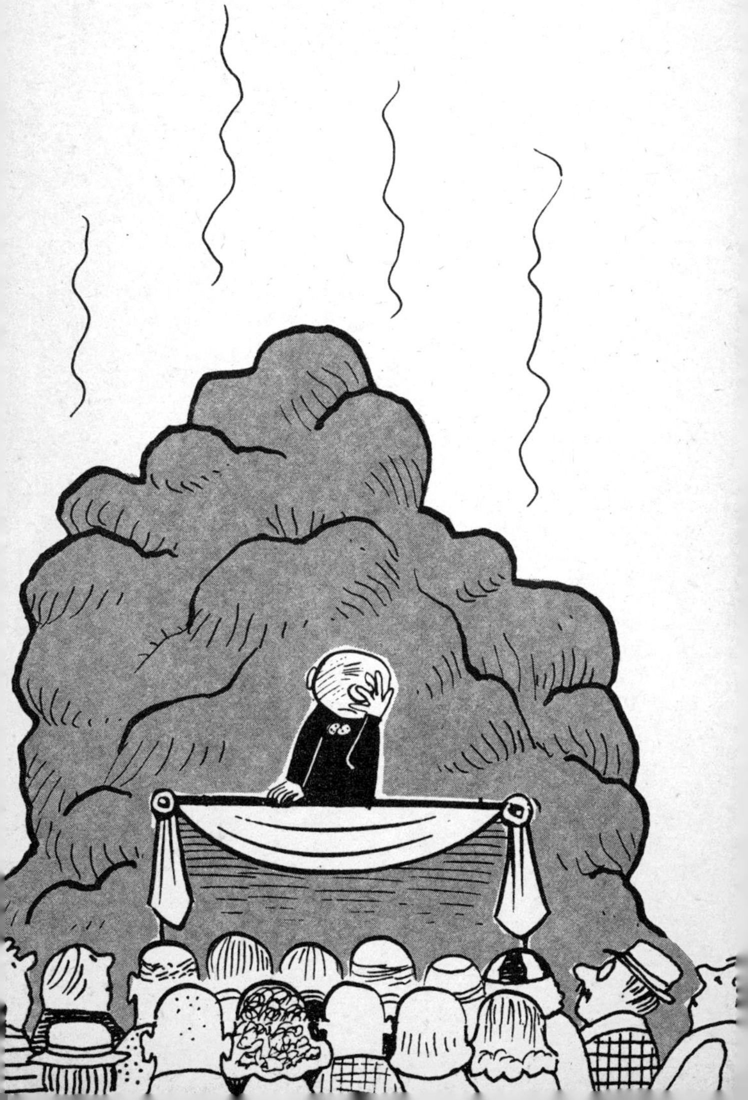

Cartoon Folio Number Three

I'd have to be off my rocker to read the next chapter in this book.

THUP!

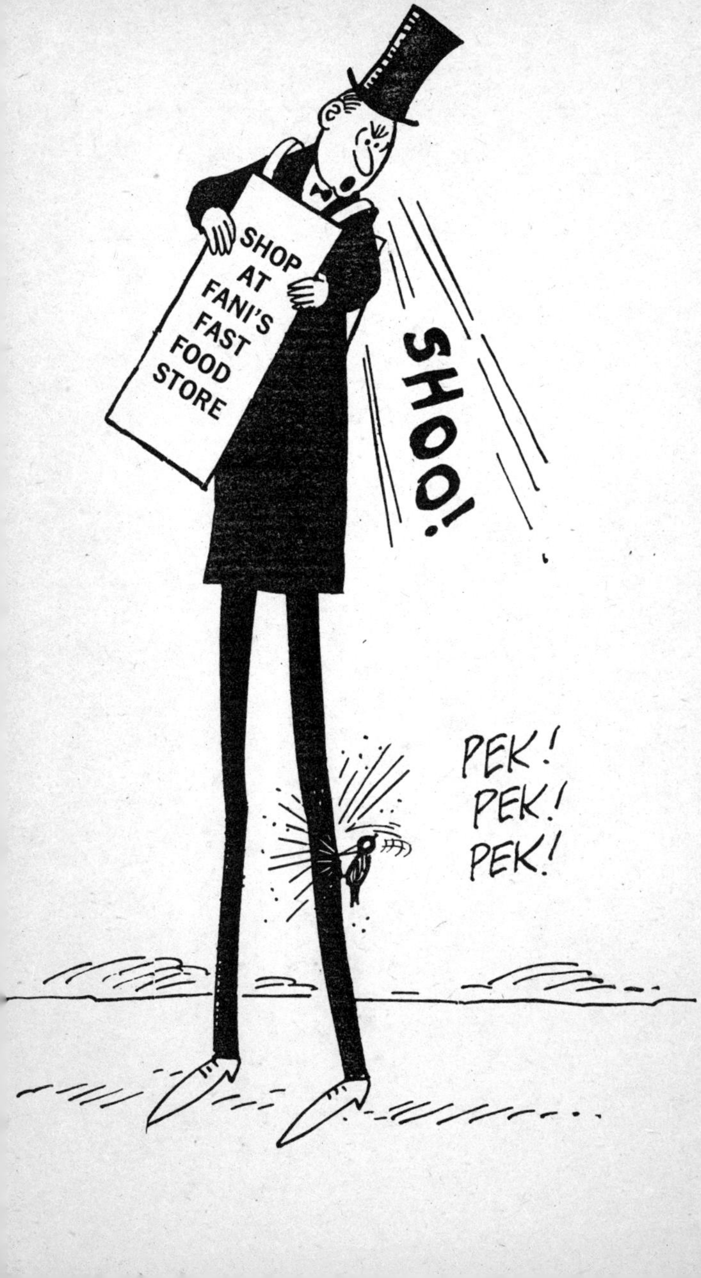
SHOP
AT
FANI'S
FAST
FOOD
STORE
SHOO!
PEK!
PEK!
PEK!

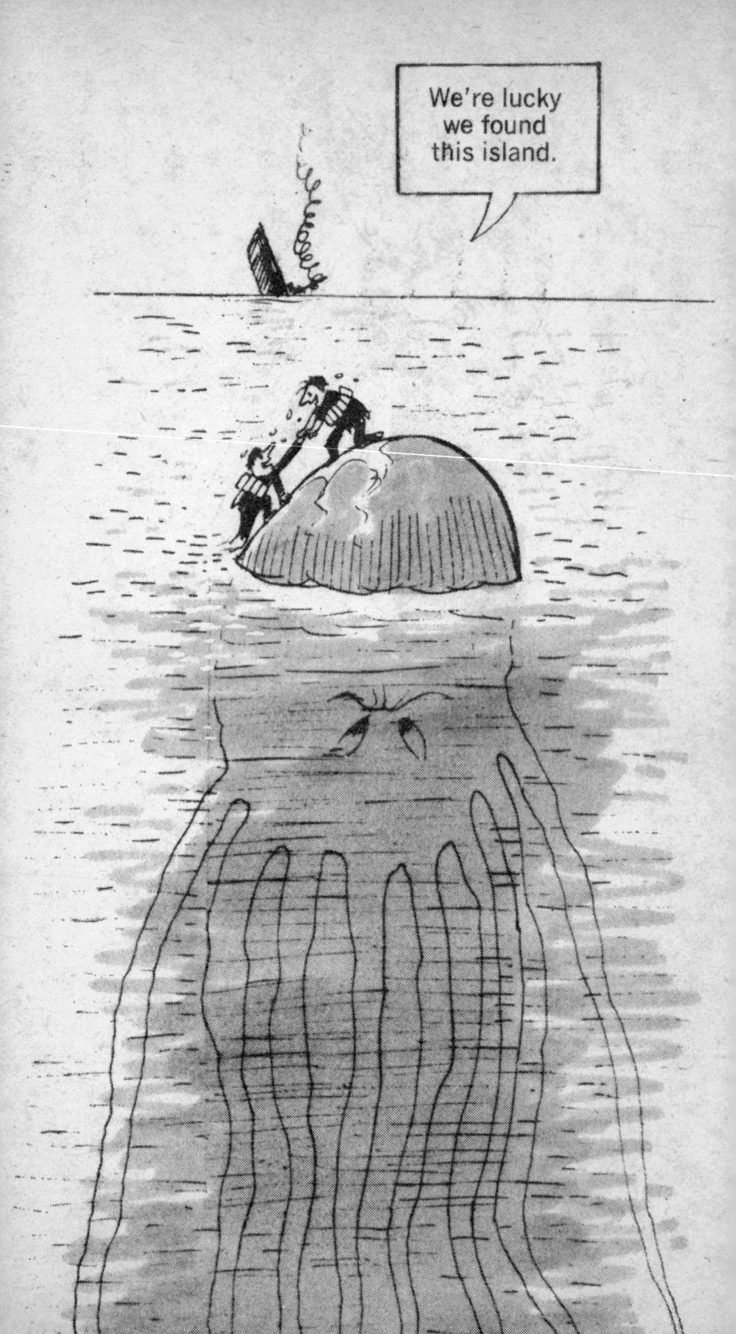
We're lucky we found this island.

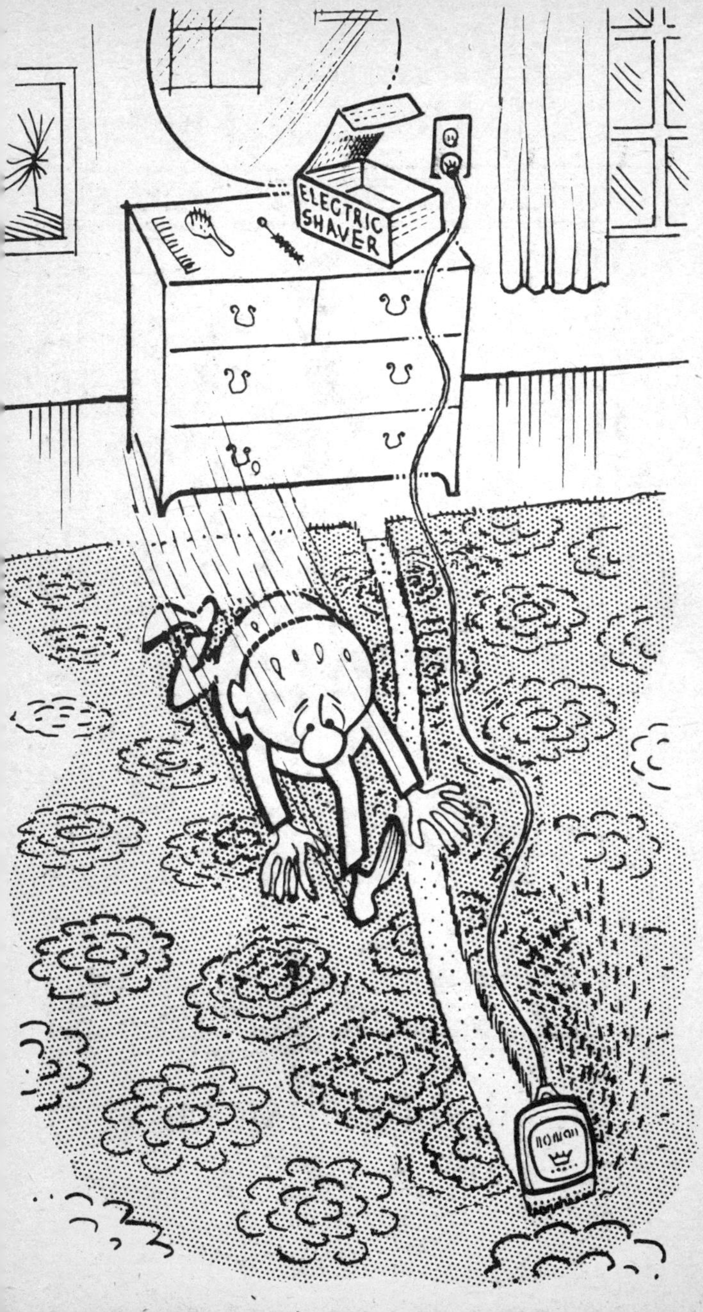
ELECTRIC SHAVER

A GALLERY OF INFAMOUS JAFFEES

DR. HERBERT UMGLICK JAFFEE
Developer of the first practical eating method for people with upside-down stomachs.

A FIRE-FIGHTING SAGA THAT'LL DRIVE YOU QUITE GAGA

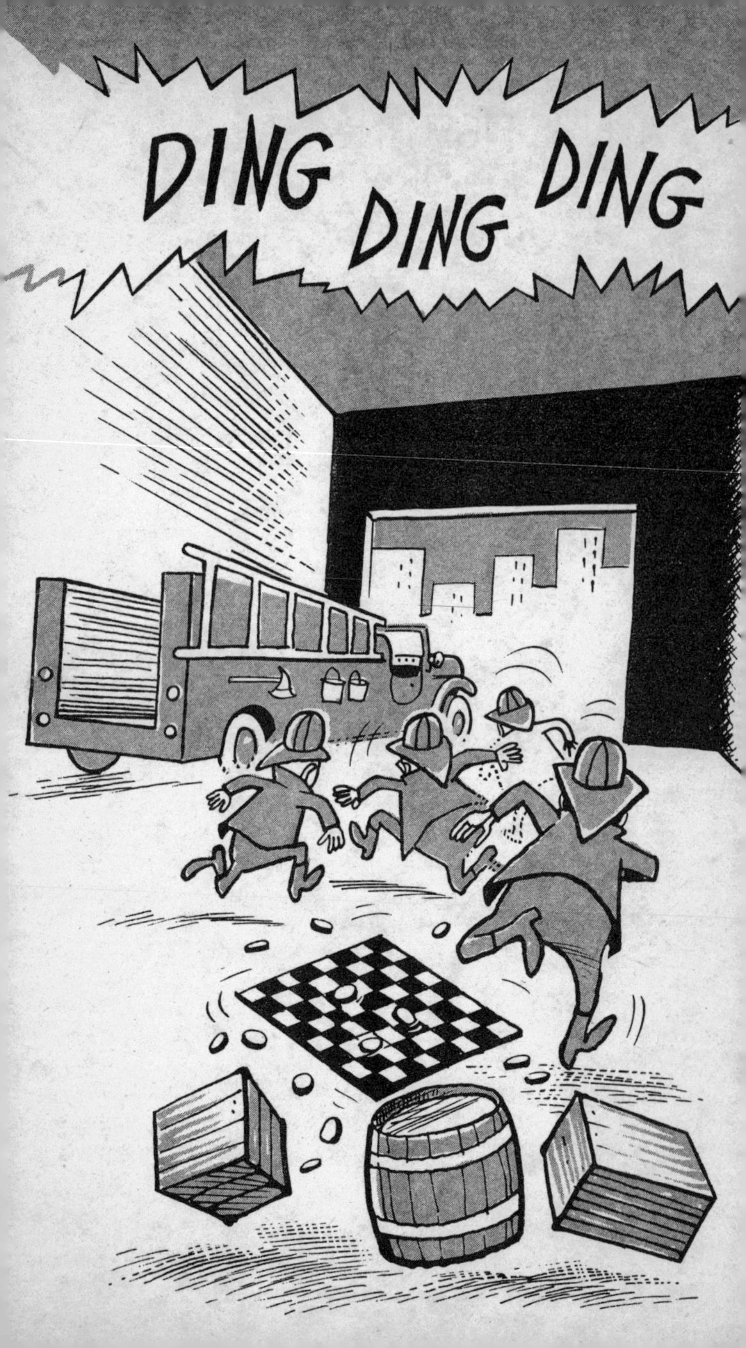
DING
DING
DING

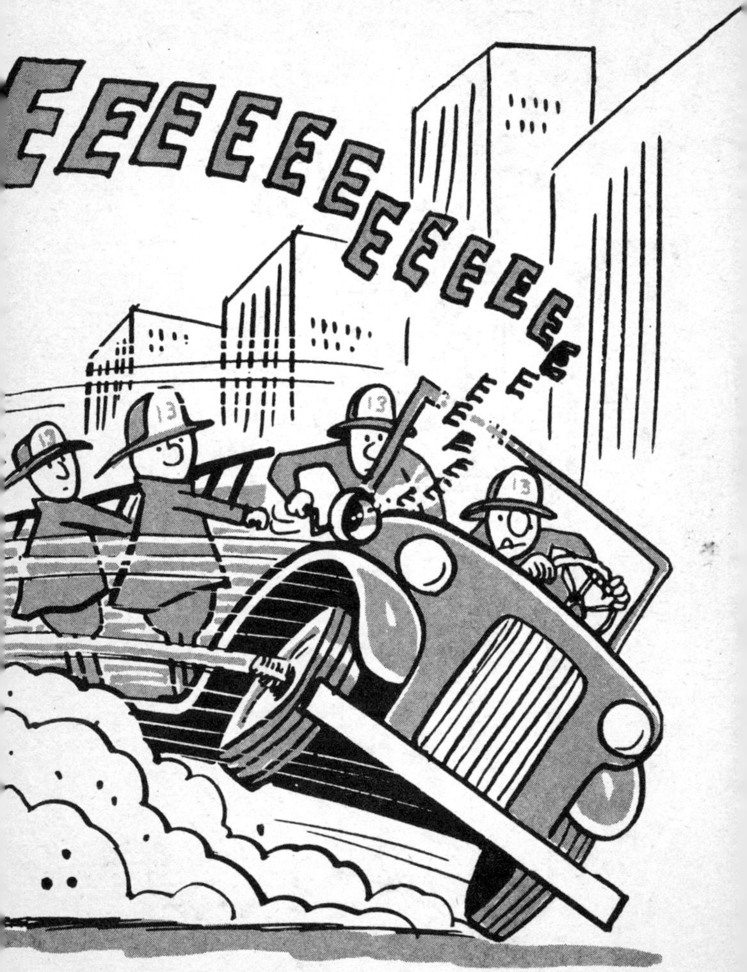
EEEEEEEEEEEE
13
13
13
13

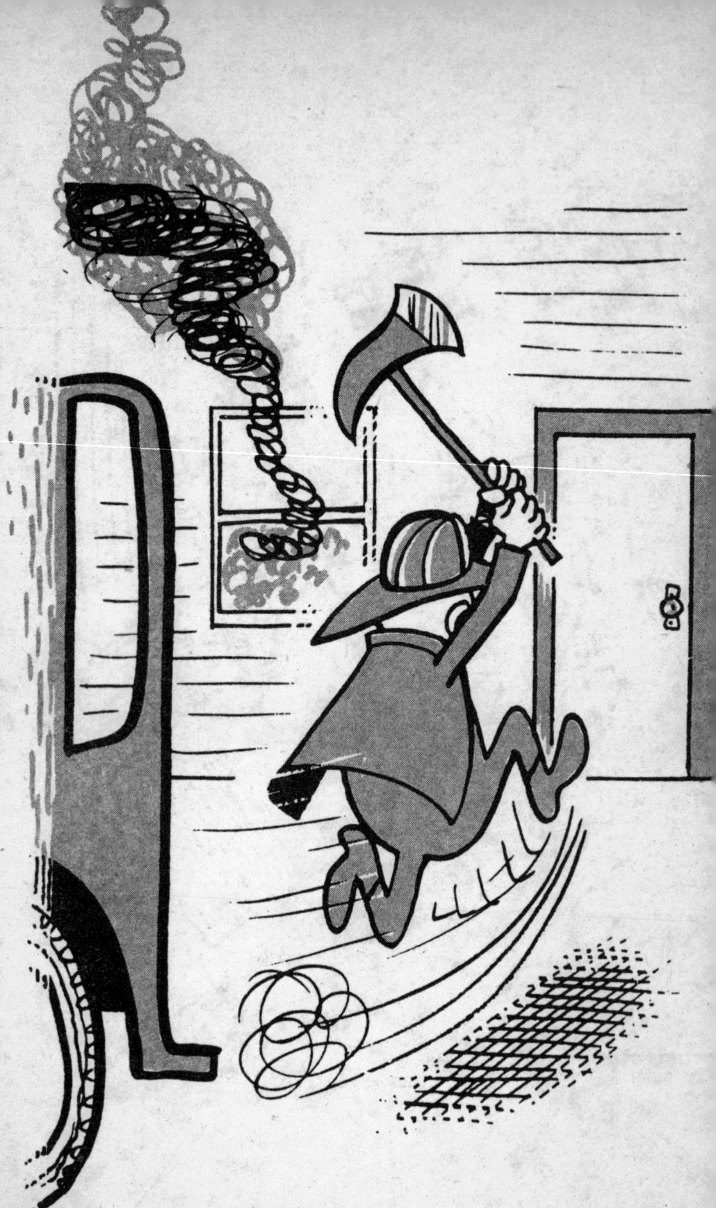

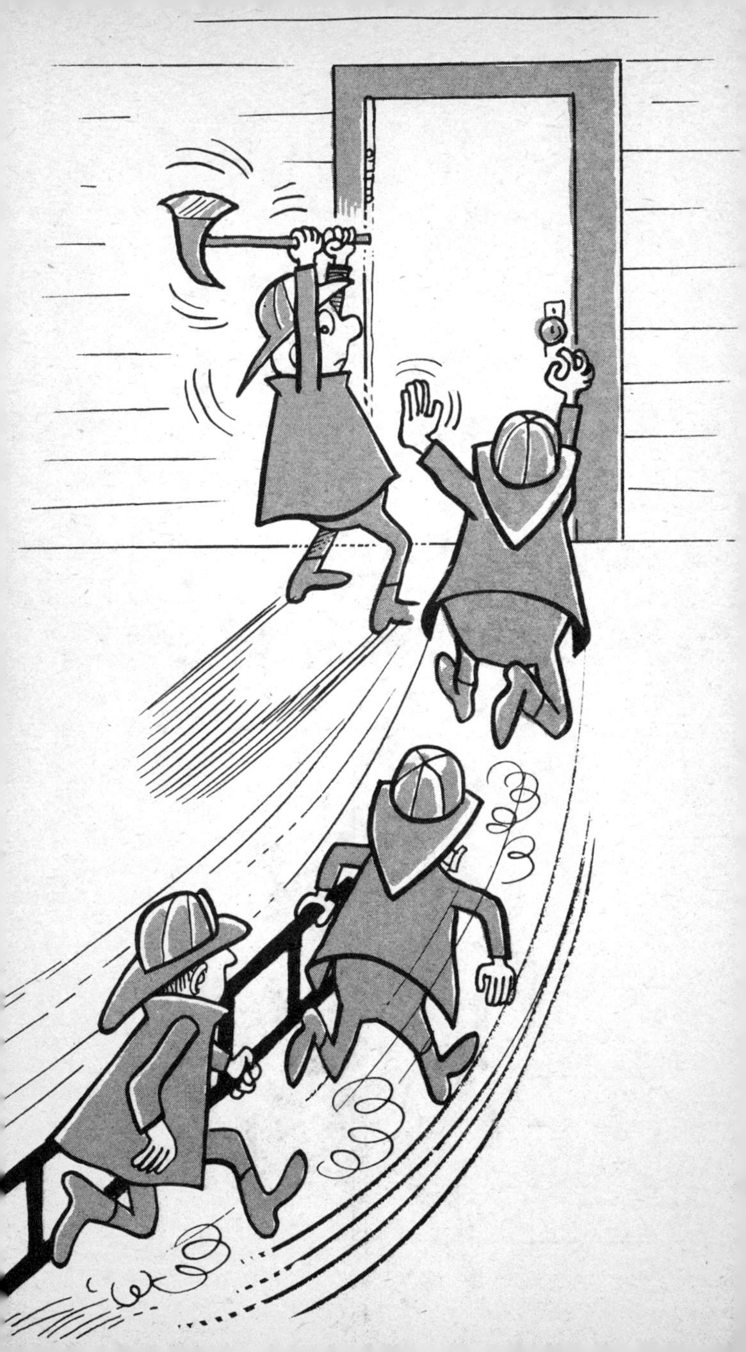

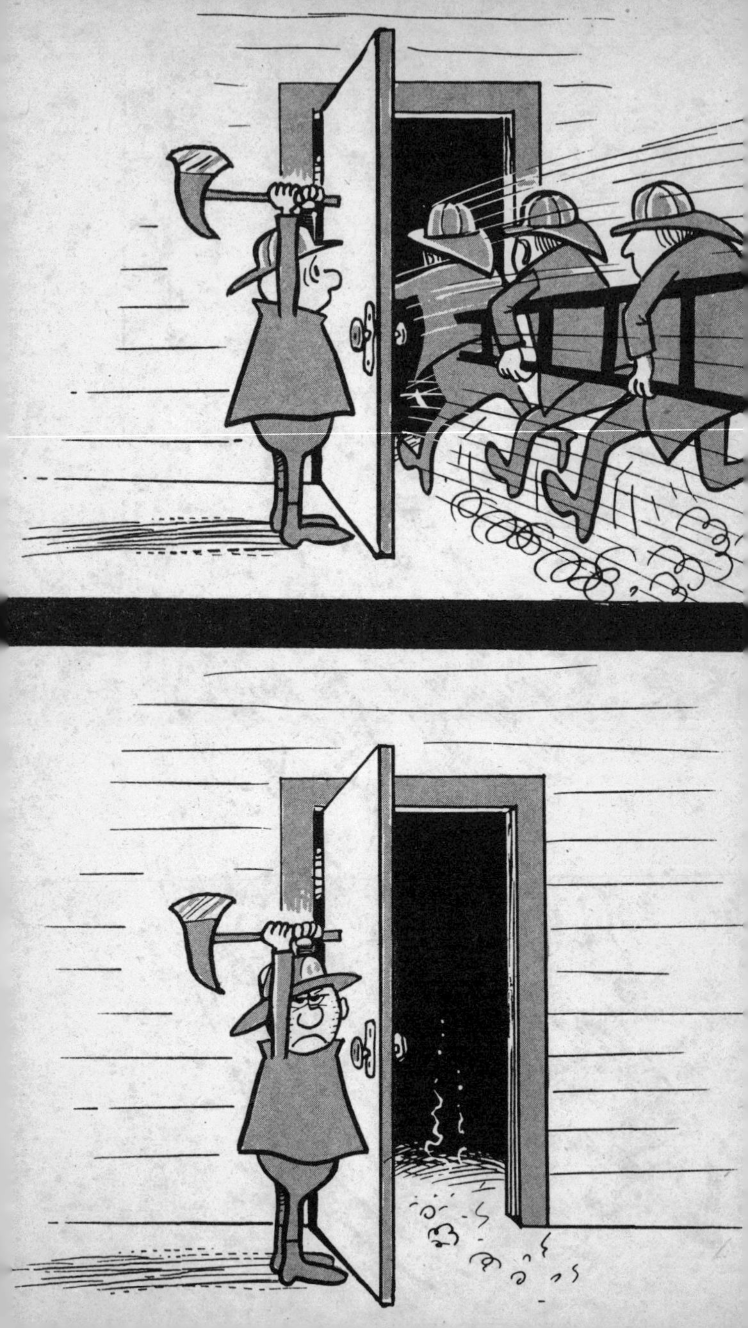

SLAM

CHOP
CHOP
CHOP
CHOP
CHOP
CHOP
CHOP
CHOP
CHOP
CHOP
CHOP
CHOP
CHOP
CHOP
CHOP
CHOP
CHOP
CHOP
CHOP
CHOP
CHOP
CHOP
CHOP

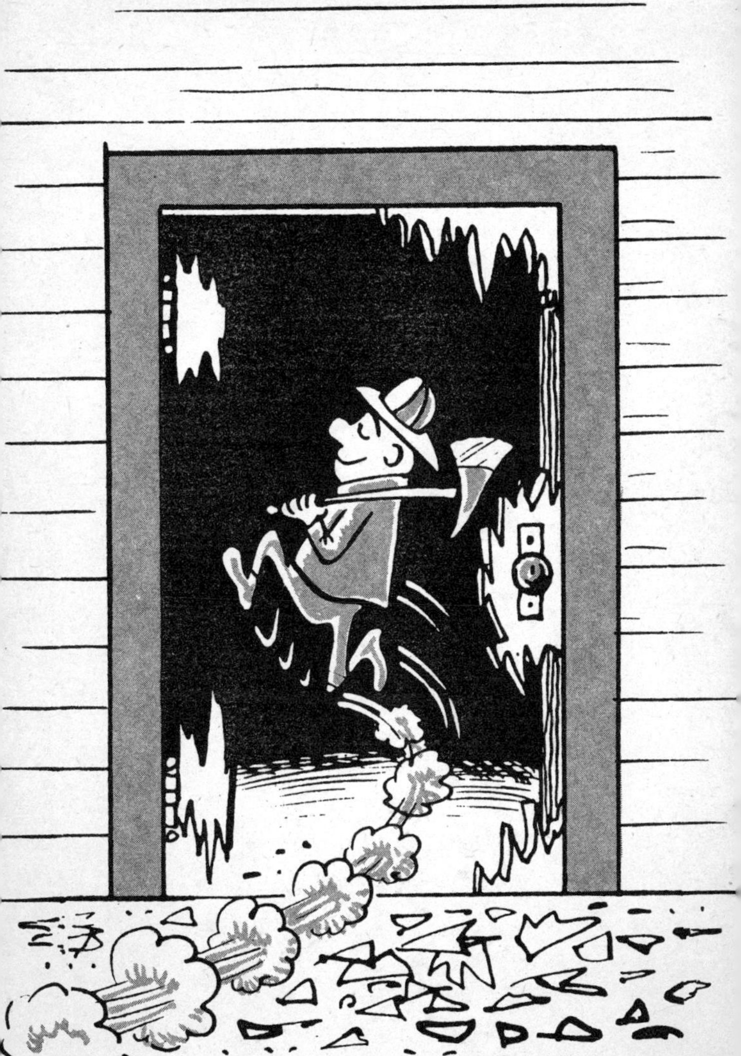

Cartoon Folio Number Four

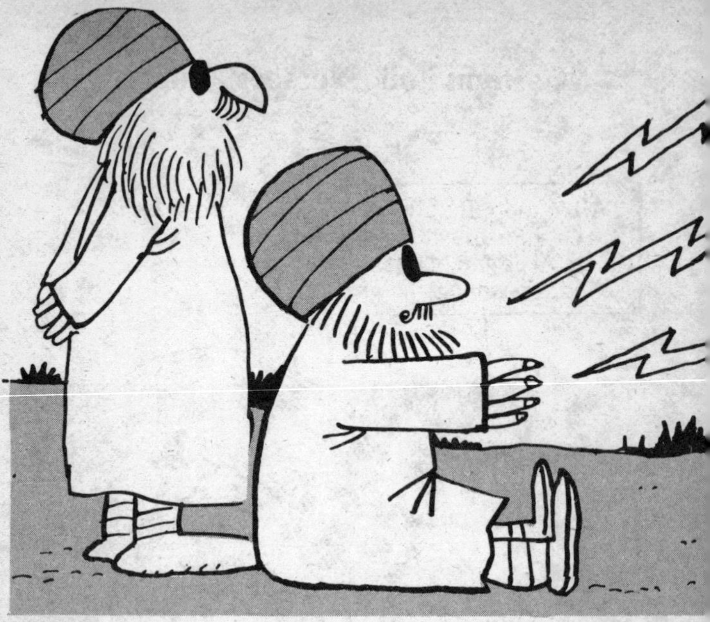

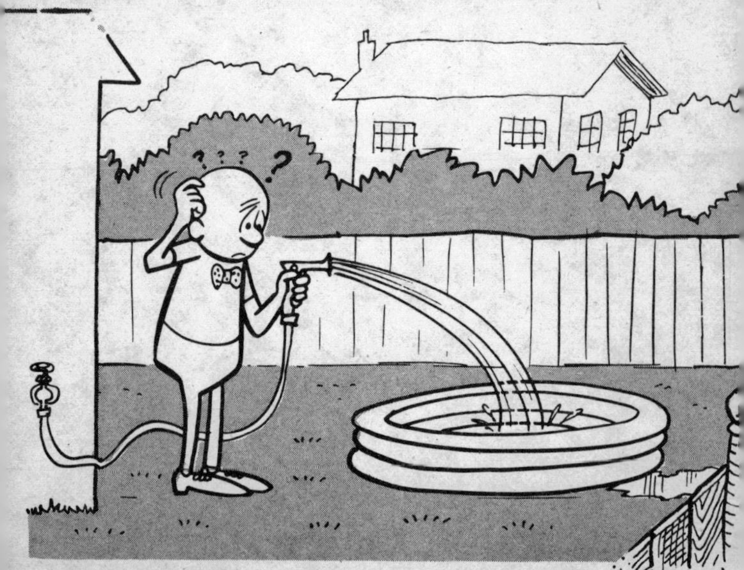

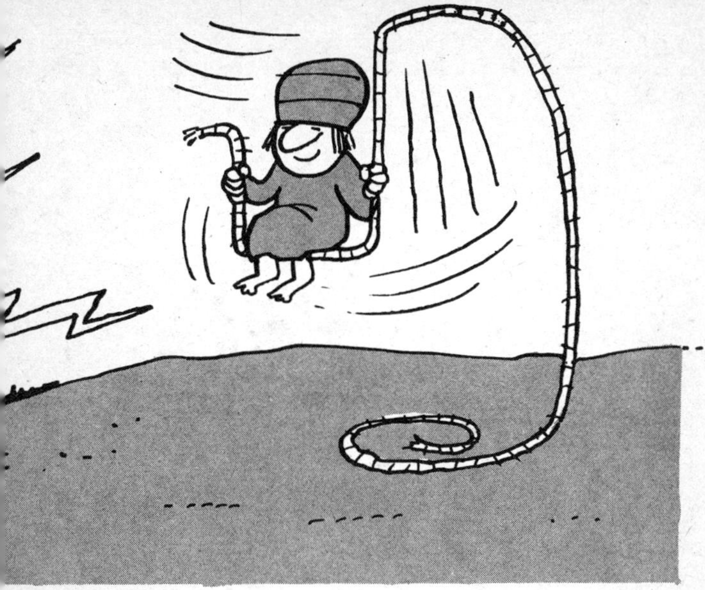

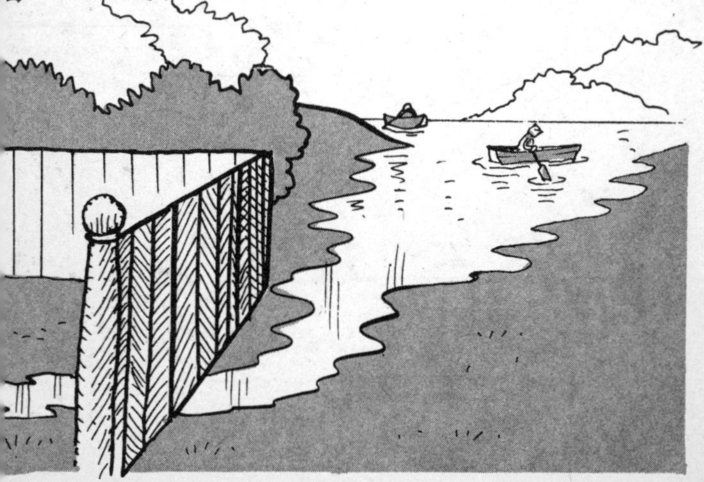

P.S. 122

CLICK!

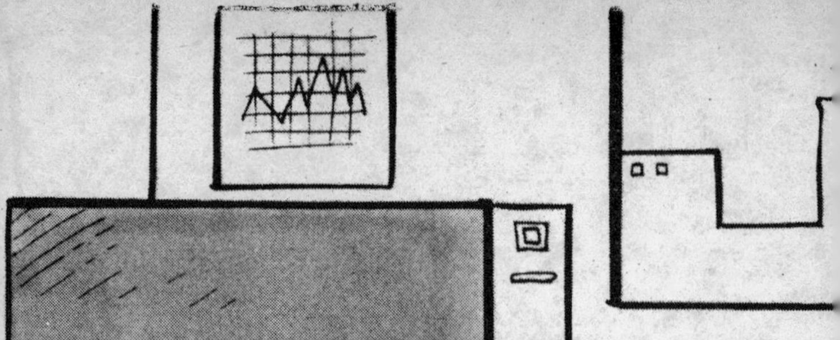

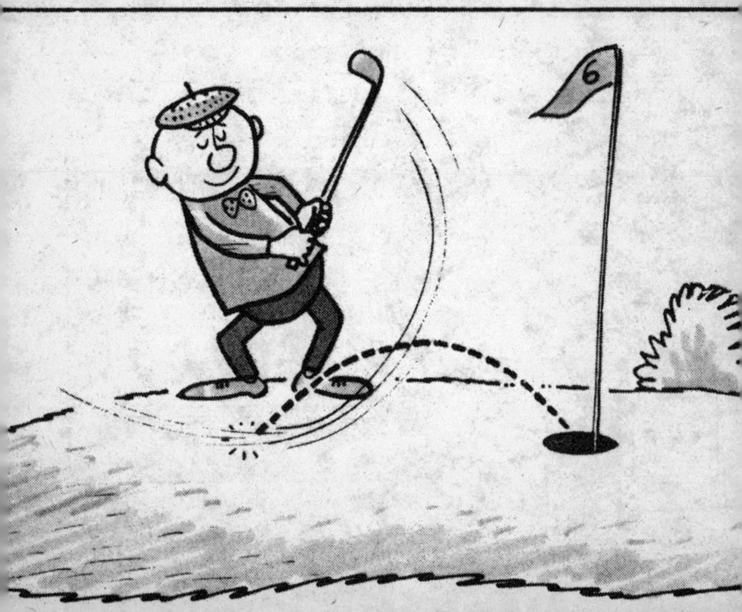
6

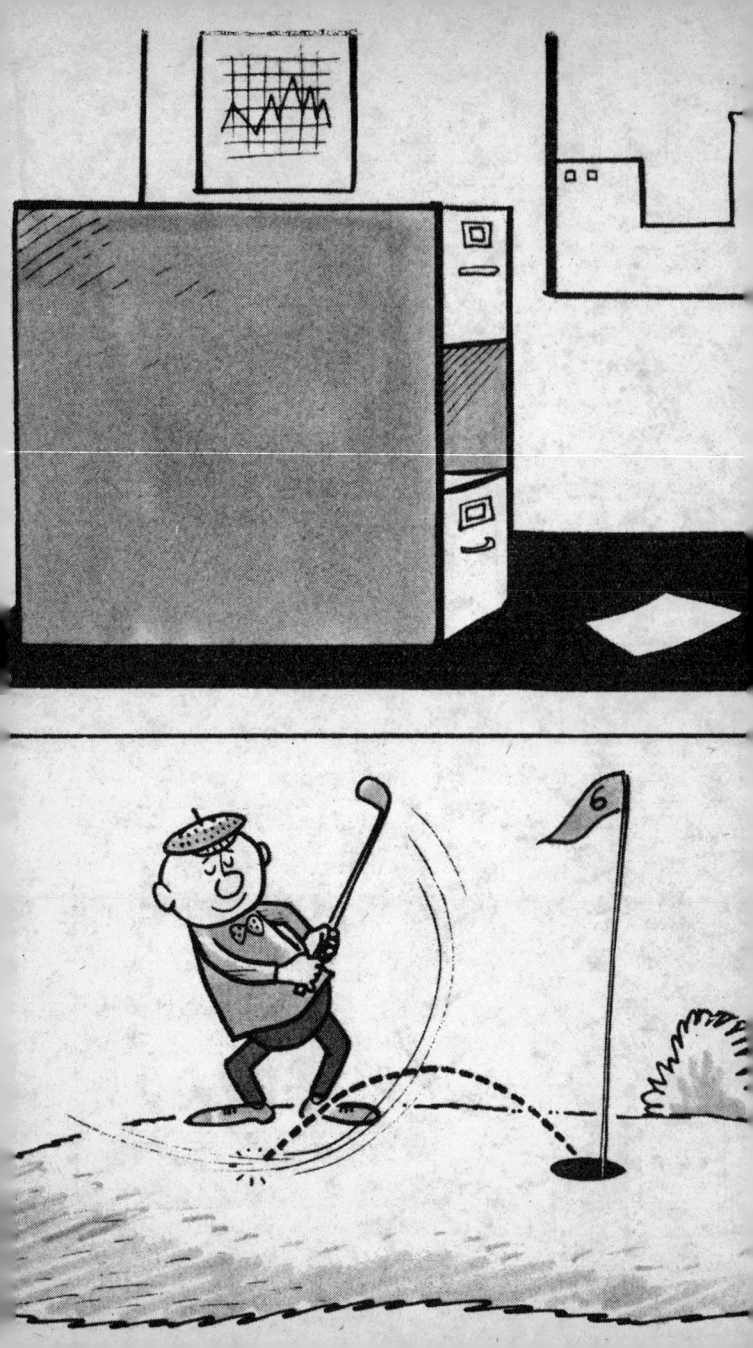

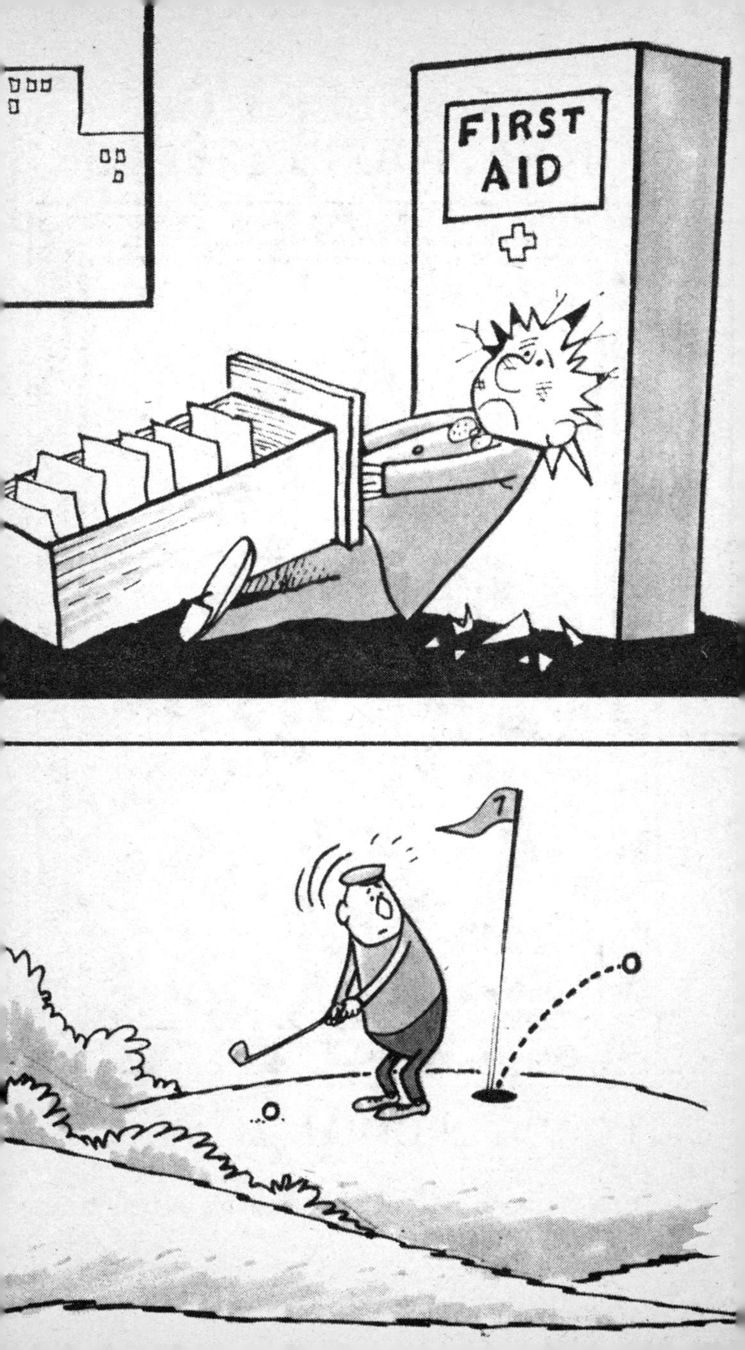
FIRST AID
7

A GALLERY OF INFAMOUS JAFFEES

LORD PERCIVAL ZITSBATH JAFFEE
First person to grow his own hair into a full-length overcoat.

A STORY OF WINE
THAT'S AWFUL, NOT FINE

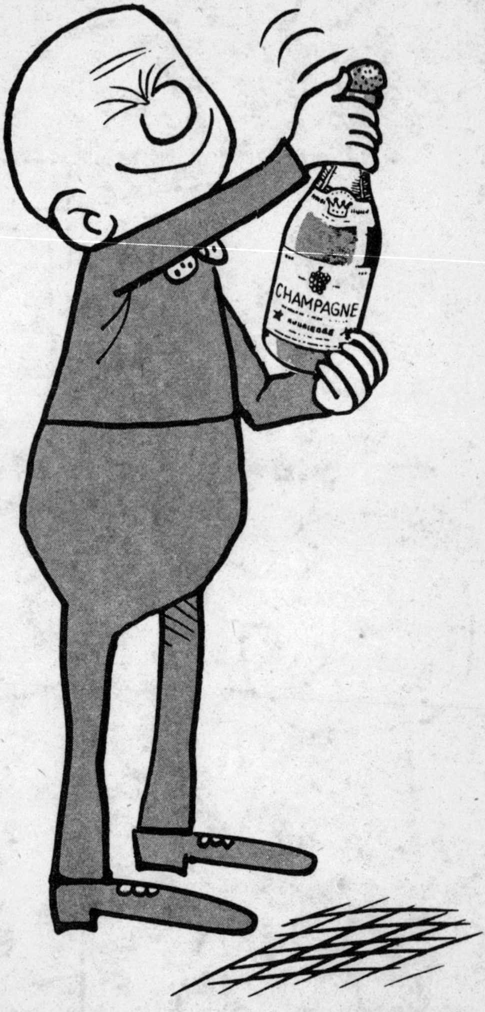
CHAMPAGNE

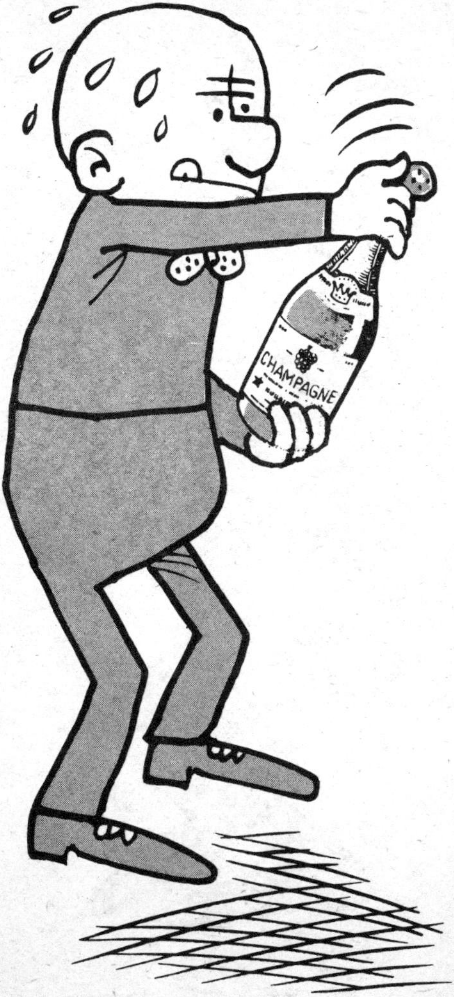
CHAMPAGNE

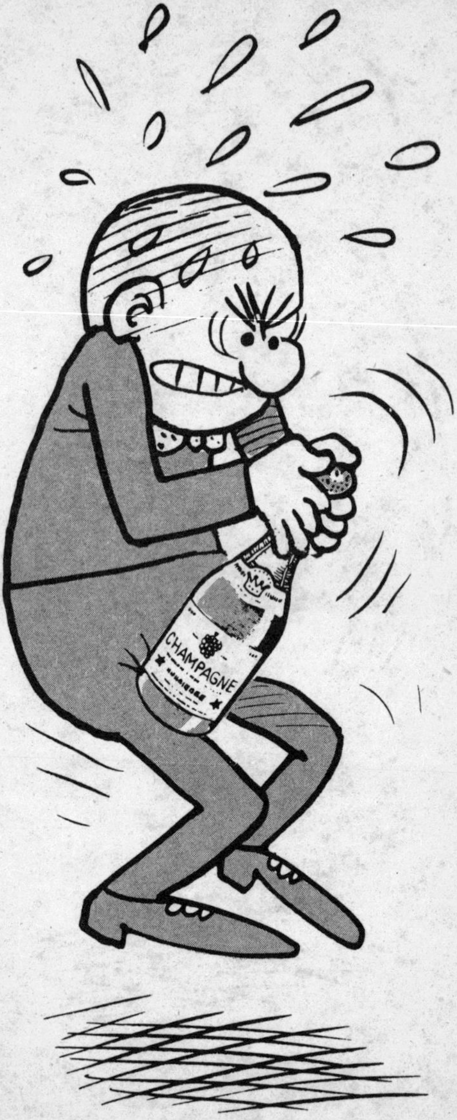
CHAMPAGNE

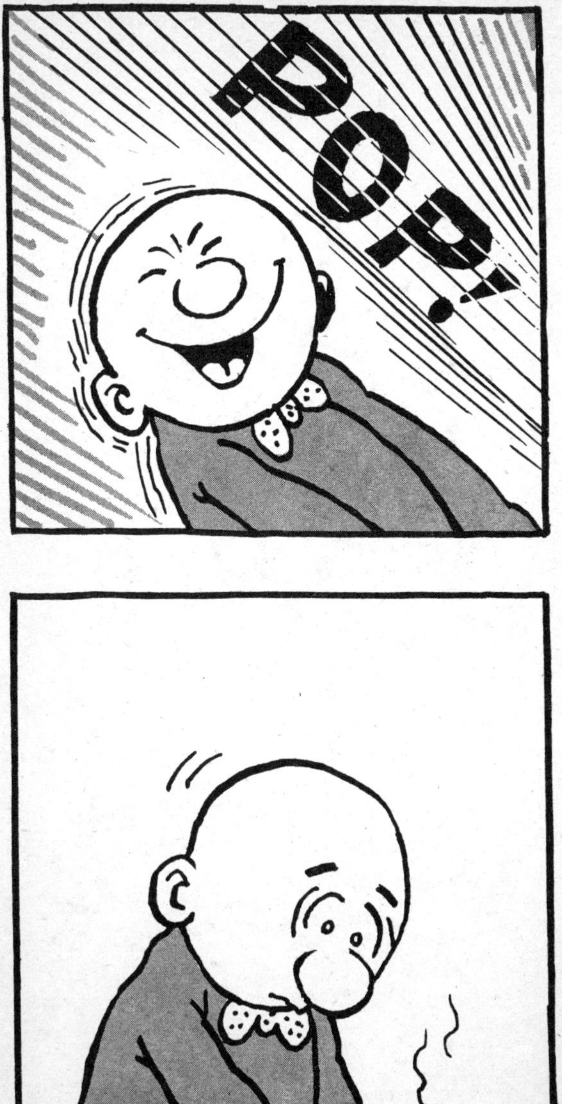
POP!

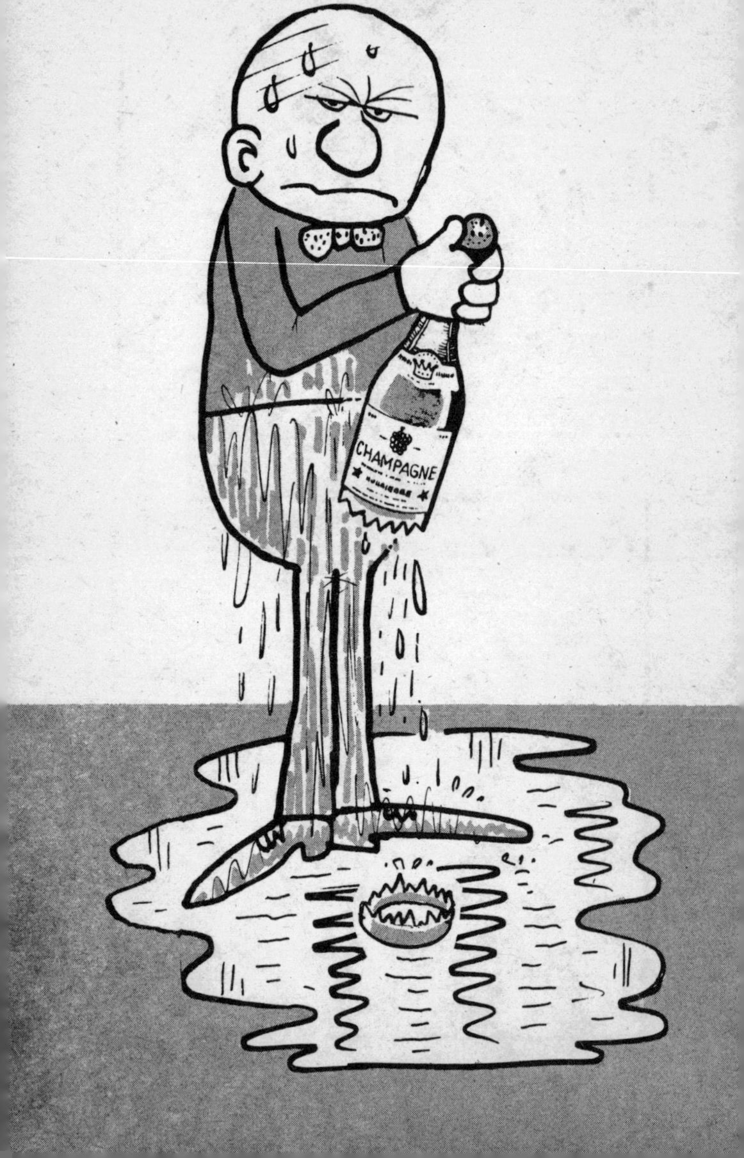
CHAMPAGNE

Cartoon Folio Number Five

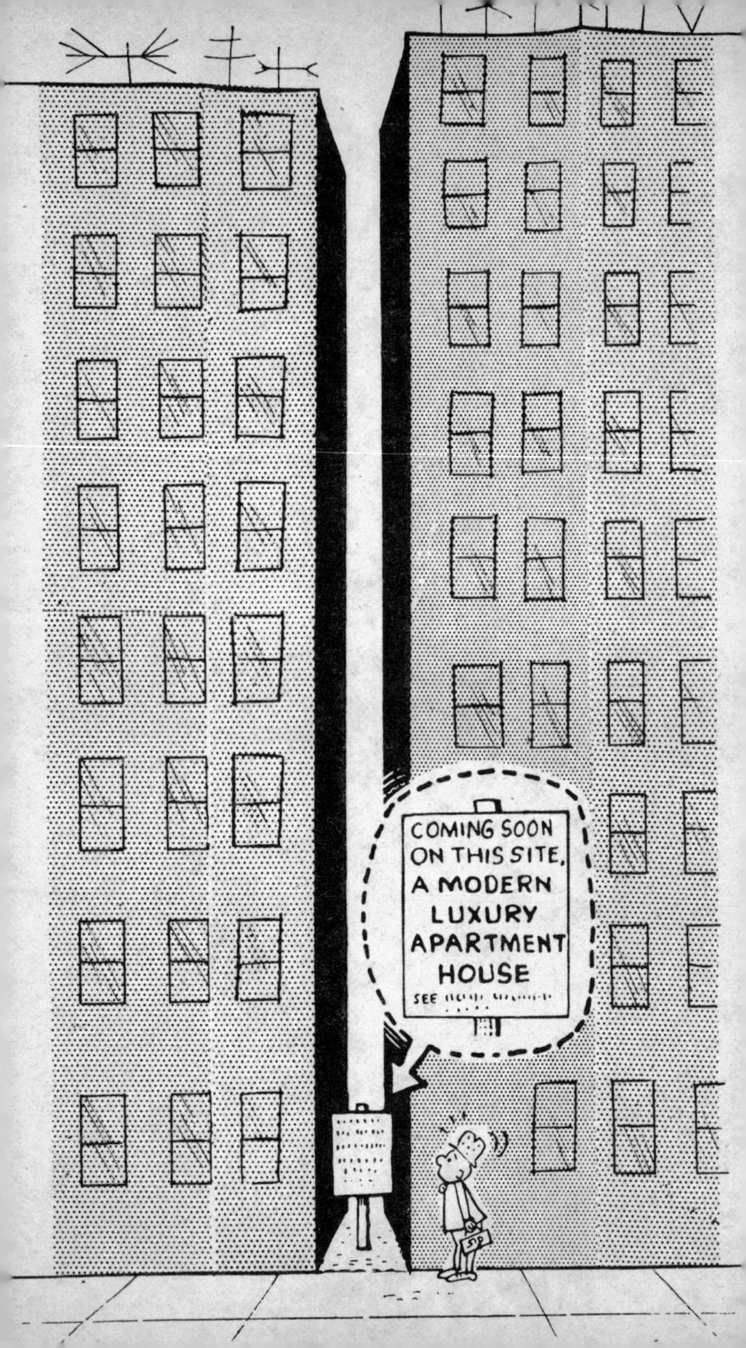
COMING SOON ON THIS SITE, A MODERN LUXURY APARTMENT HOUSE

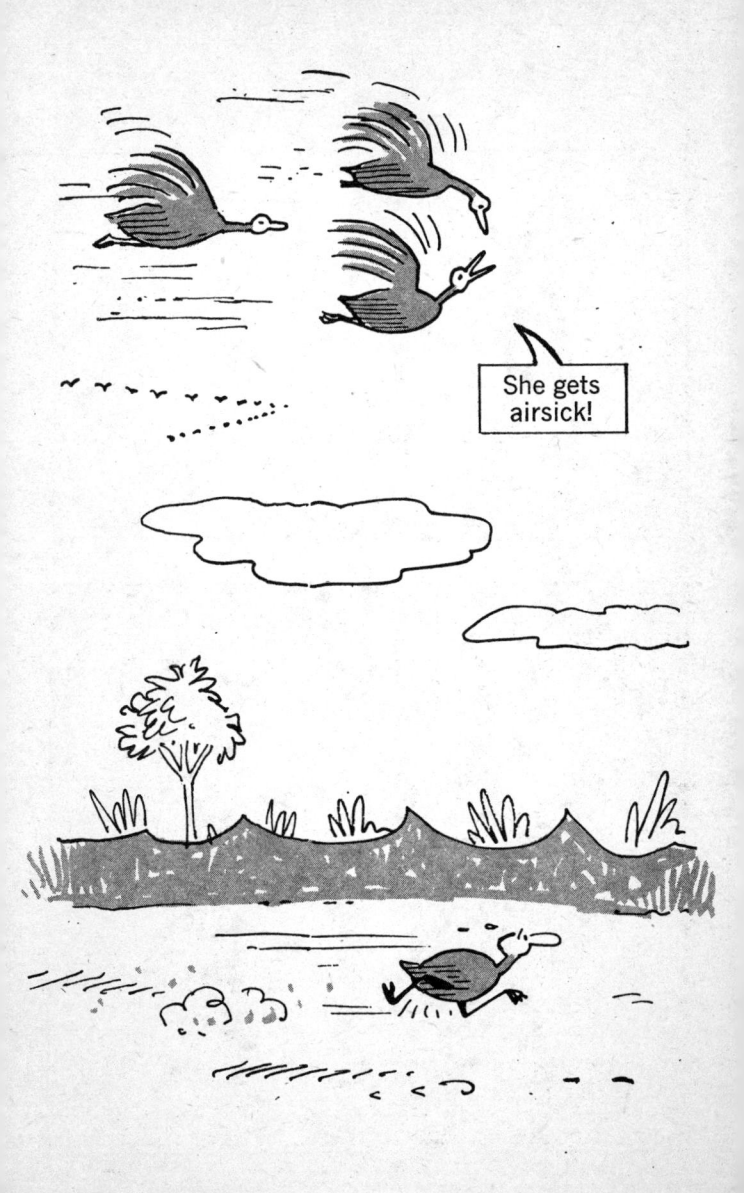
She gets airsick!

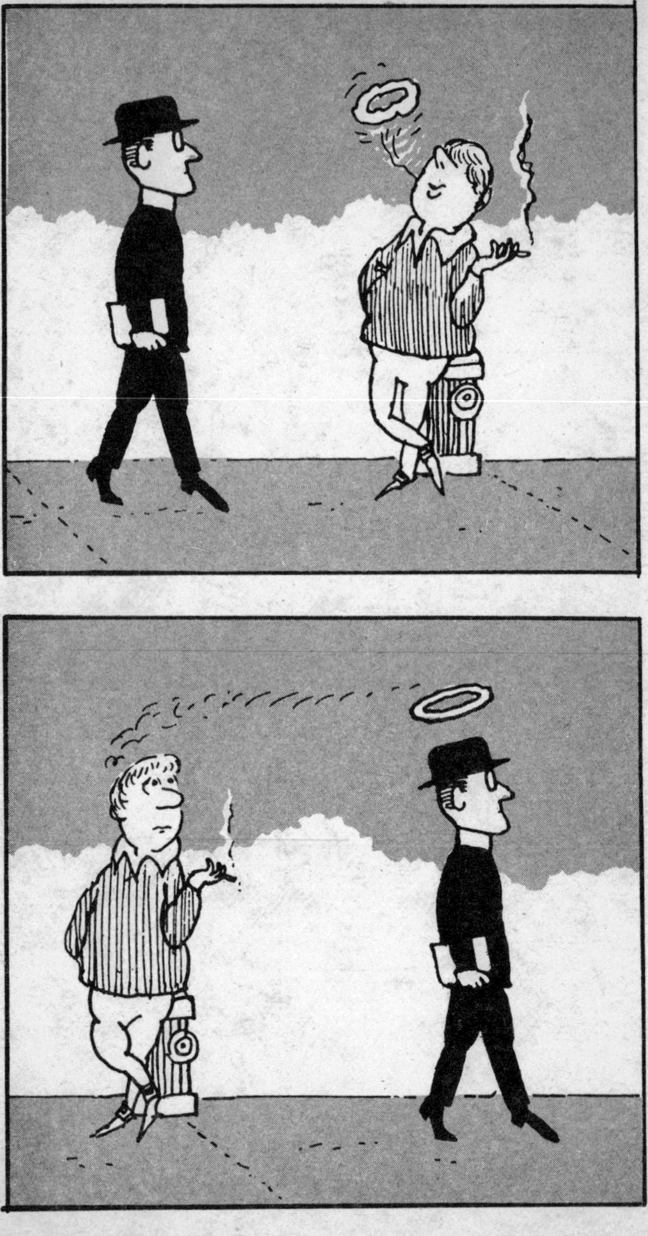

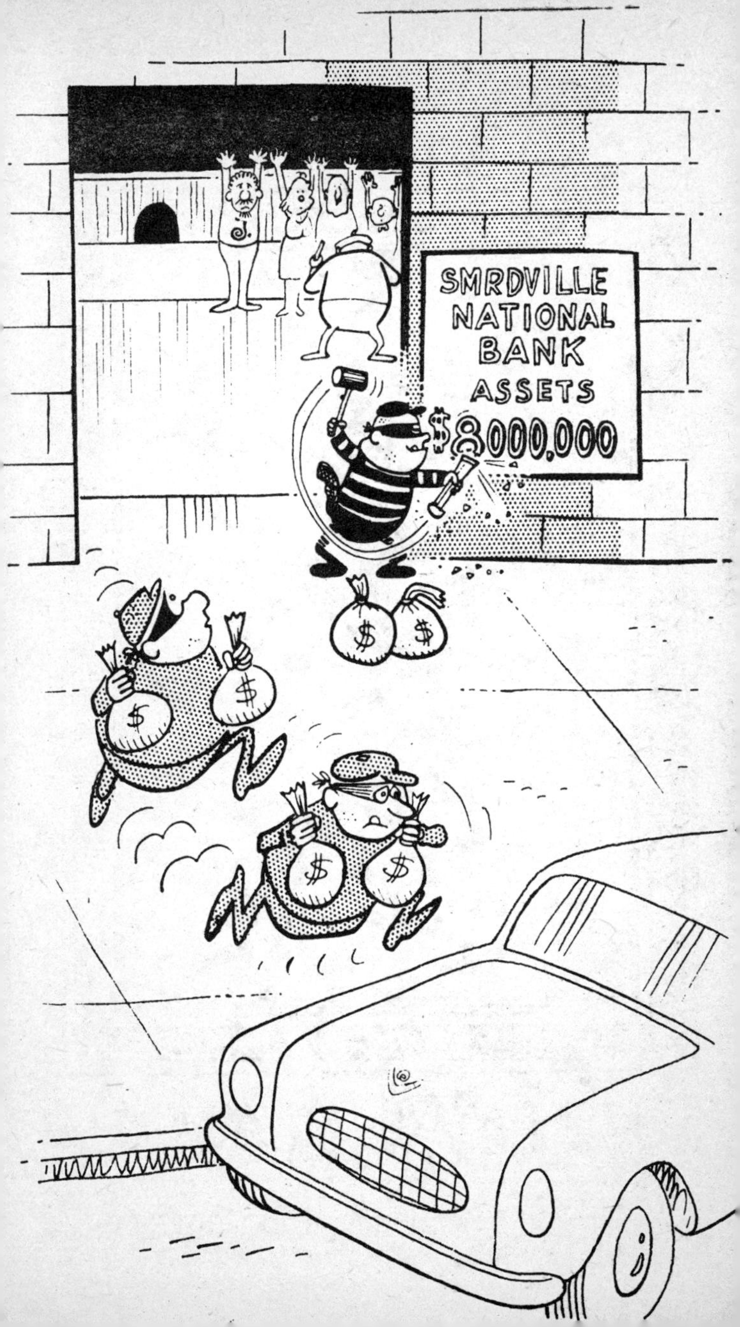
SMRDVILLE
NATIONAL
BANK
ASSETS
$8,000,000

A GALLERY OF INFAMOUS JAFFEES

FIFI HAYWIRE JAFFEE
Juggler, tightrope walker, and stupid idiot.

A JUNGLE MISCUE THAT'S DREARY, IF TRUE

HELP

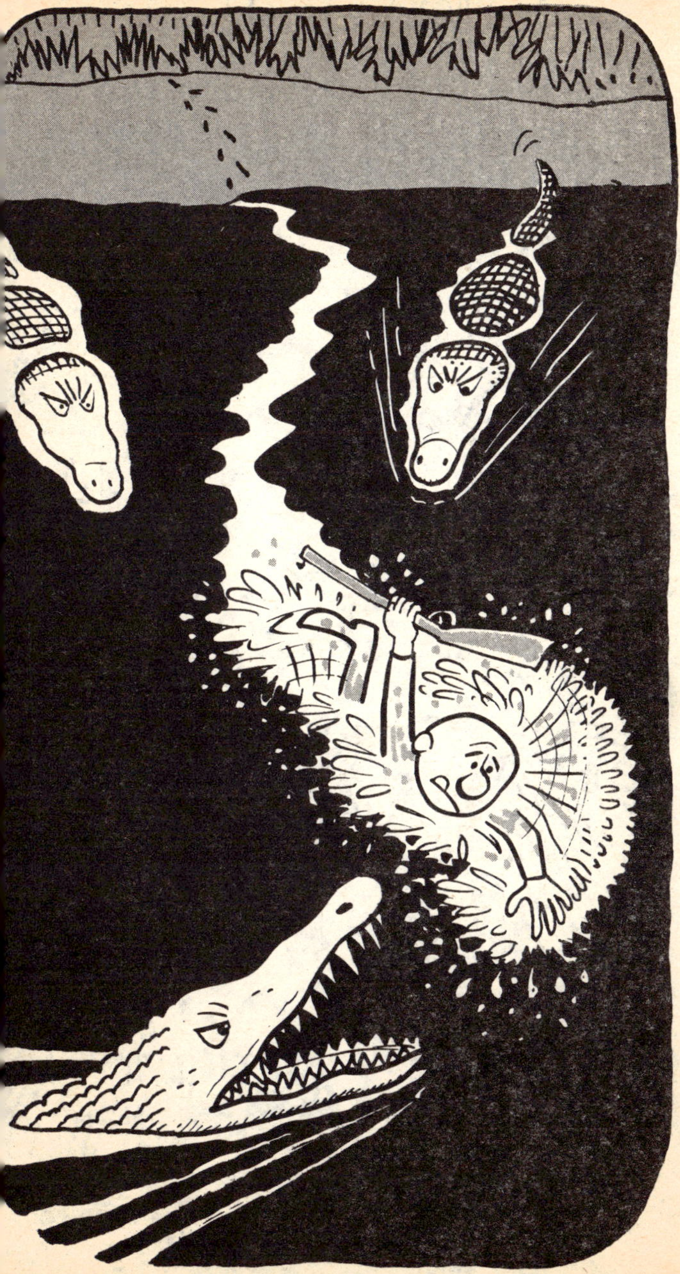

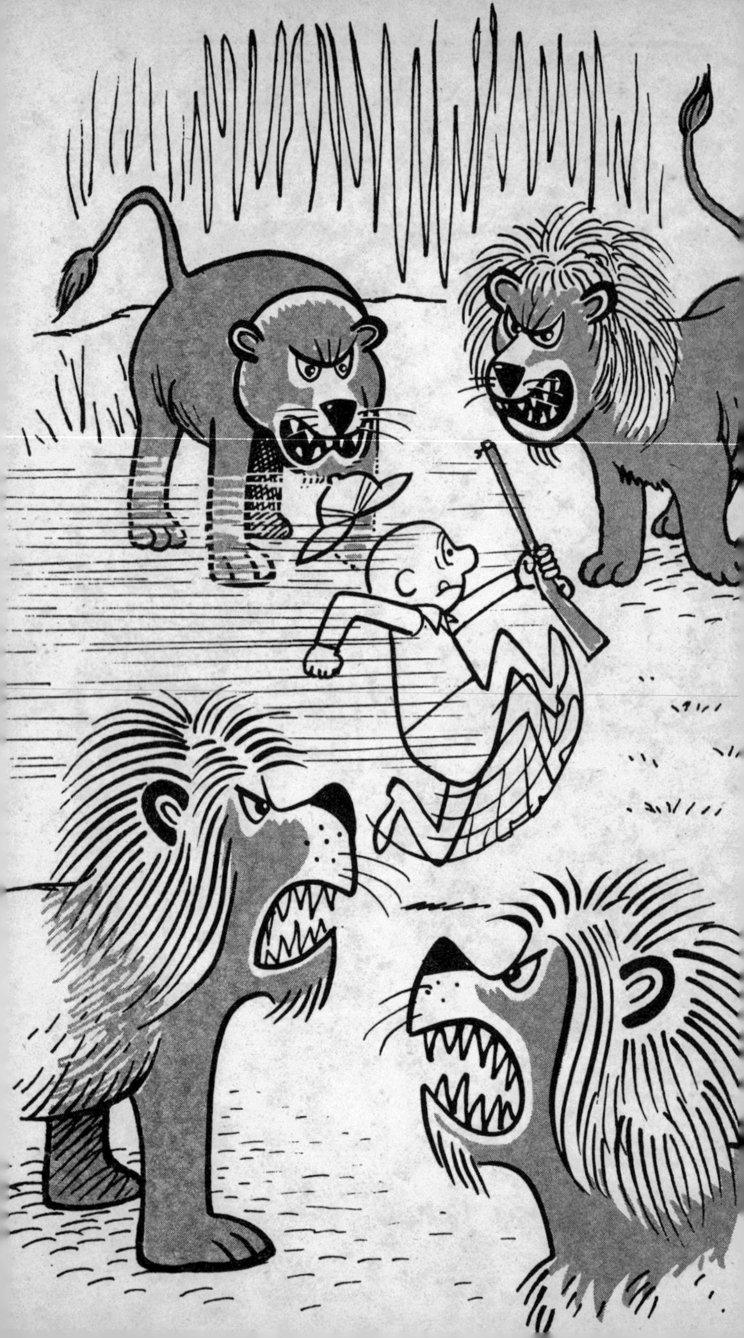

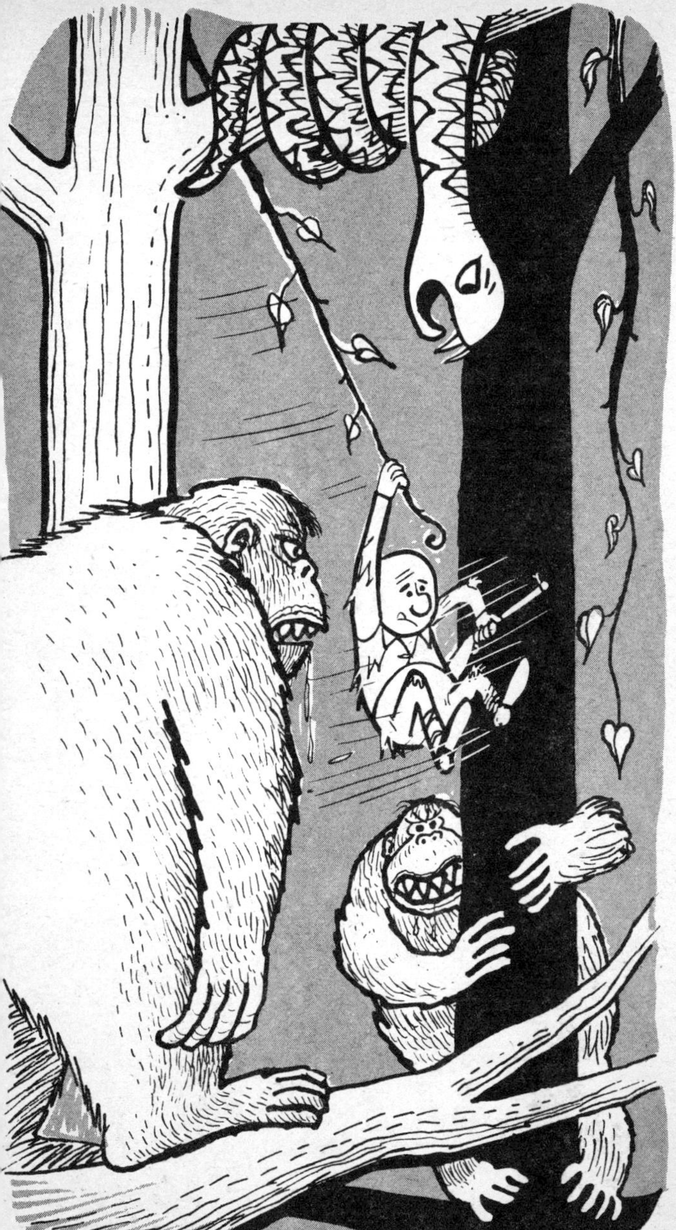

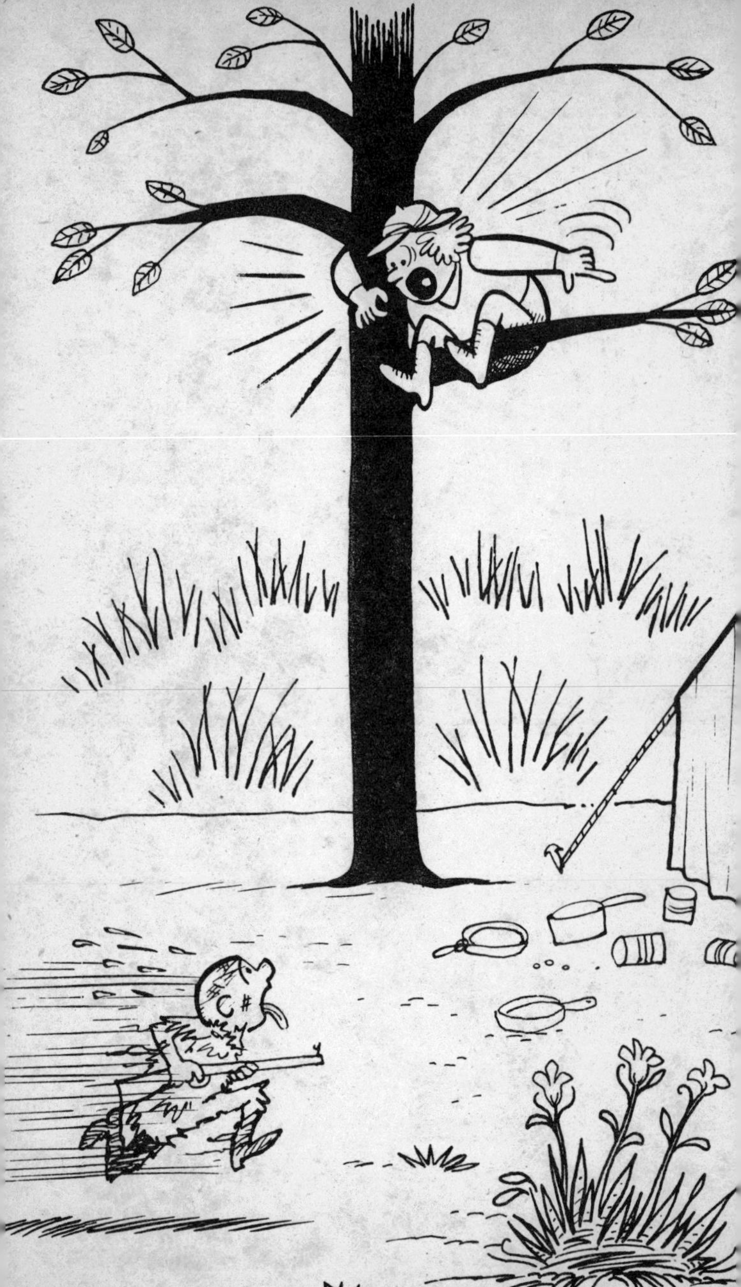

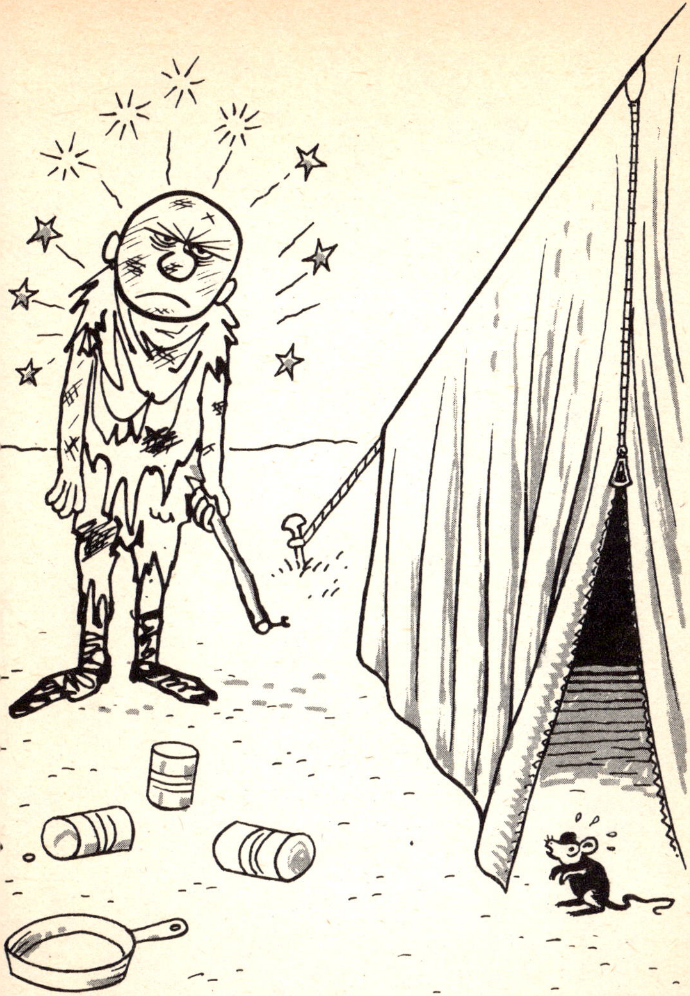

Cartoon Folio Number Six

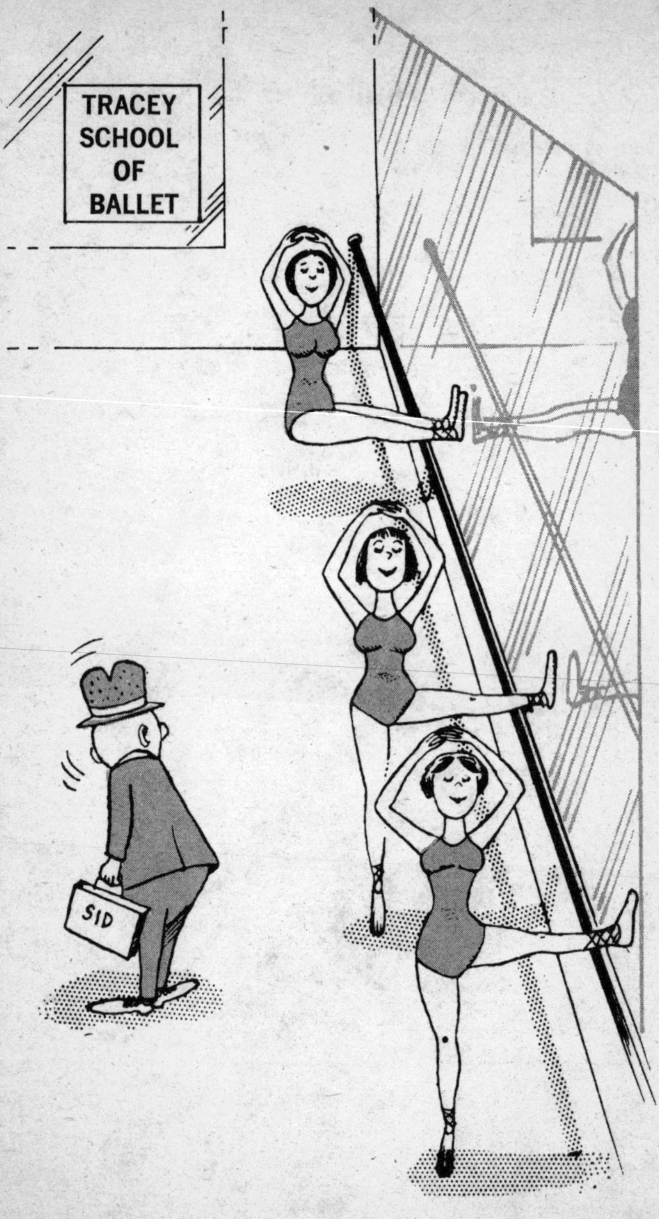
TRACEY SCHOOL OF BALLET
SID

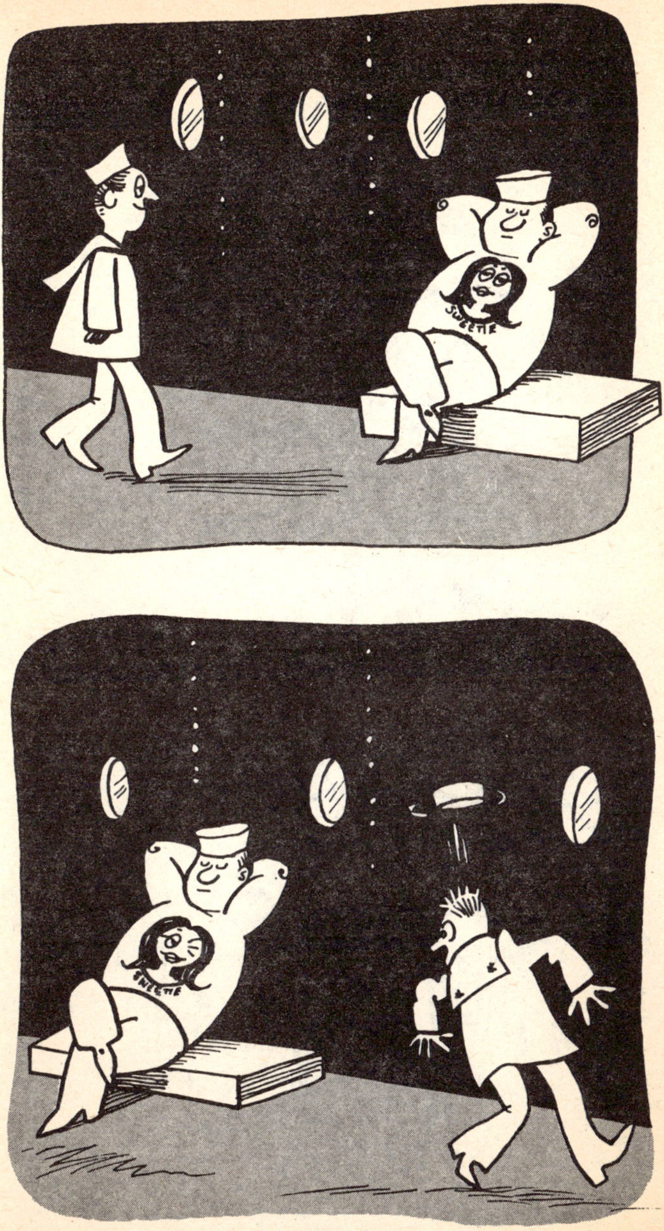
SWEETIE
SWEETIE

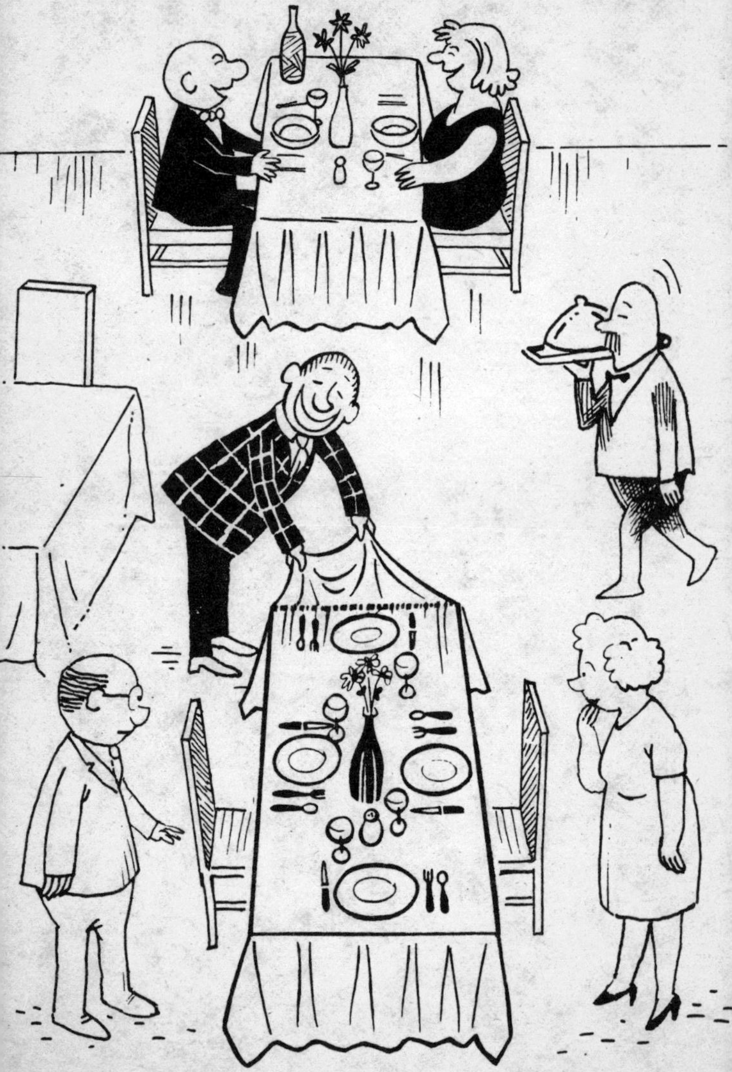

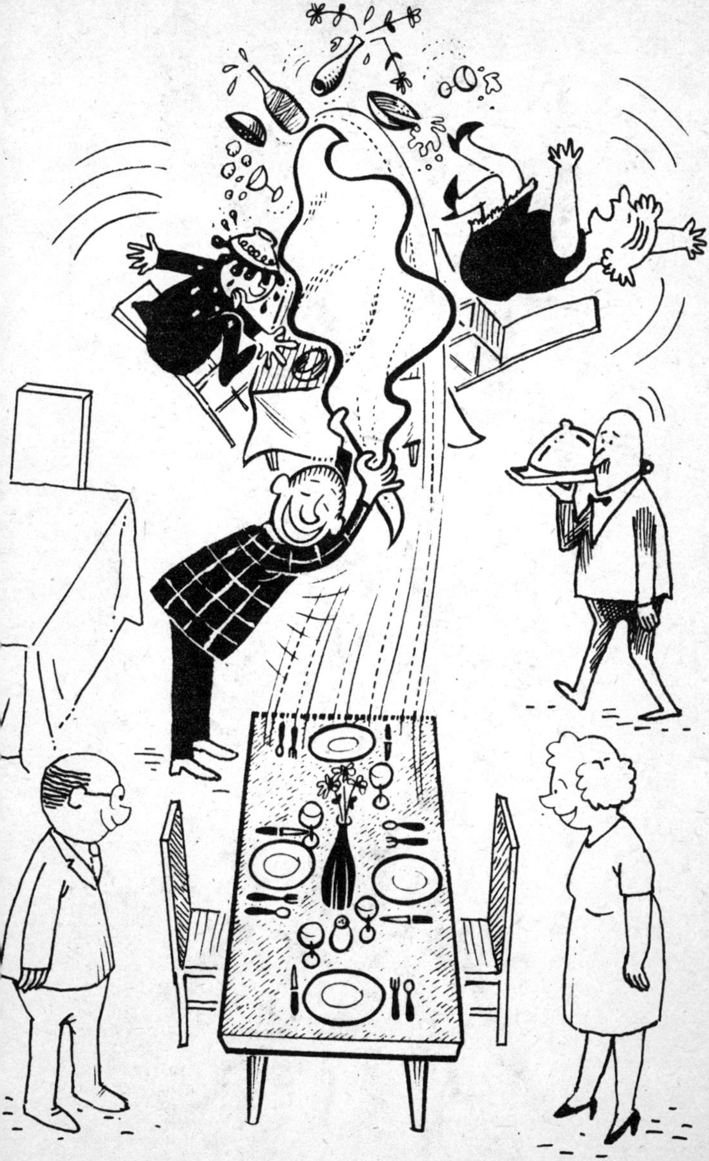

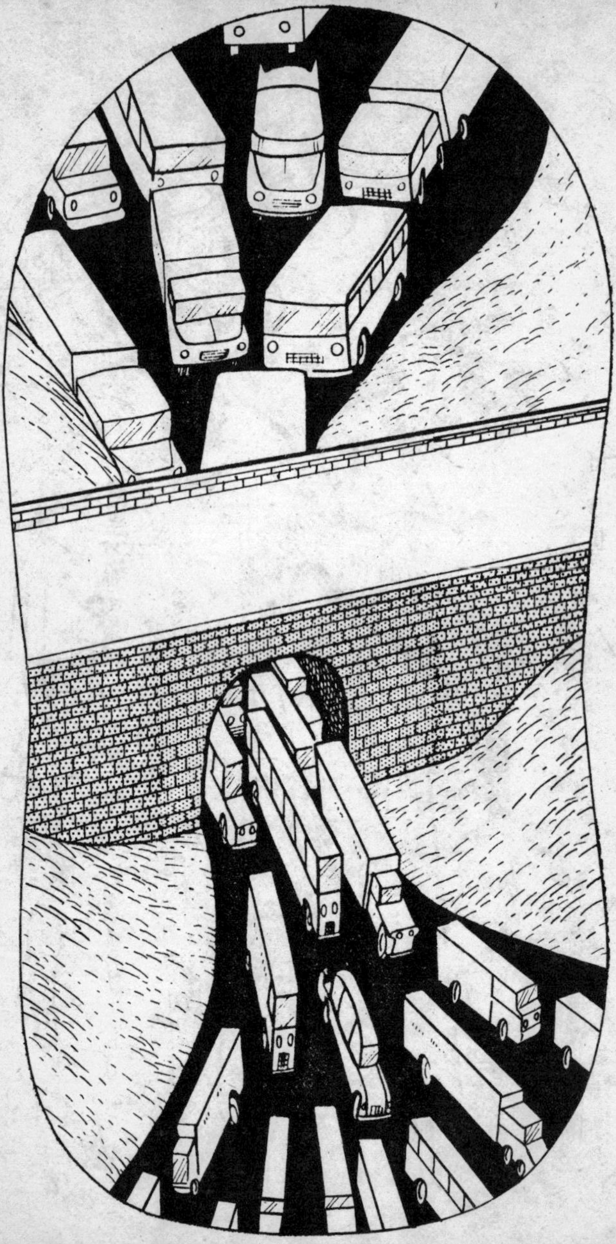

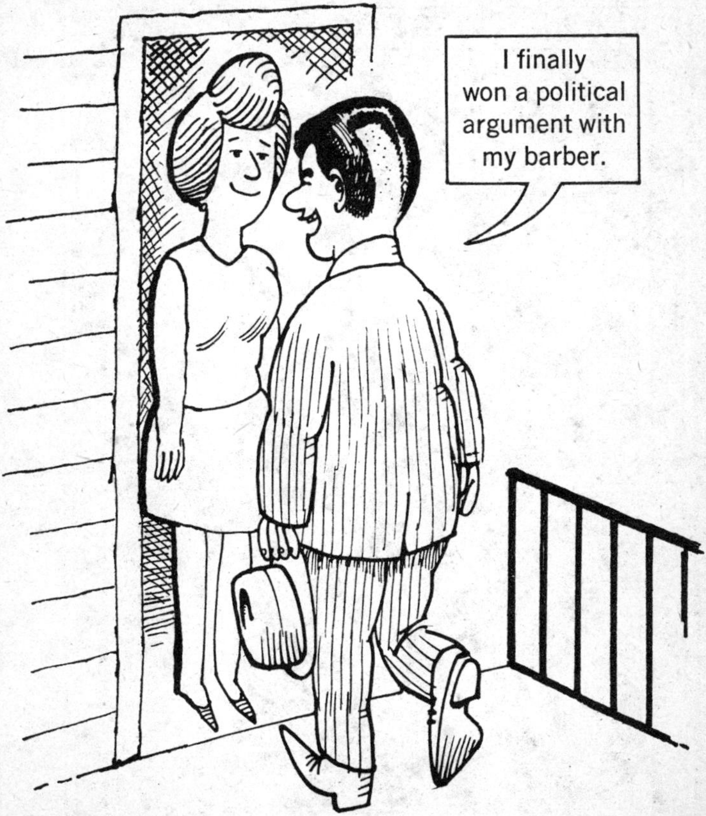
I finally won a political argument with my barber.

A GALLERY OF INFAMOUS JAFFEES

CYRIL LUSTIG JAFFEE
Shepherd, poet, and passionate animal lover.
Denounced by the ASPCA.

A SHARPSHOOTING TRYOUT THAT DOESN'T QUITE PAN OUT

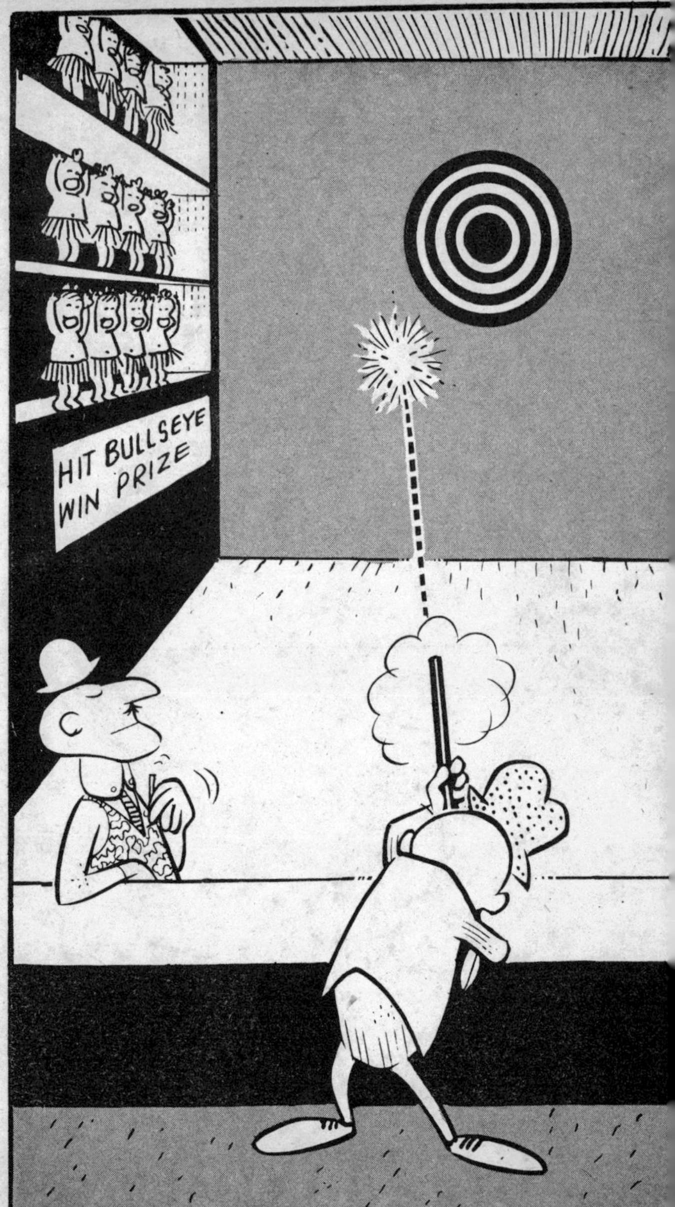
HIT BULLSEYE
WIN PRIZE

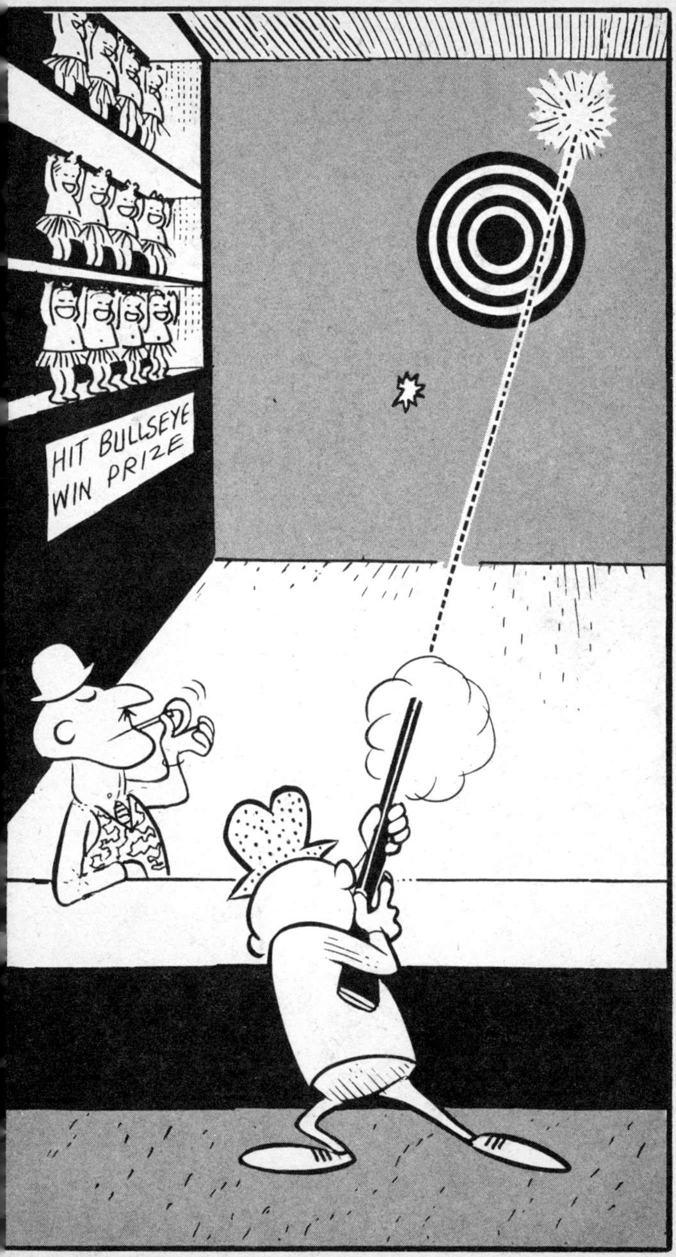
HIT BULLSEYE
WIN PRIZE

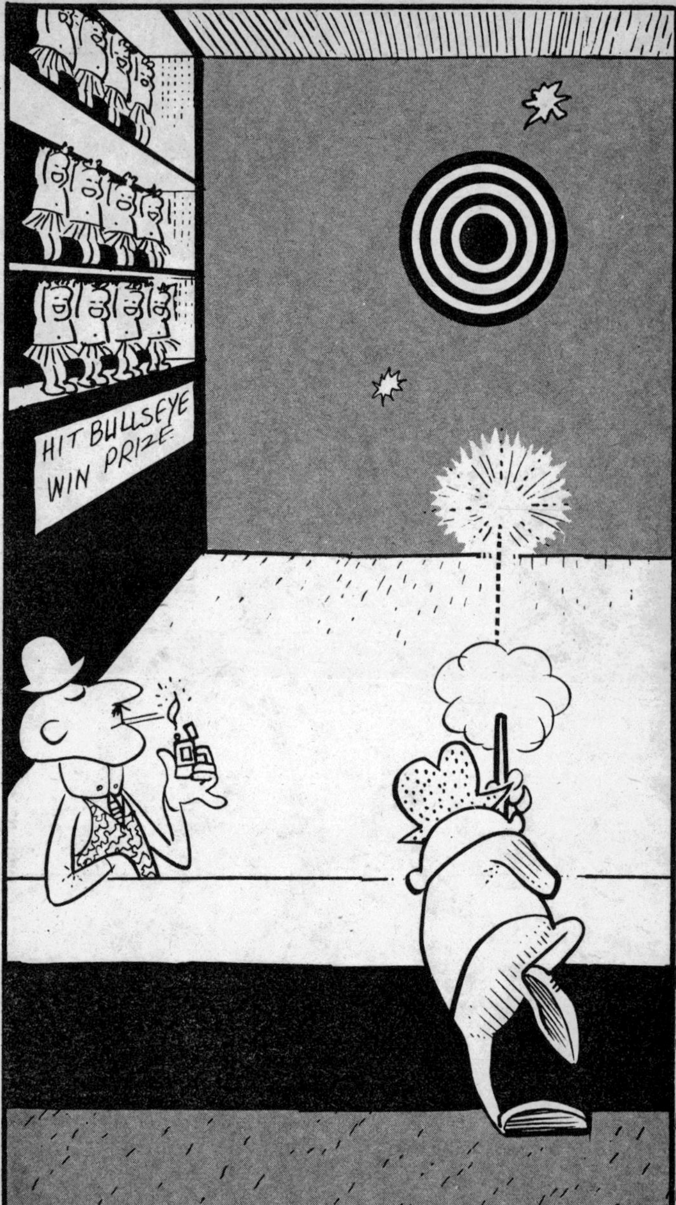
HIT BULLSEYE
WIN PRIZE

HIT BULLSEYE
WIN PRIZE

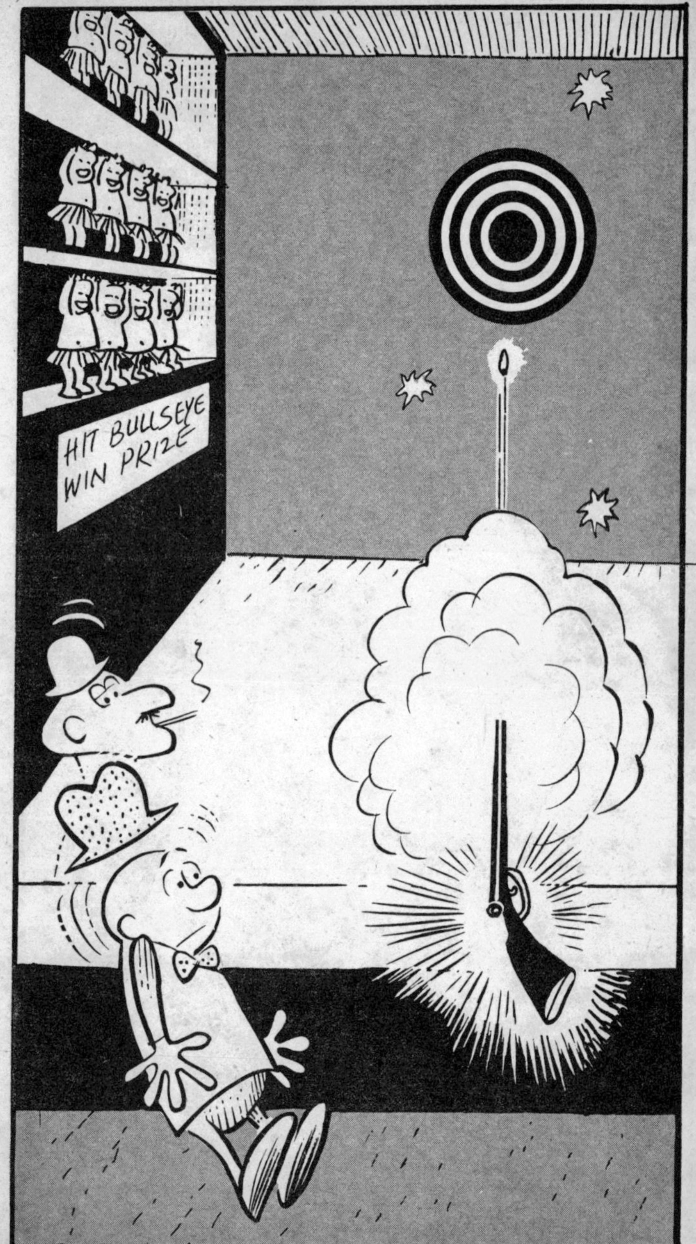
HIT BULLSEYE
WIN PRIZE

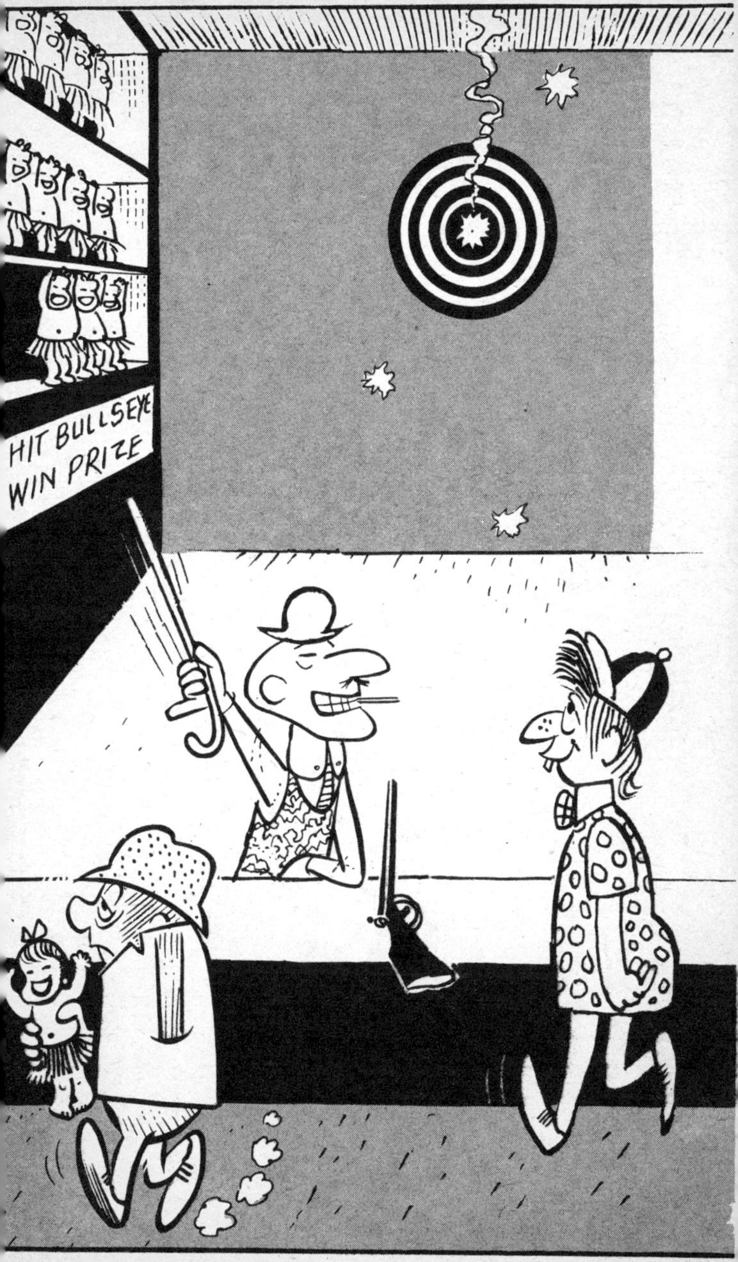
HIT BULLSEYE
WIN PRIZE

Cartoon Folio Number Seven

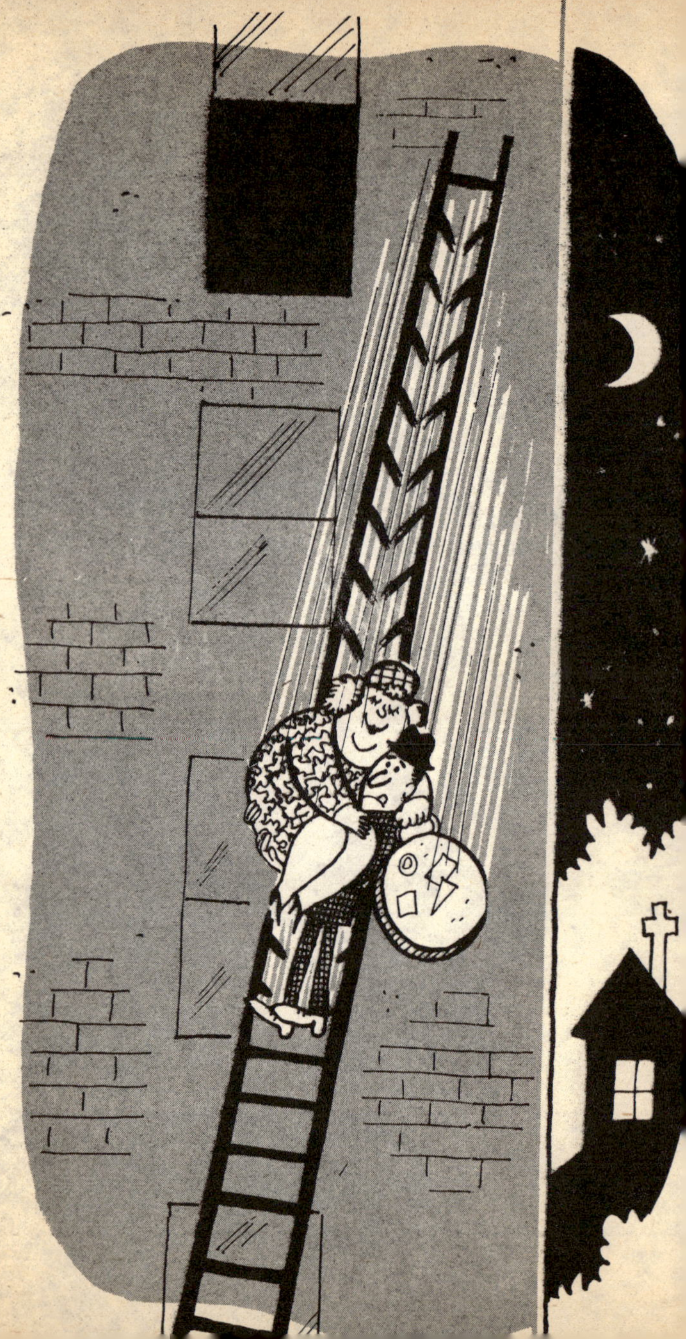

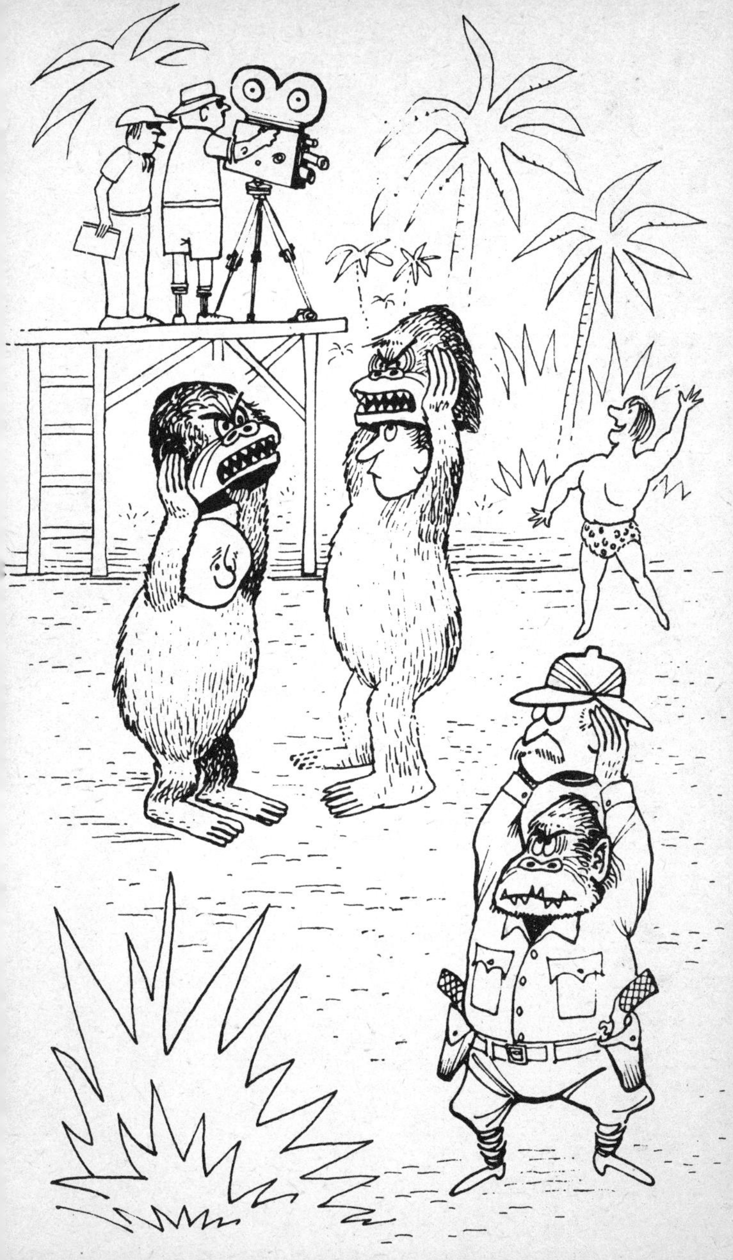

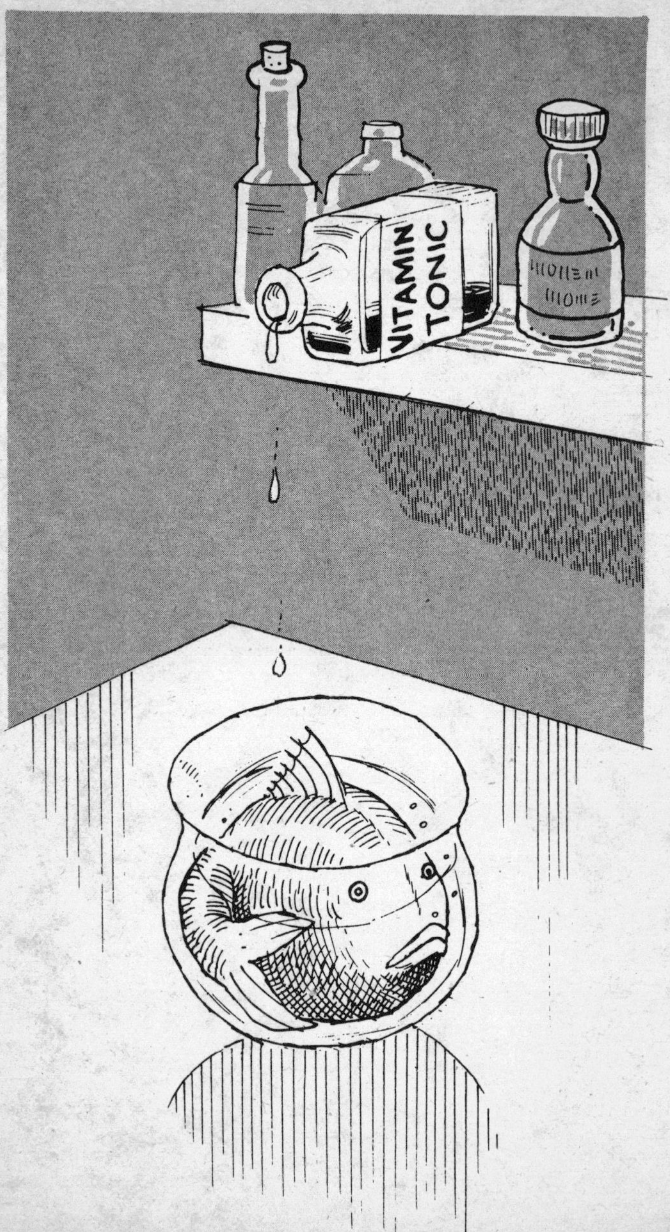
VITAMIN TONIC

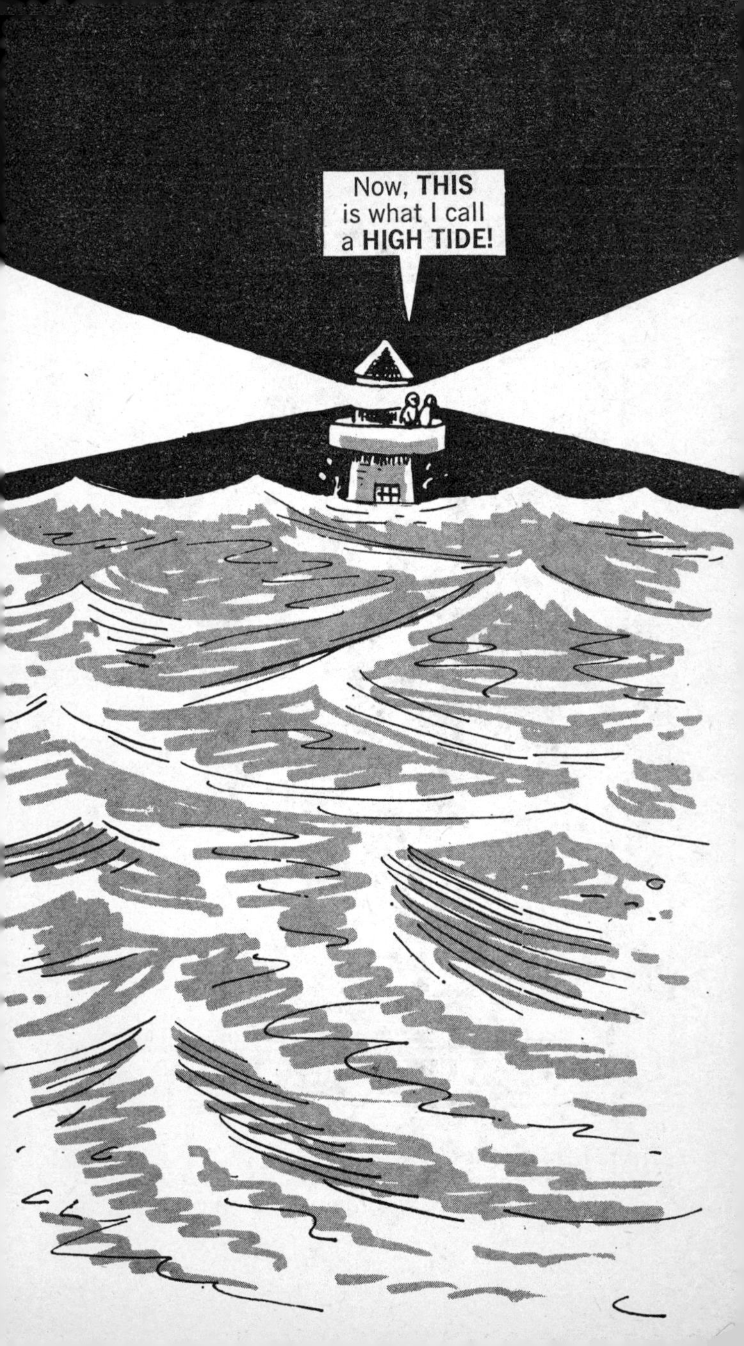
Now, THIS is what I call a HIGH TIDE!

A GALLERY OF INFAMOUS JAFFEES

DELBERT SNOOKER JAFFEE
Renowned gameplayer; creator of lawn billiards.

A FISHING EVENT WITH TIME THAT'S ILL-SPENT

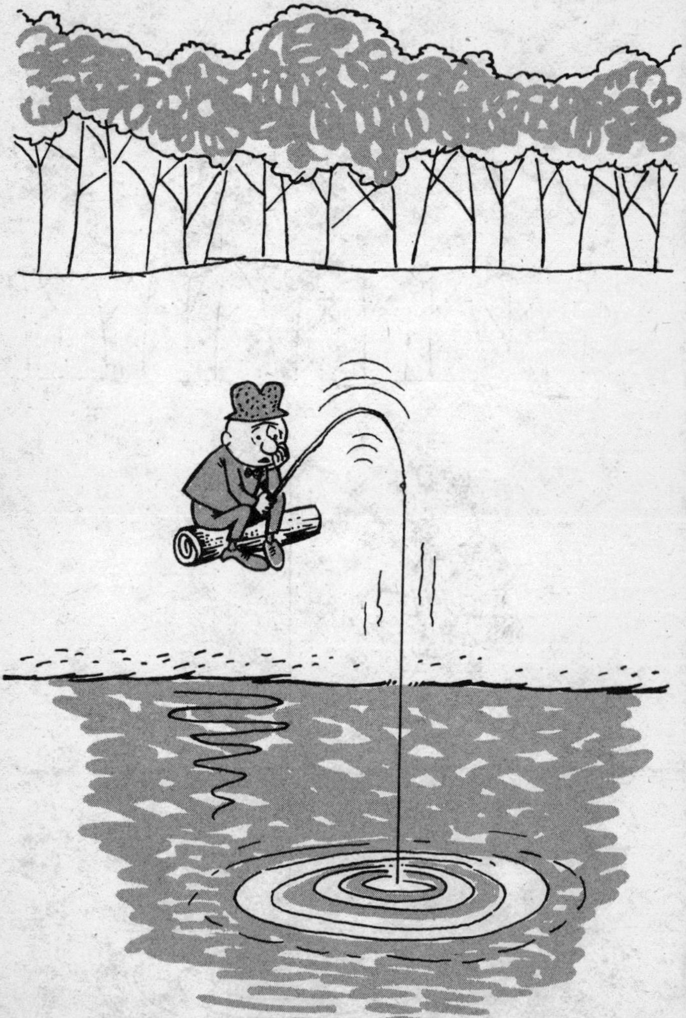

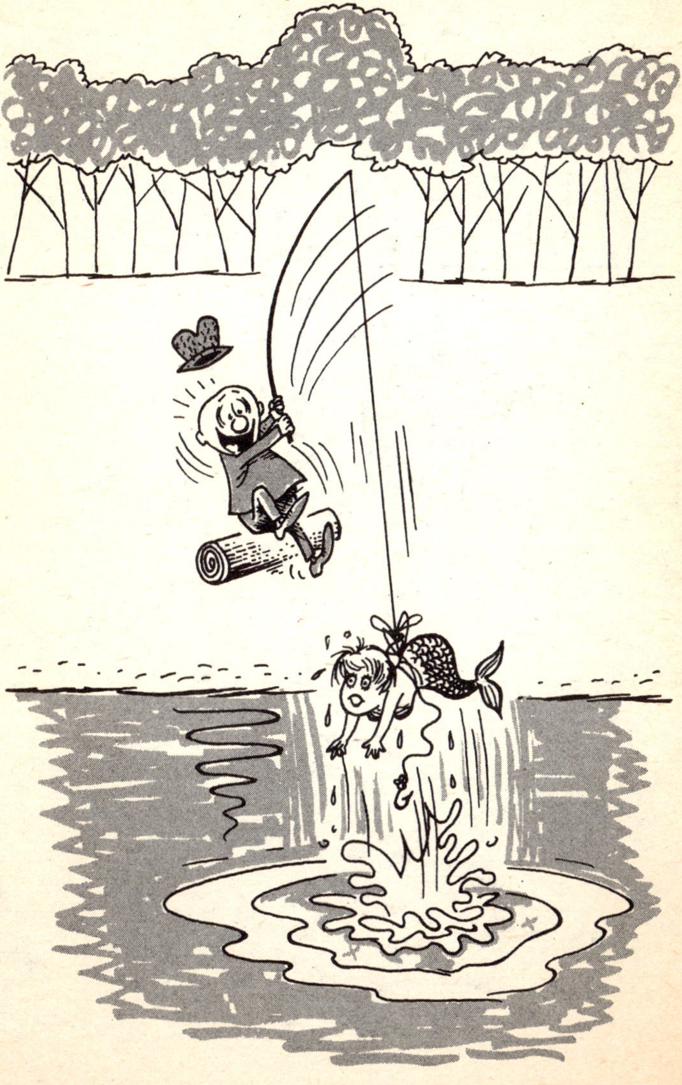

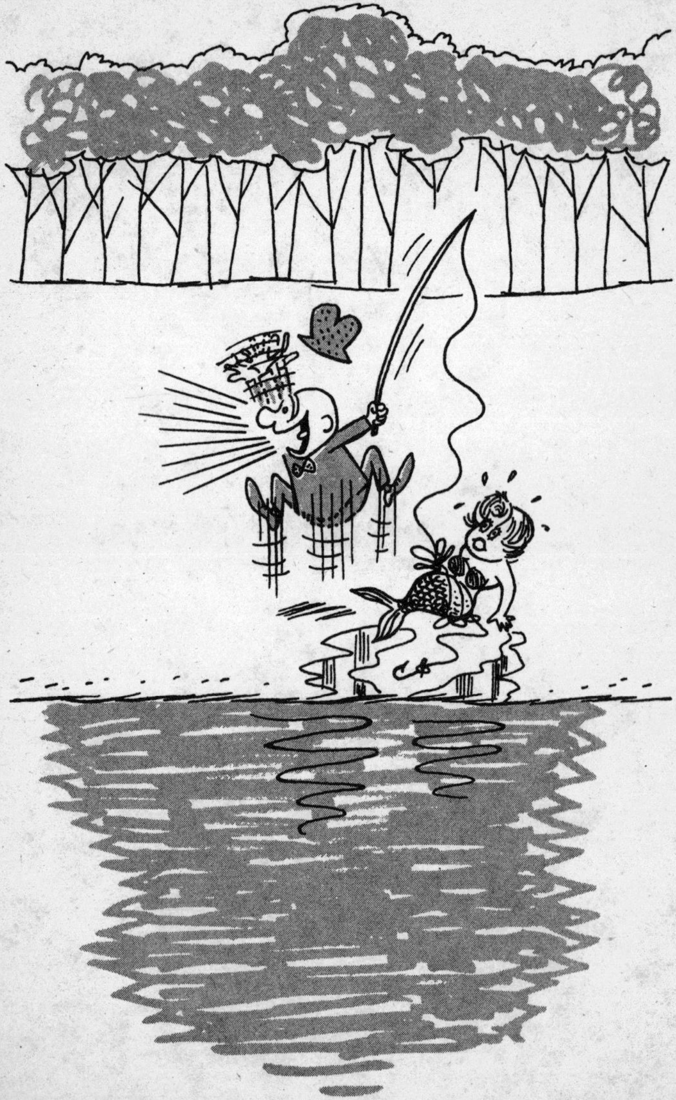

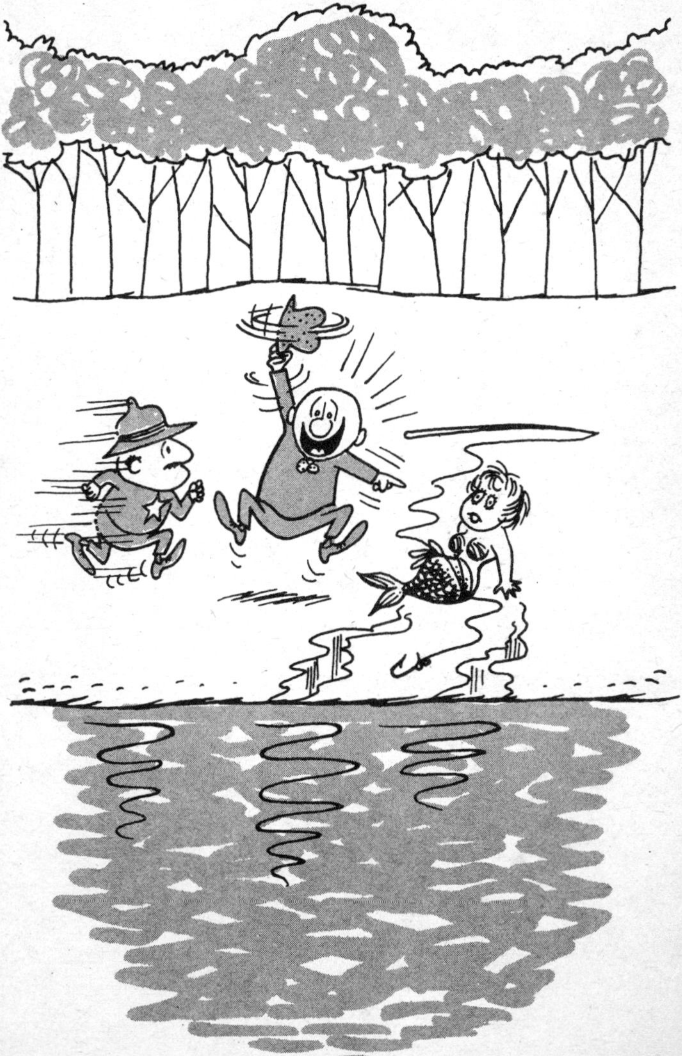

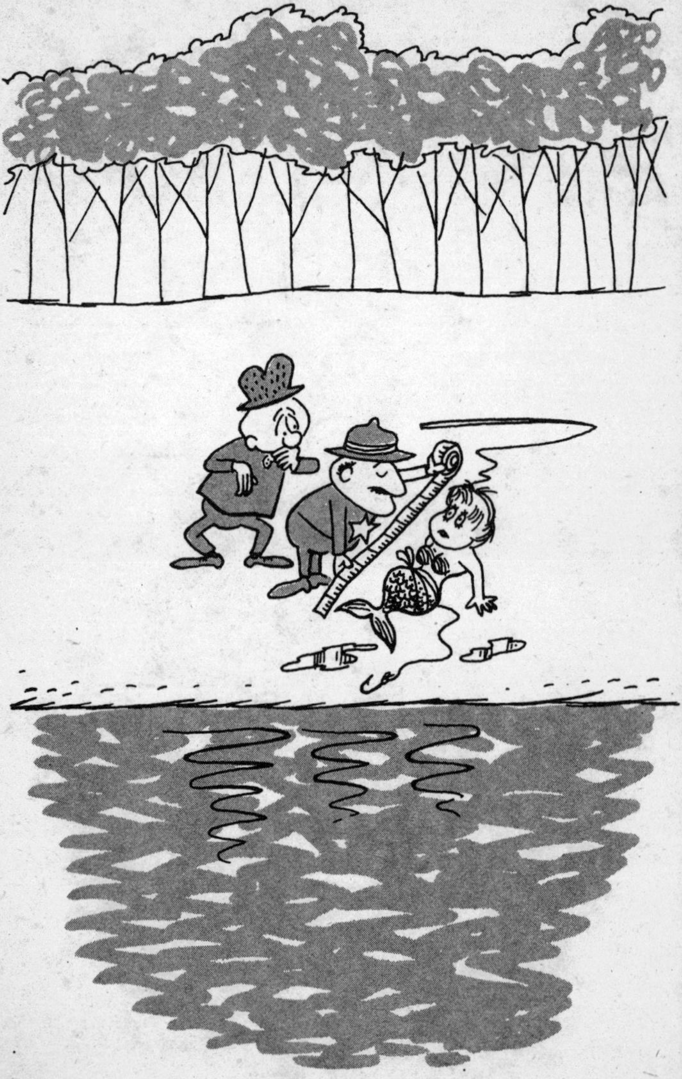

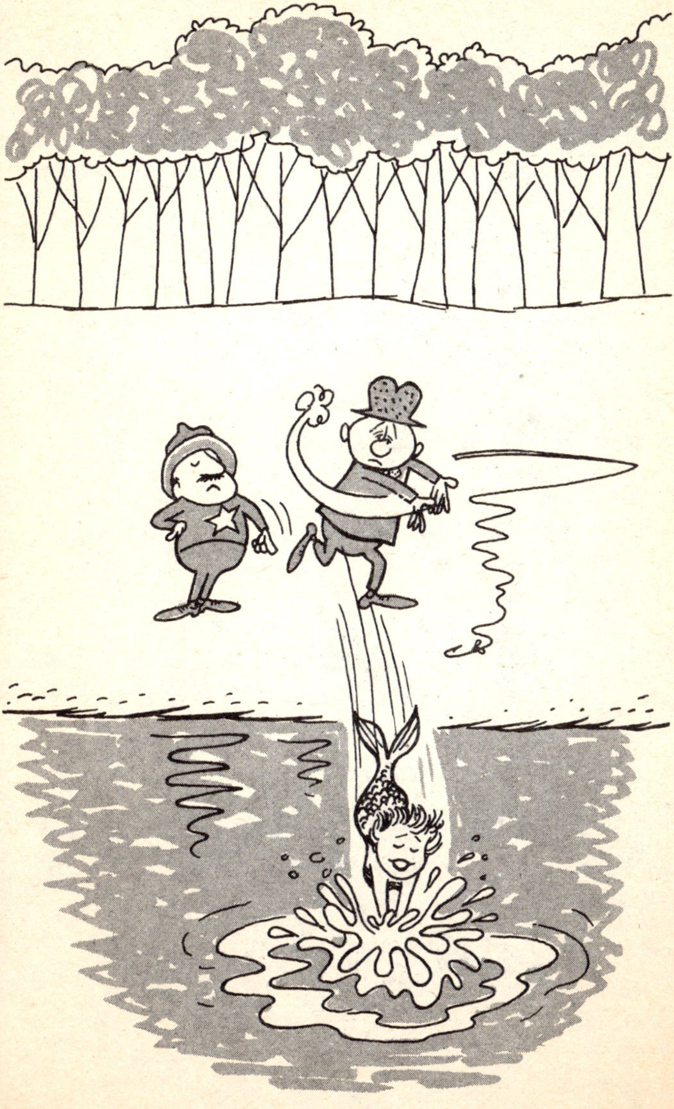

Cartoon Folio Number Eight

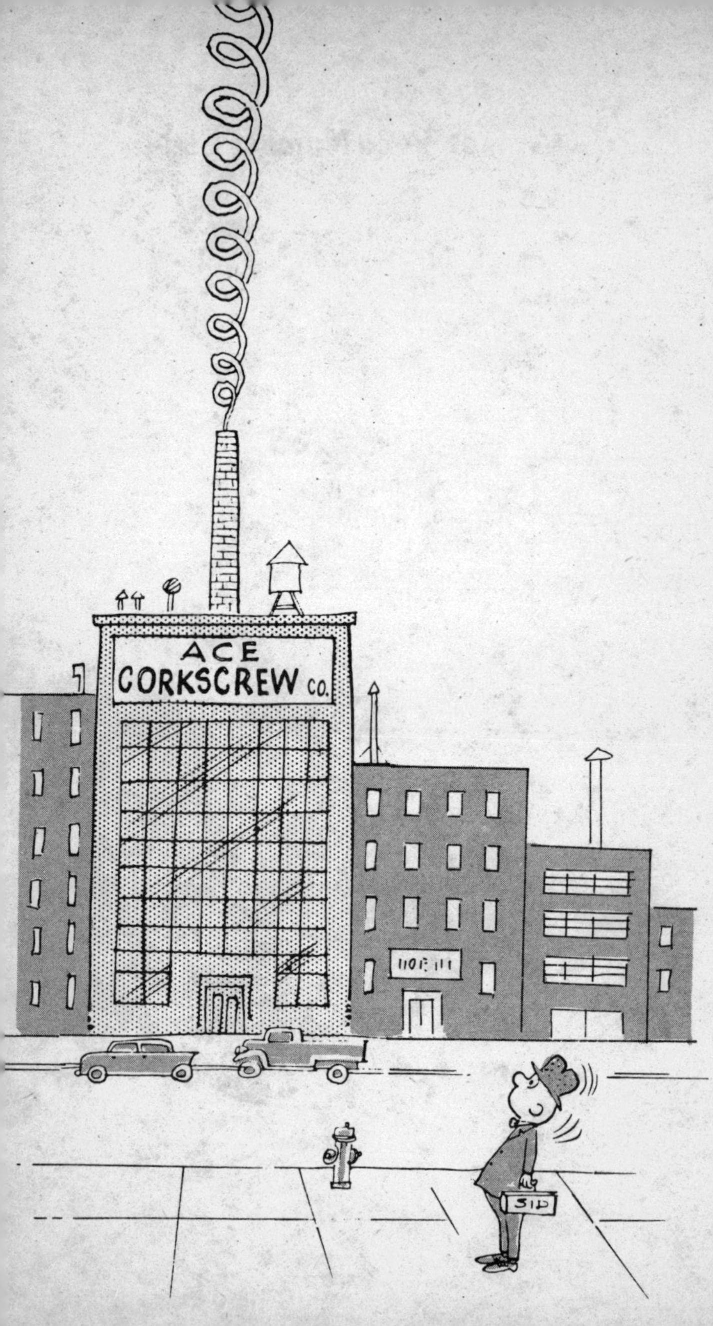
ACE
CORKSCREW CO.
SID

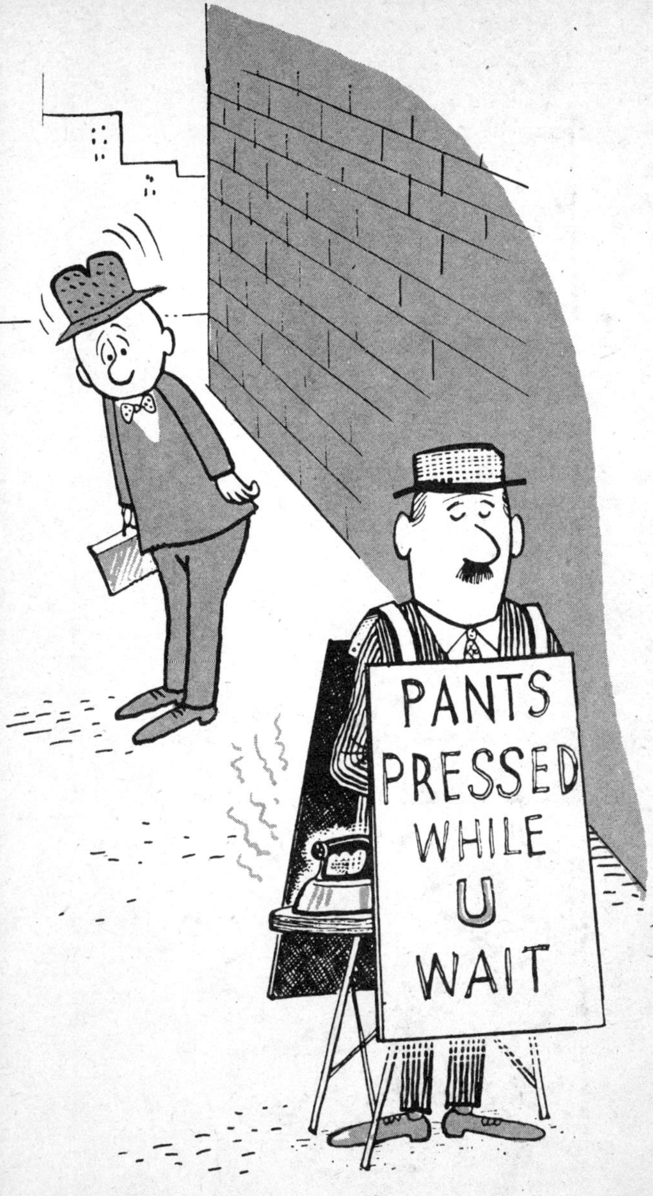
PANTS
PRESSED
WHILE
U
WAIT

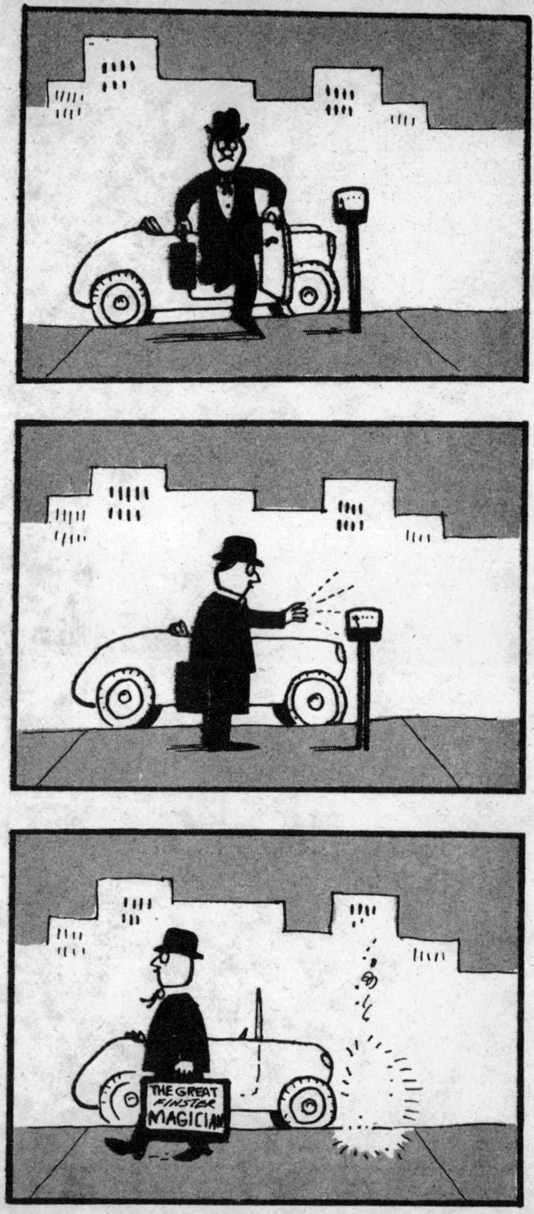
THE GREAT
FINSTER
MAGICIAN

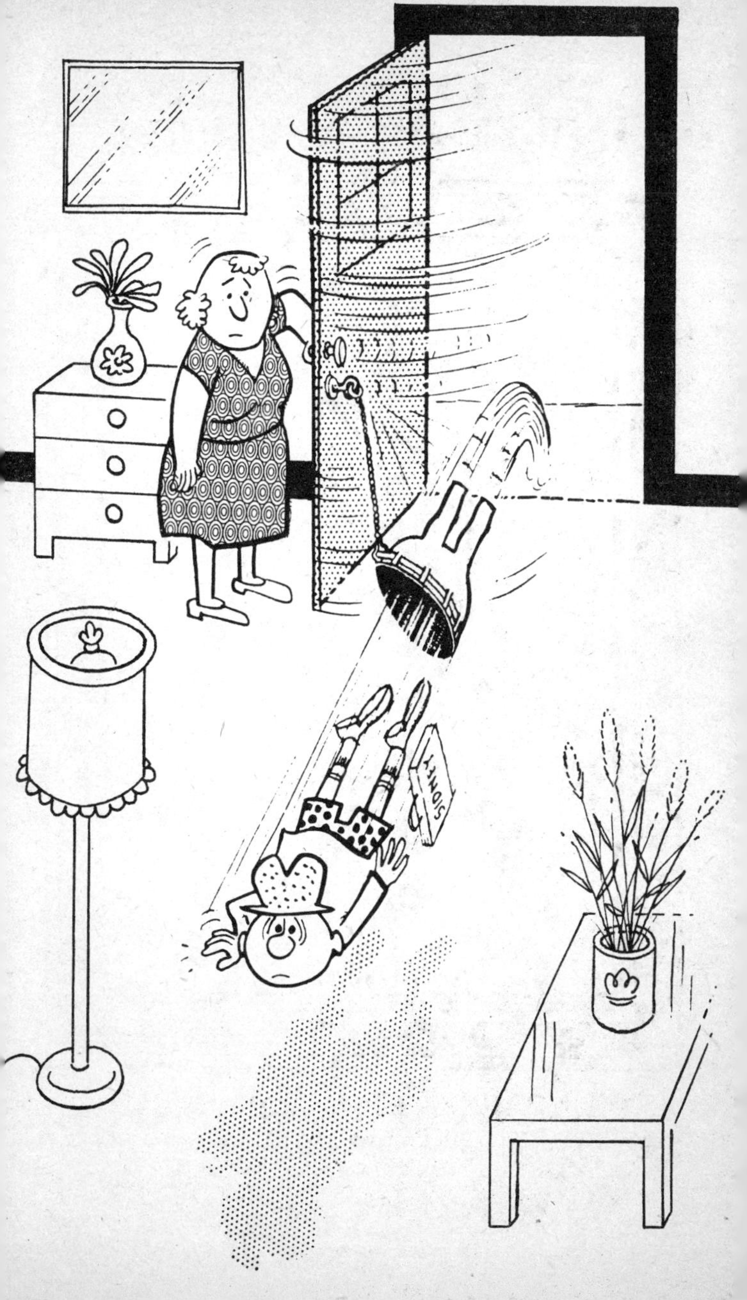
SIDNEY

A GALLERY OF INFAMOUS JAFFEES

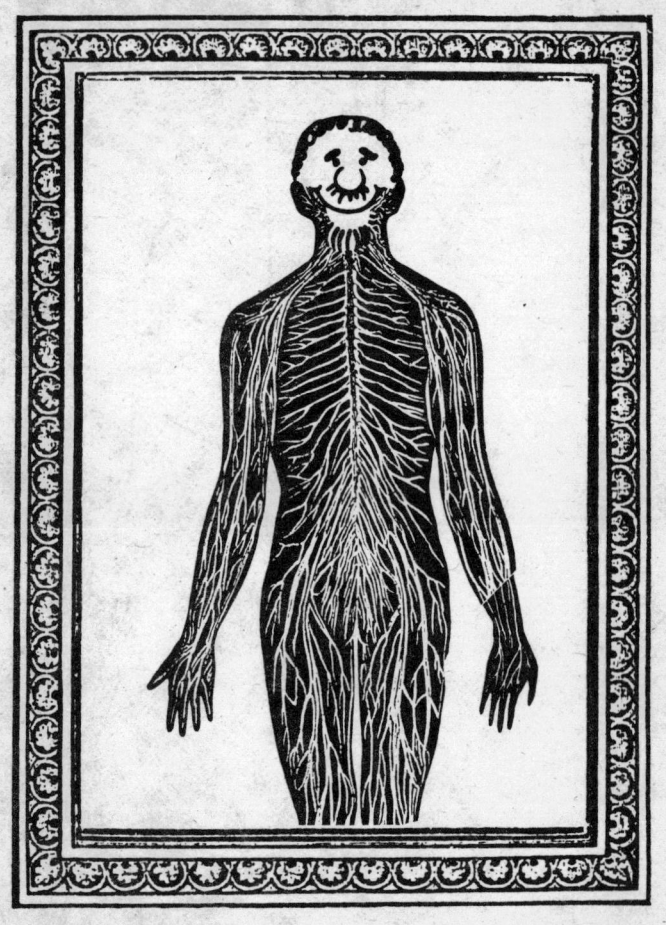

SEYMOUR "THE BOD" JAFFEE
Male medical model best known in surgical textbooks.

A SPACE TRIP ABOVE
THAT NO ONE CAN LOVE

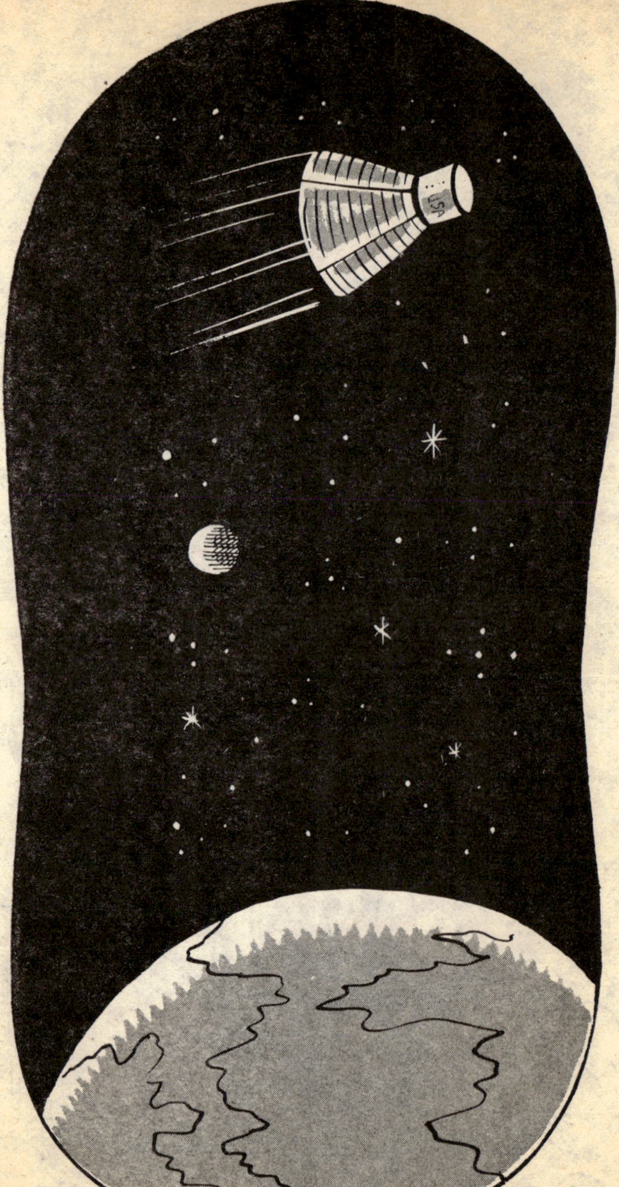
USA

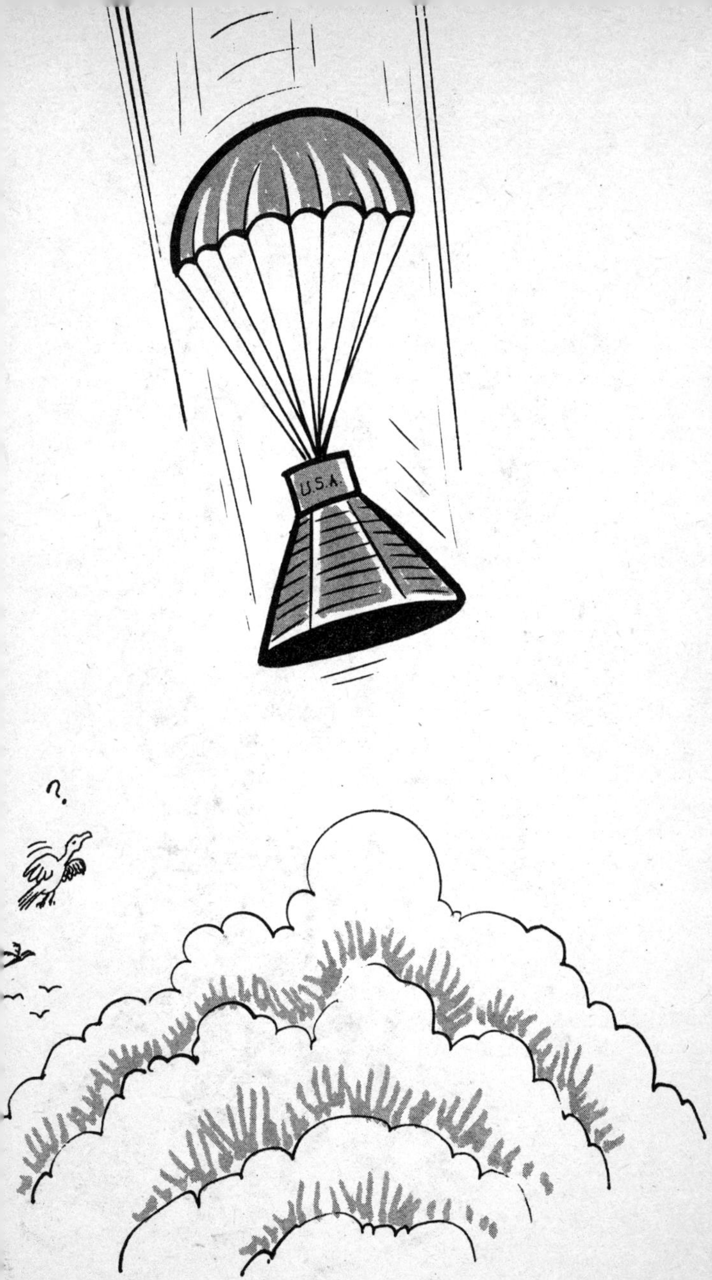
U.S.A.

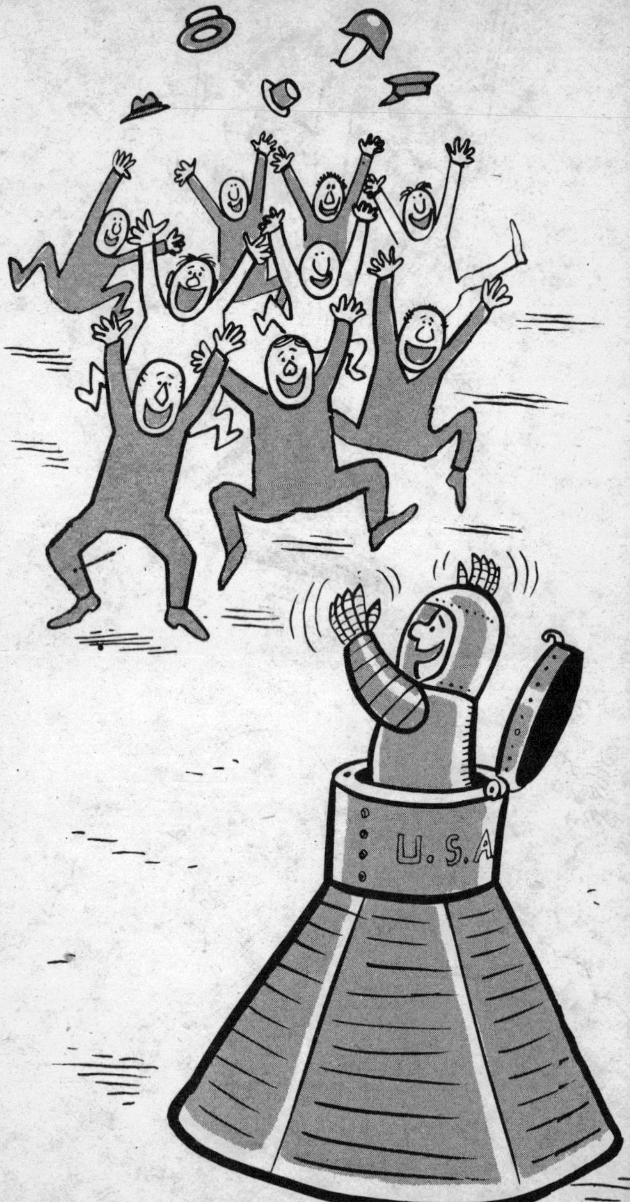
U.S.A

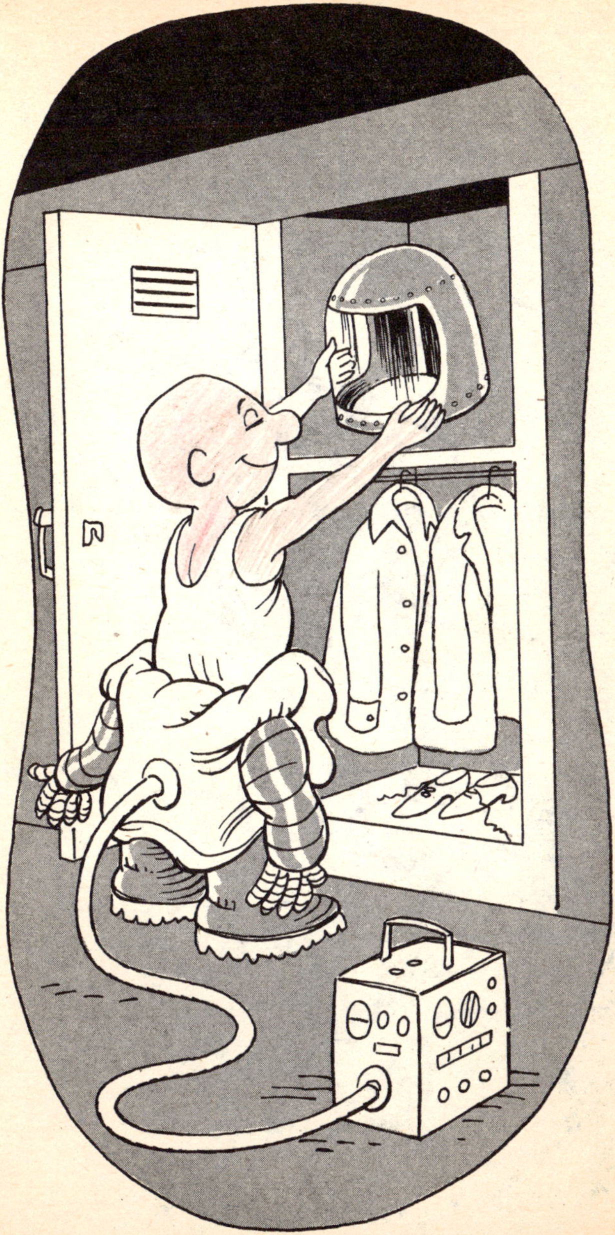

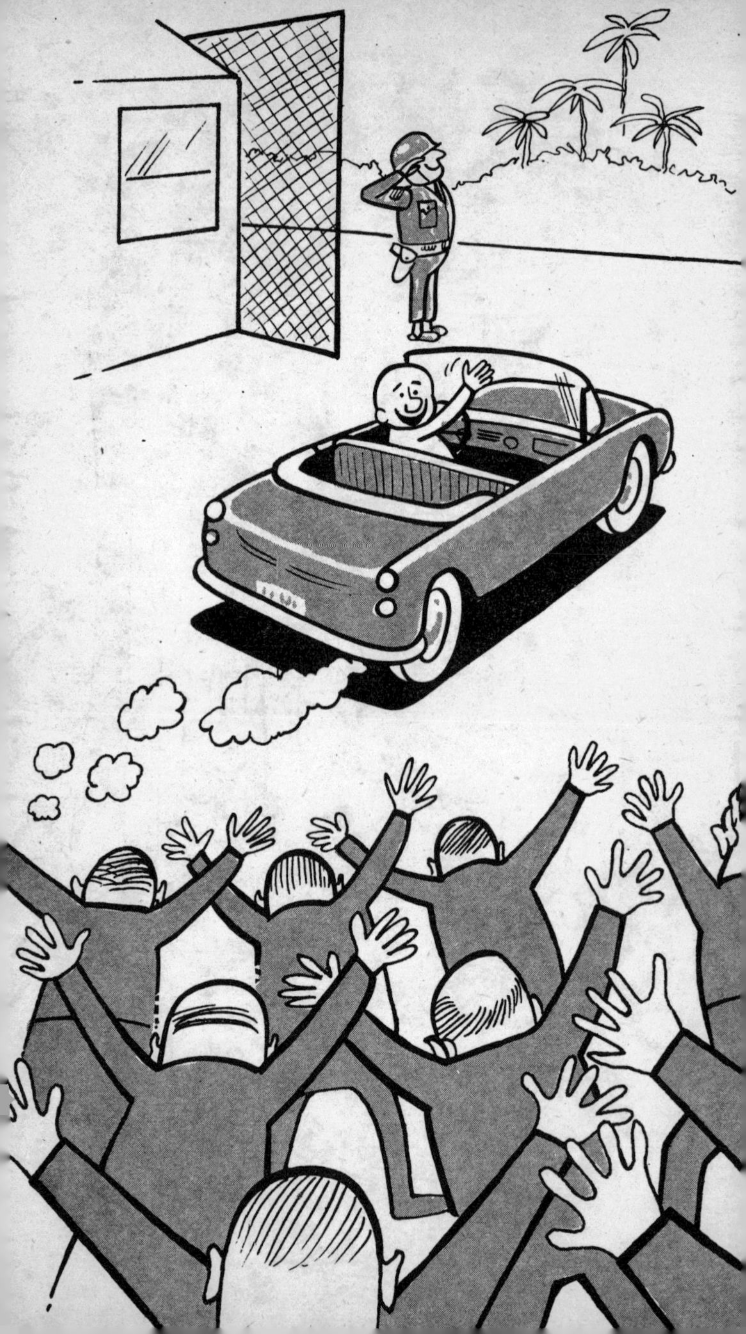

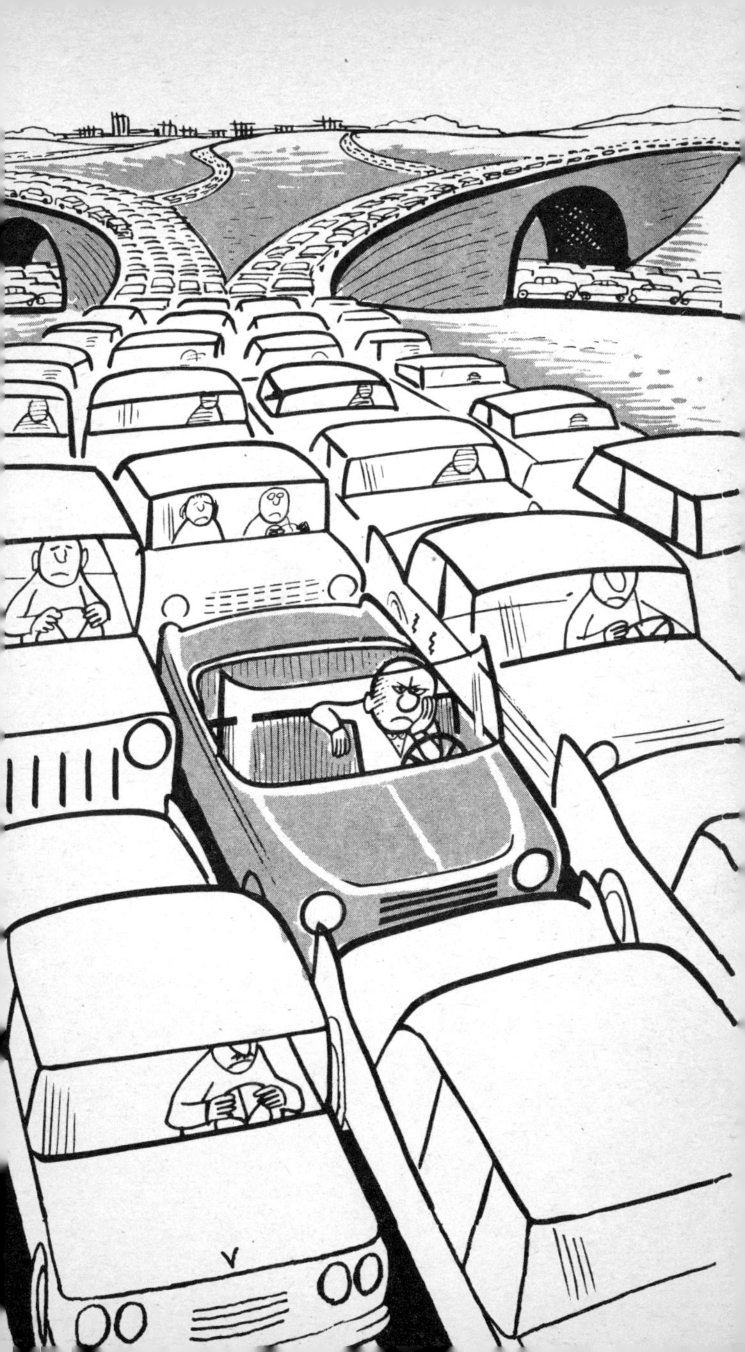

Cartoon Folio Number Nine

> Professionally, we are the happiest of clowns. But after reading this book . . .

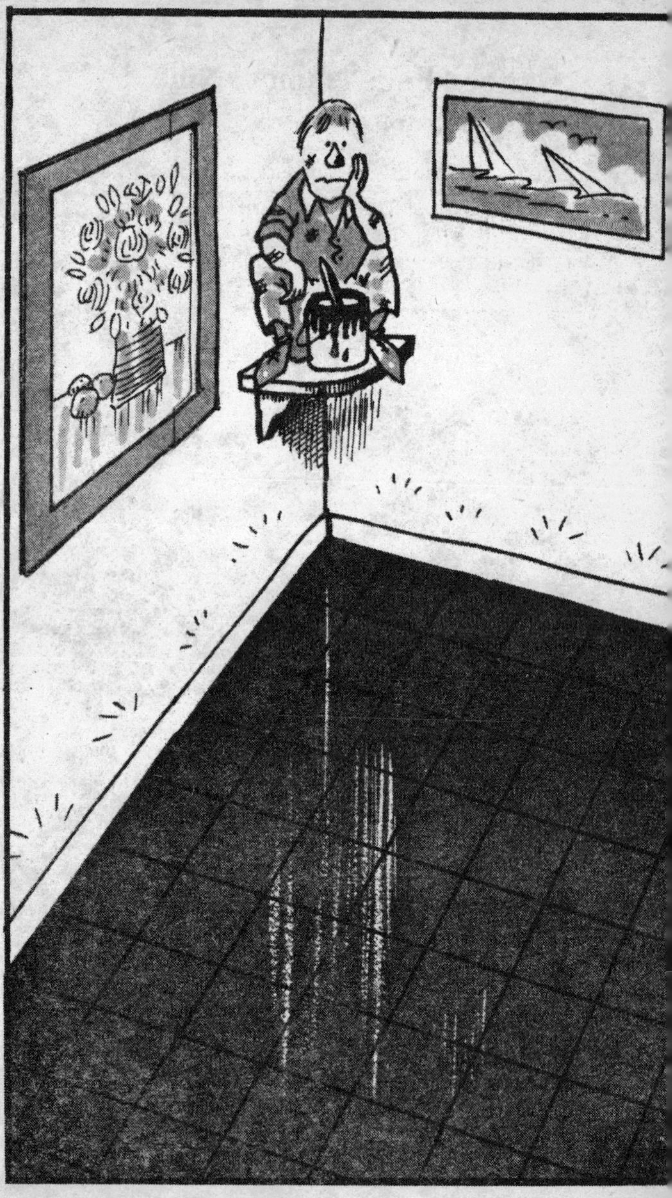

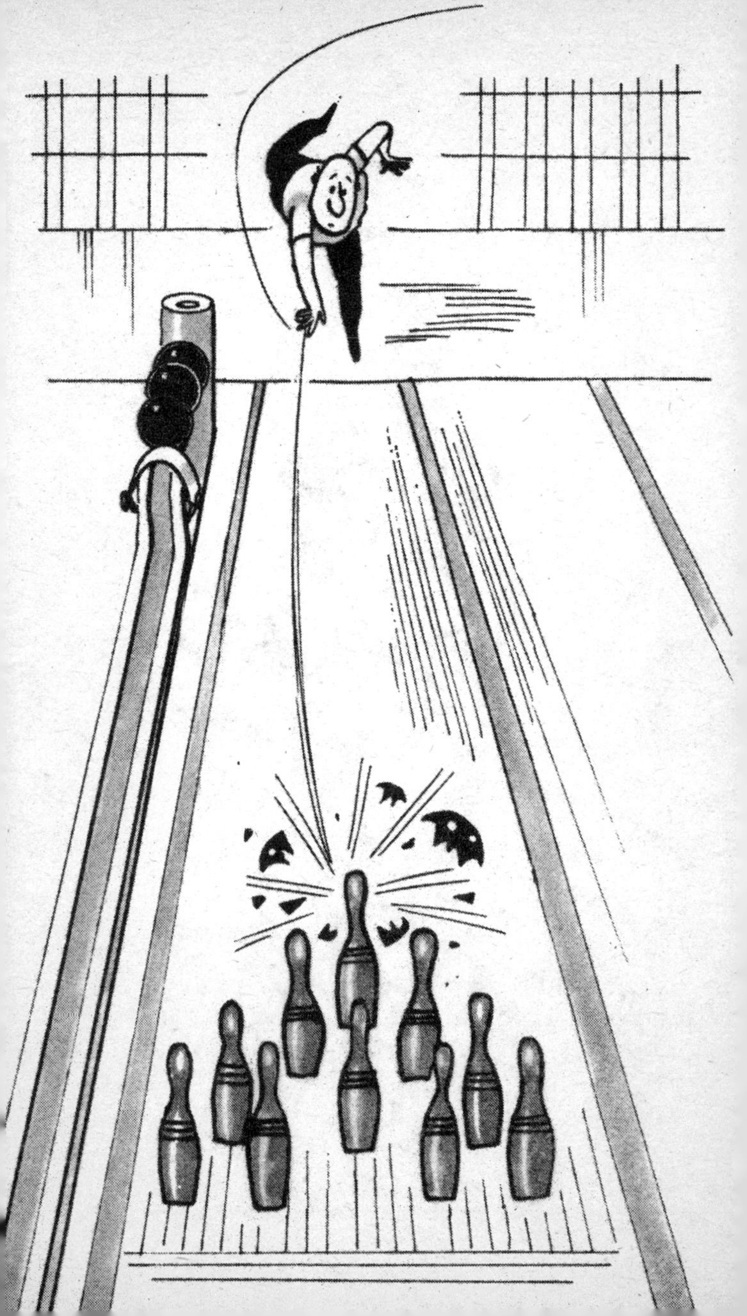

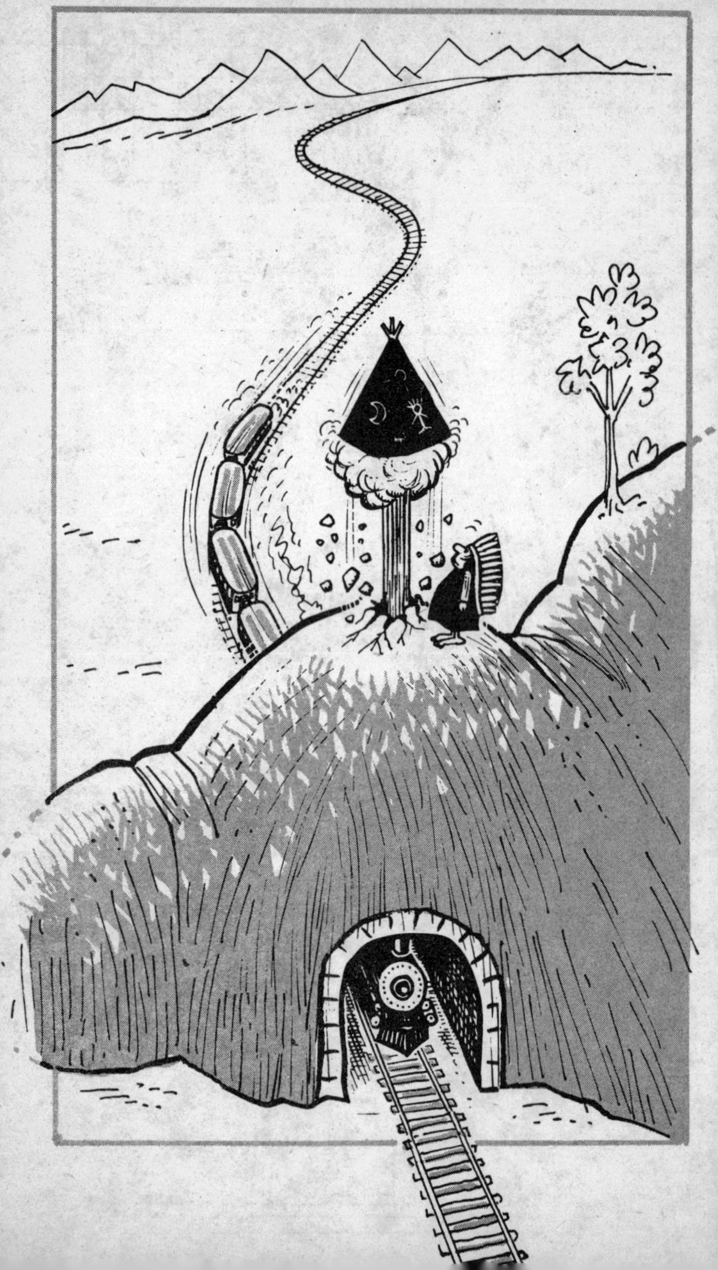

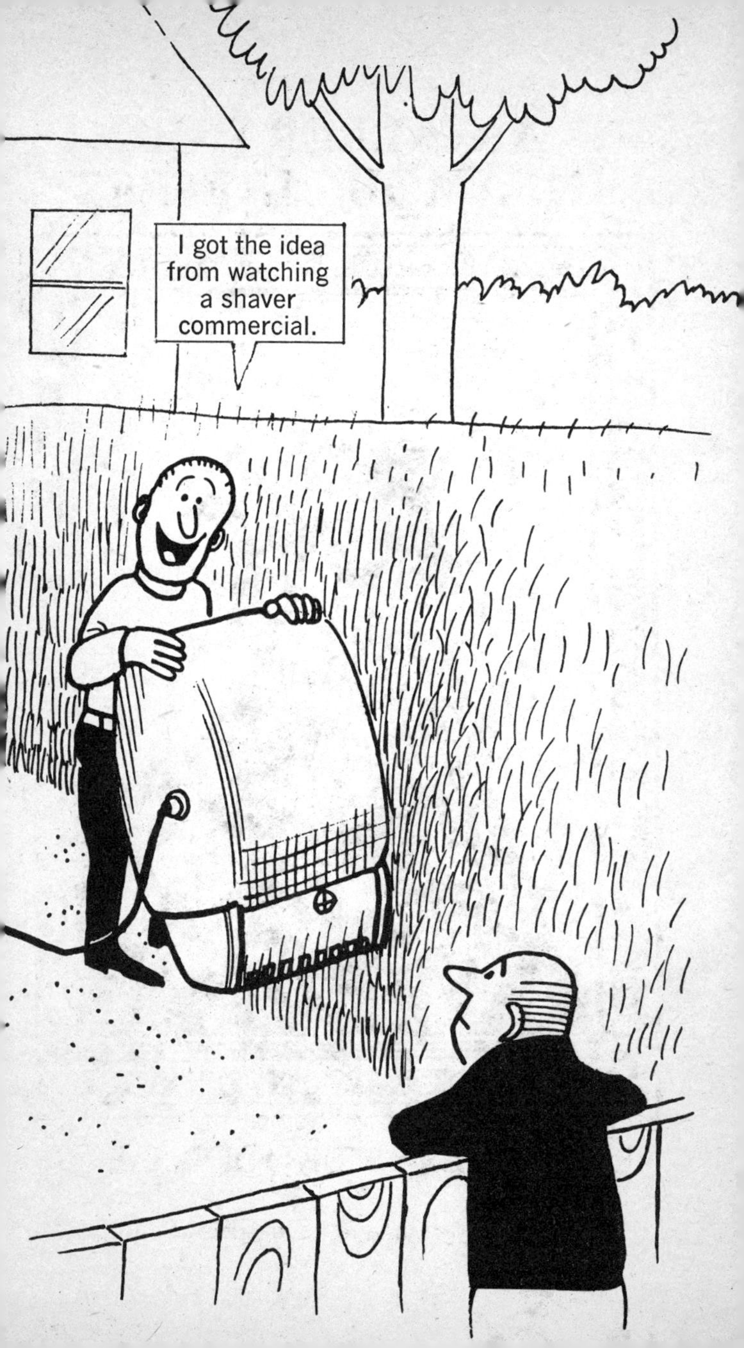
I got the idea from watching a shaver commercial.

A GALLERY OF INFAMOUS JAFFEES

RASPUTIN PASKOODNYAK JAFFEE
Mad monk, pervert, and intimate adviser to Russian czars.

AN ARCTICLIKE TREK THAT'S SILLY AS HECK

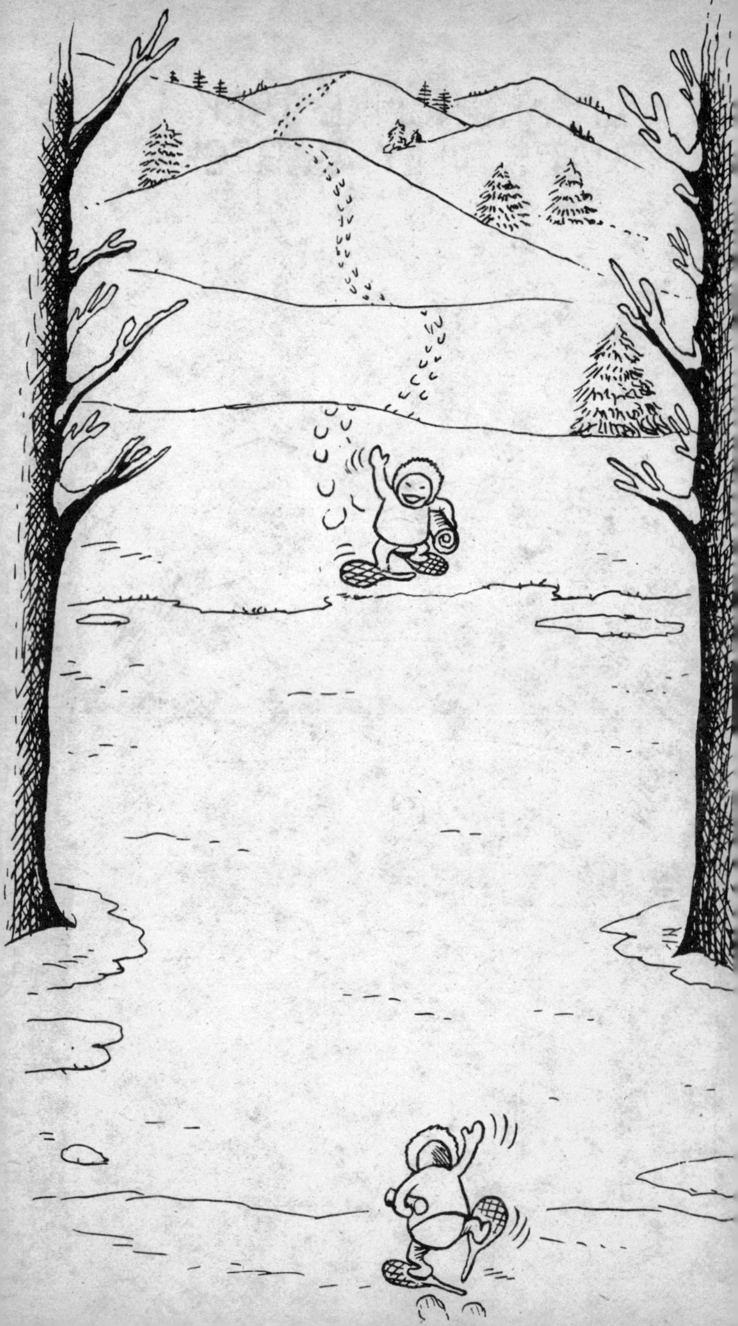

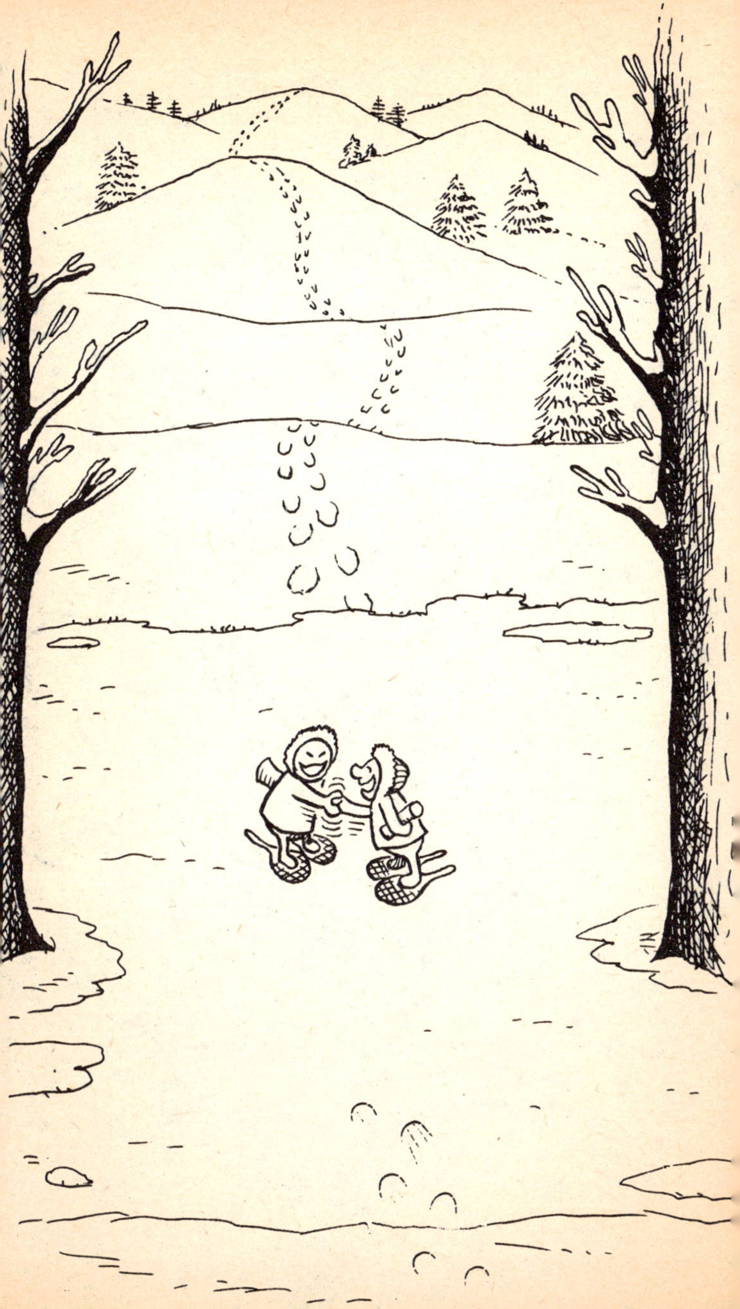

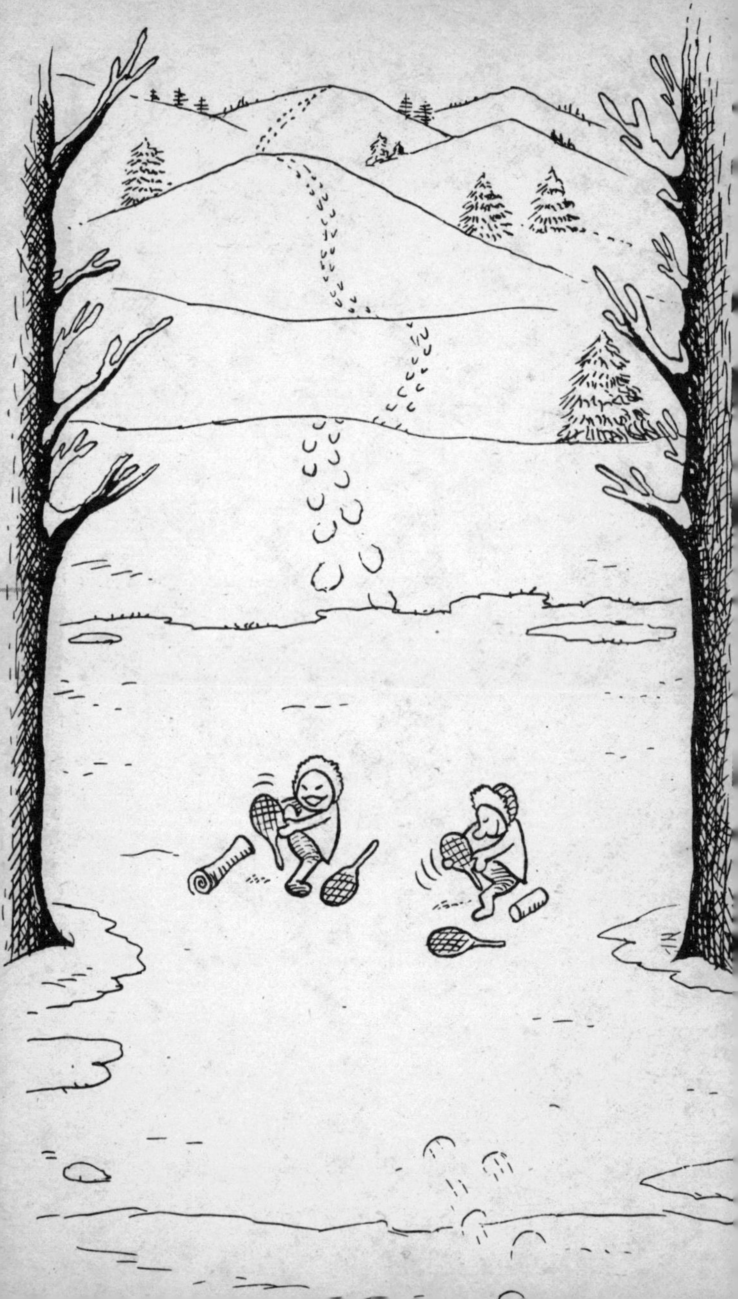

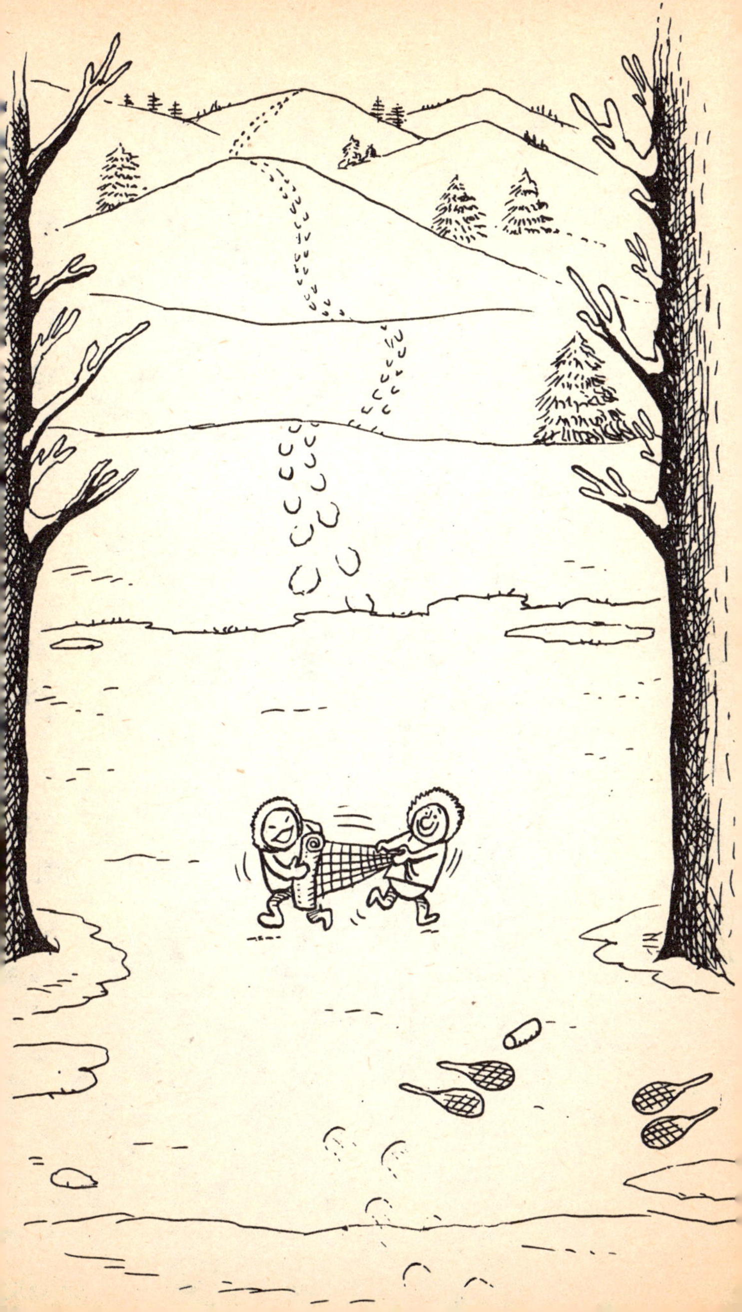

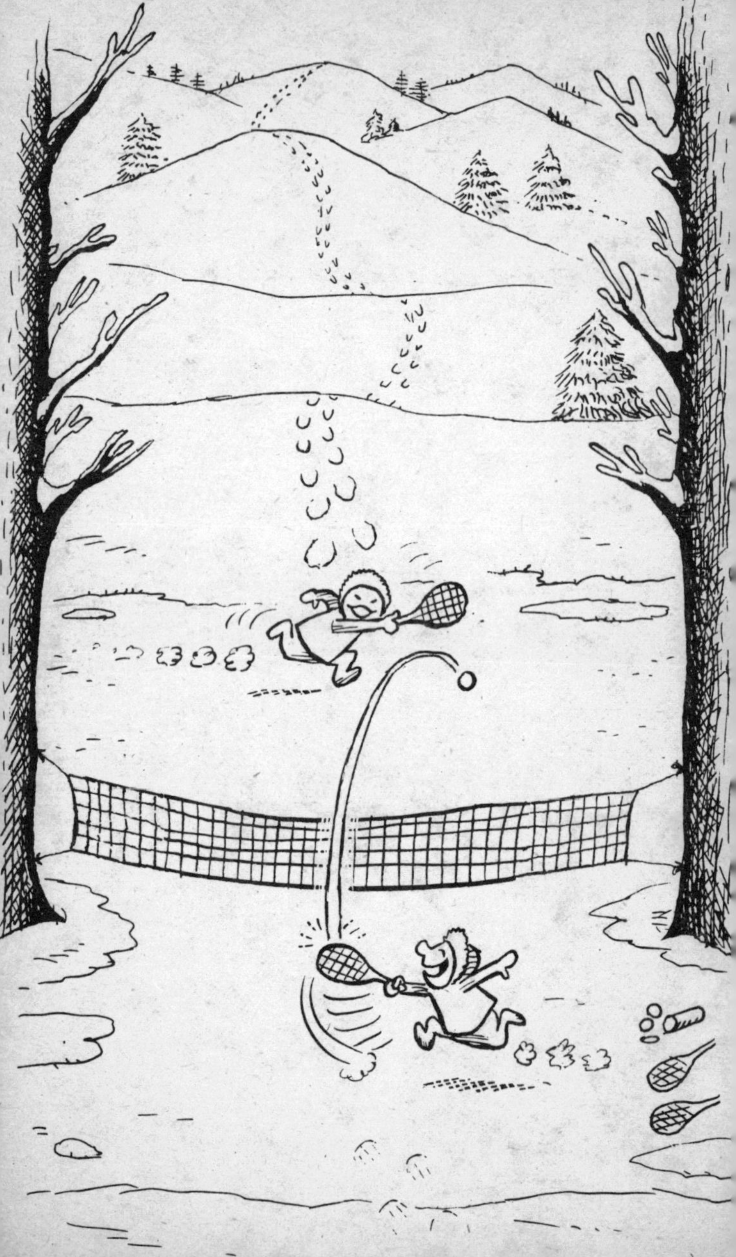

Cartoon Folio Number Ten

Yes, your brain is hopelessly scrambled. I warned you not to read this book.

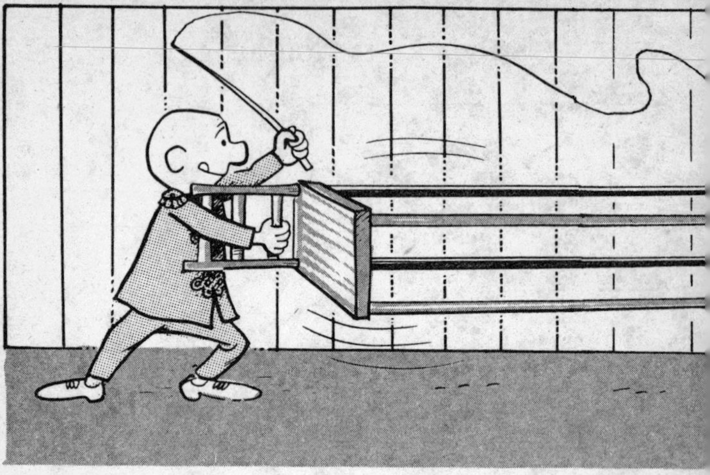

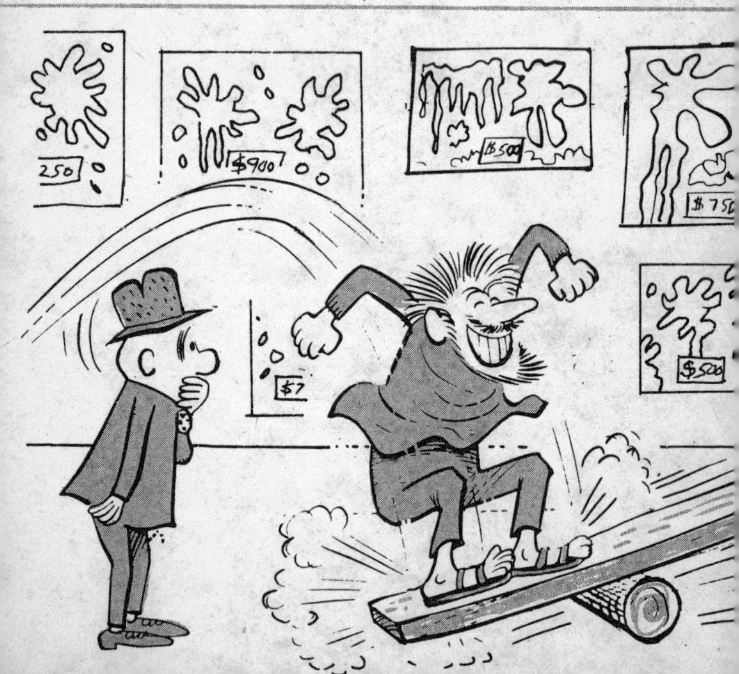

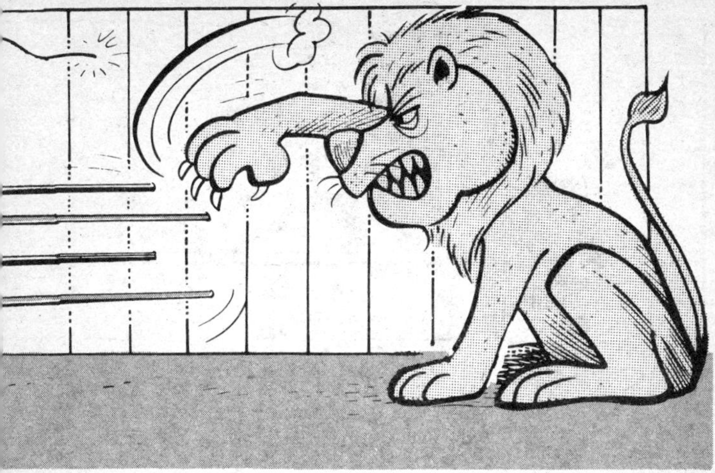

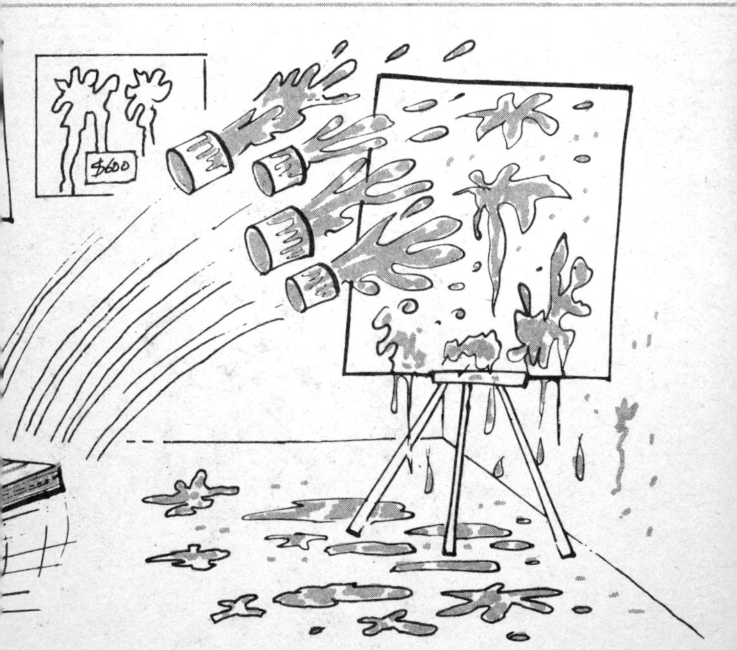
$600

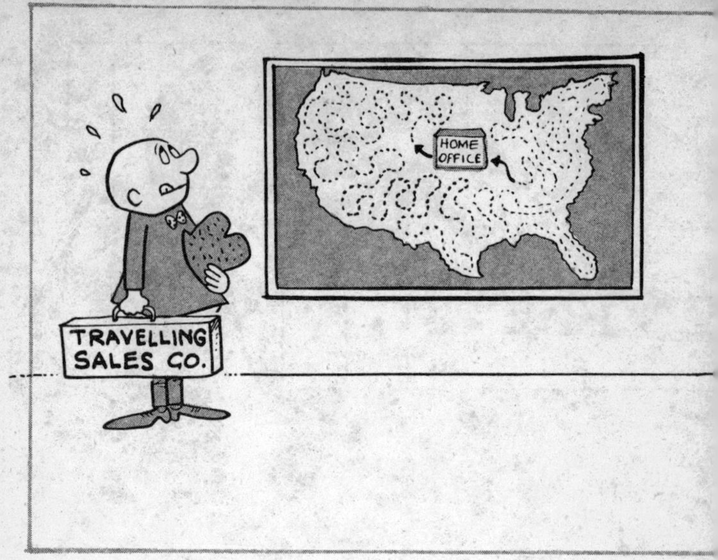
HOME
OFFICE
TRAVELLING
SALES CO.

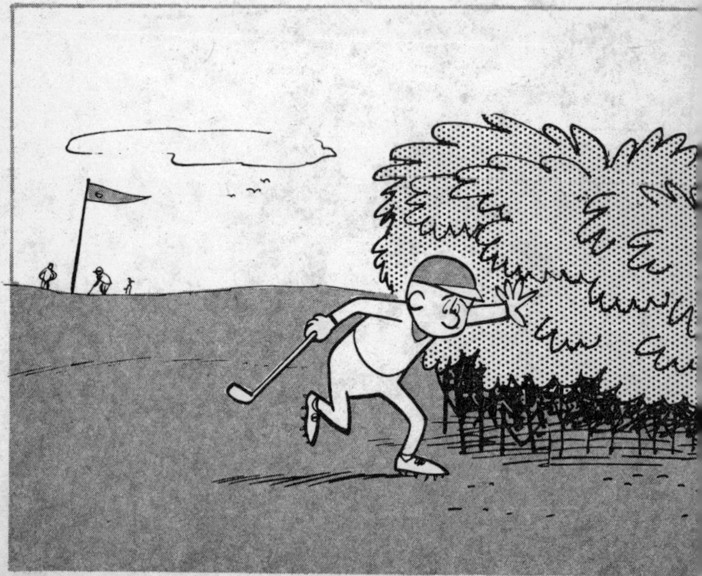

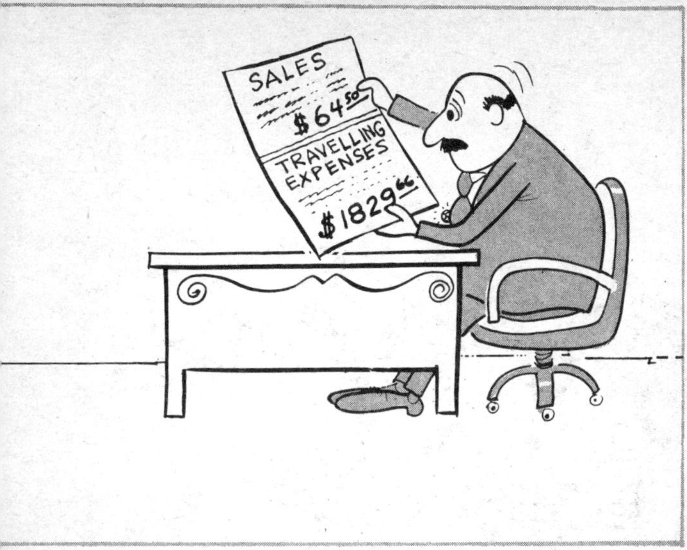
SALES
$64.50
TRAVELLING EXPENSES
$1829.66

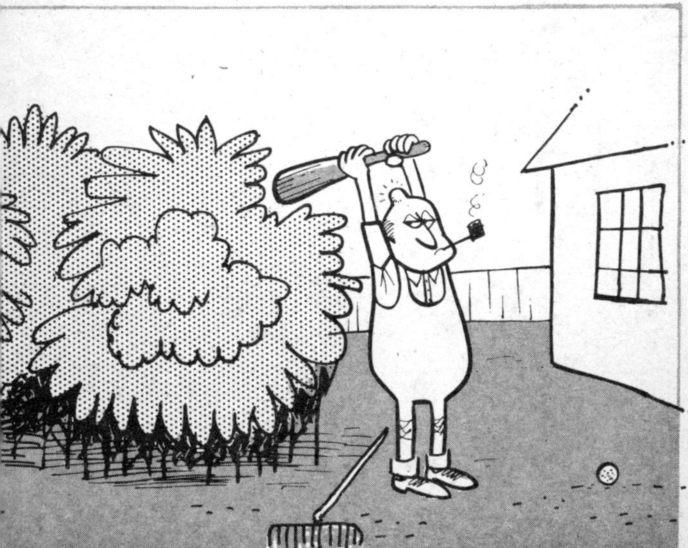

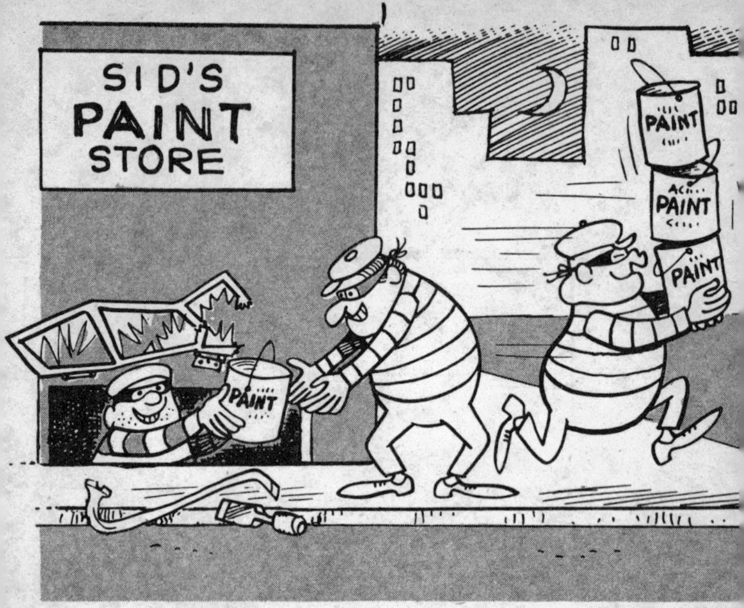
SID'S
PAINT
STORE
PAINT
PAINT
PAINT
PAINT

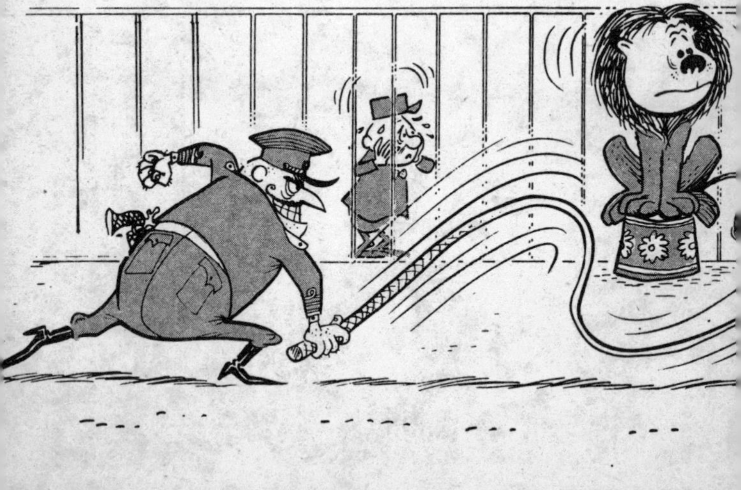

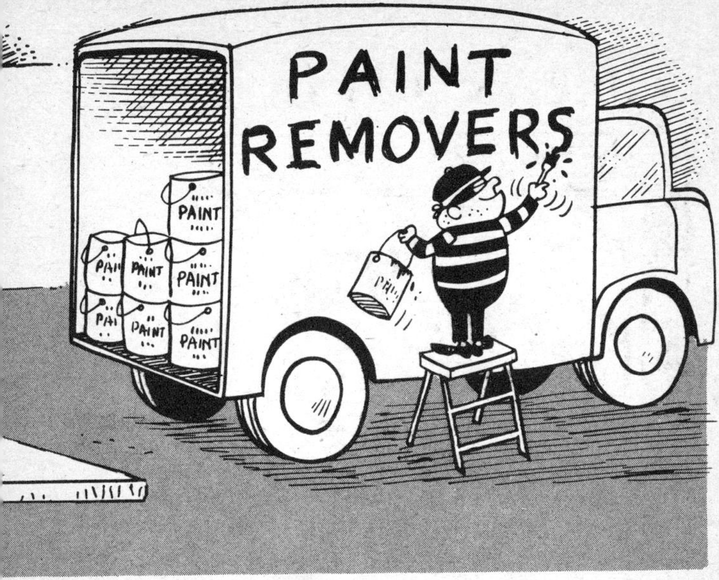
PAINT
REMOVERS
PAINT
PAINT
PAINT
PAINT

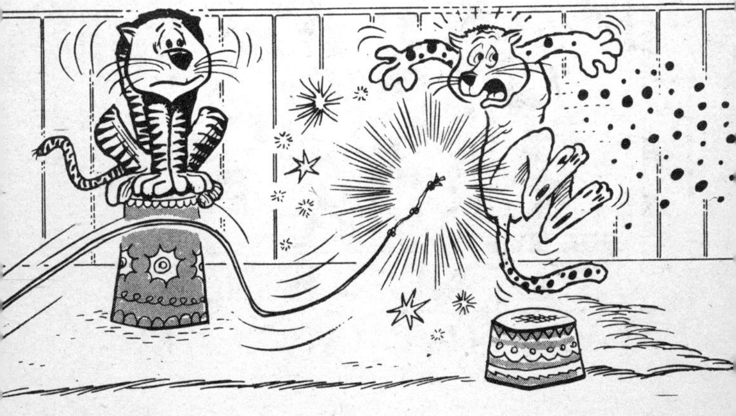

A GALLERY OF INFAMOUS JAFFEES

SWAMI HOOHAH JAFFEE
Discovered and promoted deep meditation as a substitute for work.

A RESTAURANT MEAL THAT'S NOT A BIG DEAL

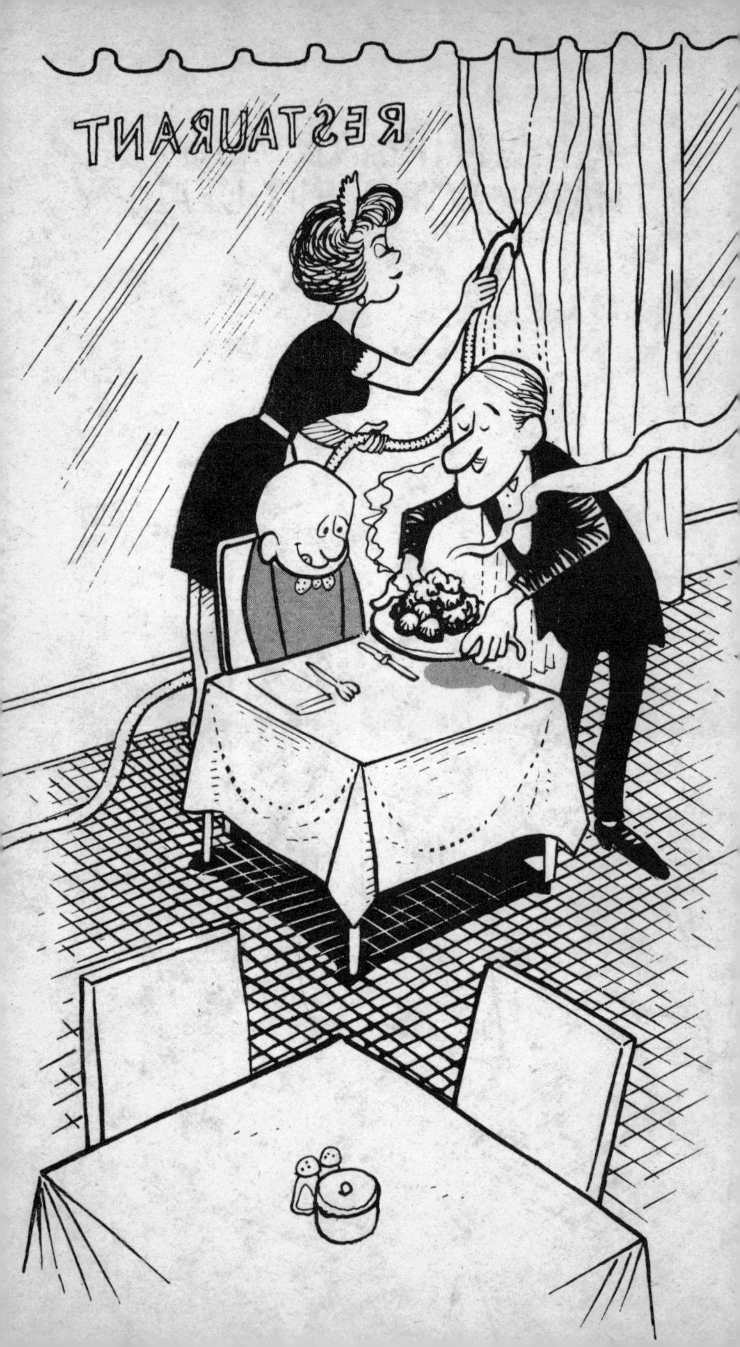
RESTAURANT

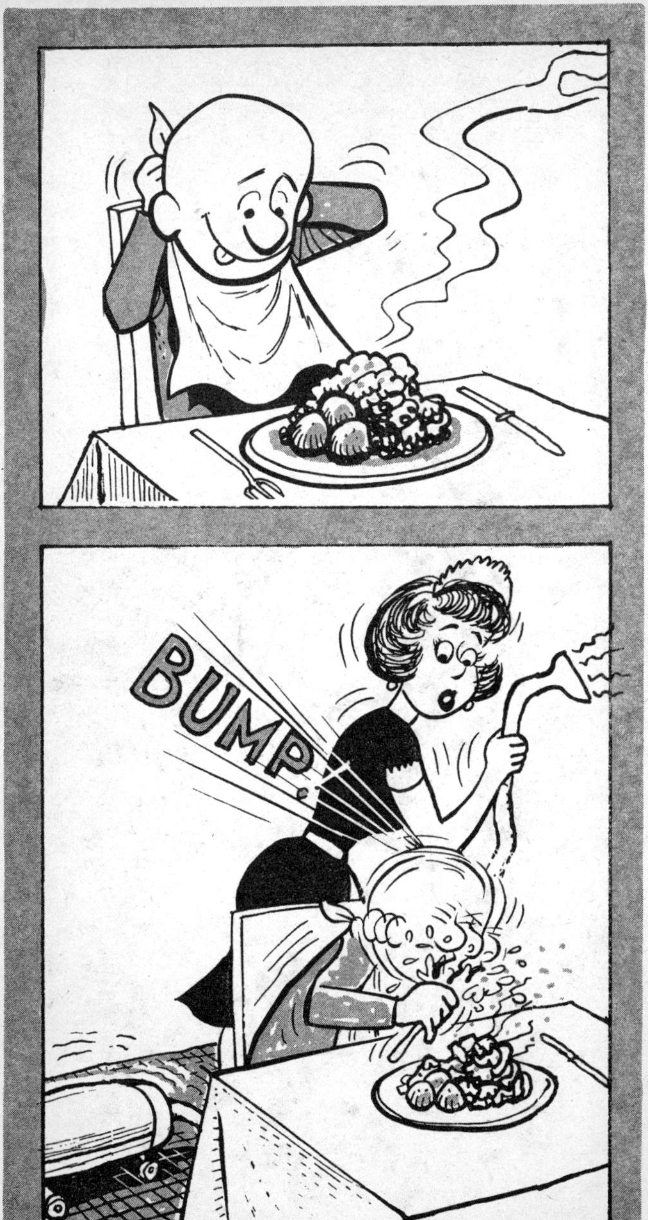
BUMP!

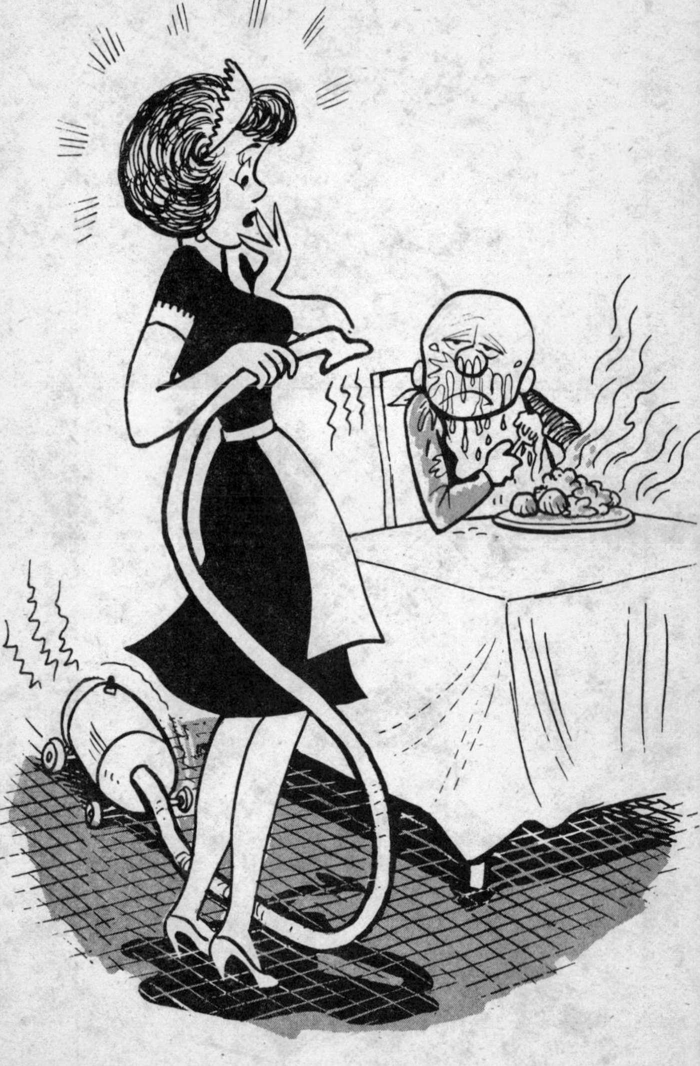

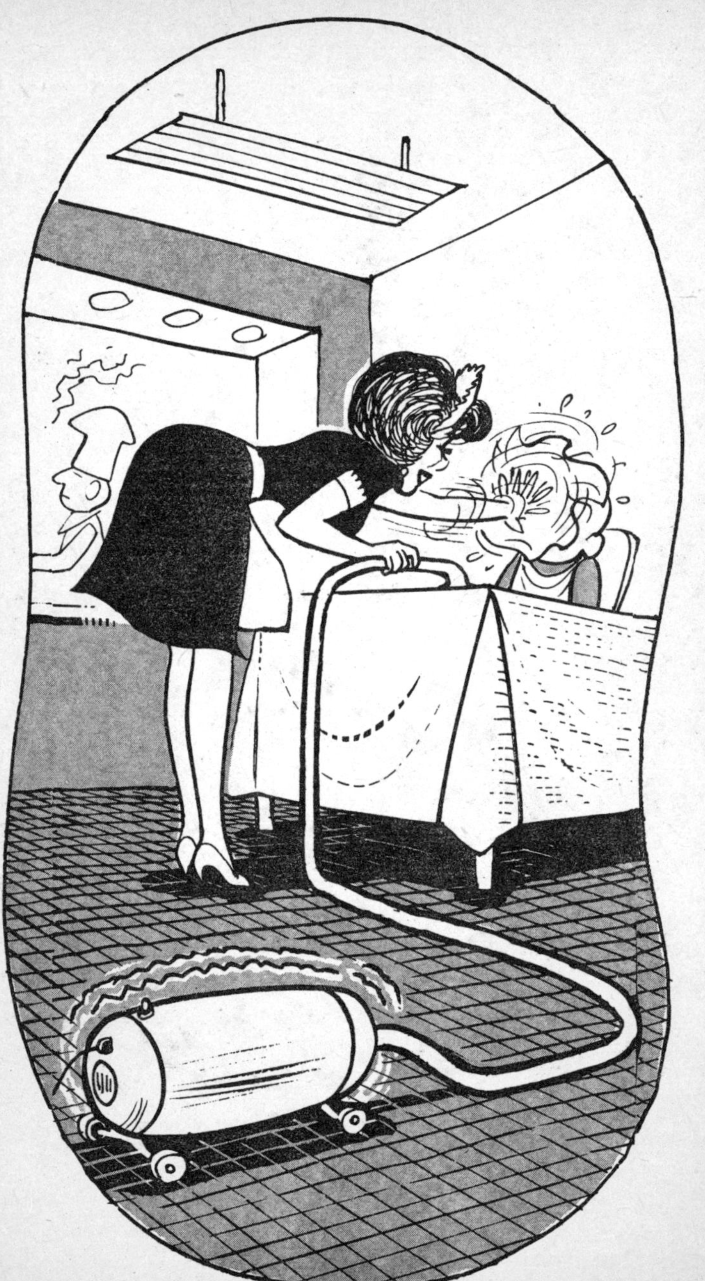

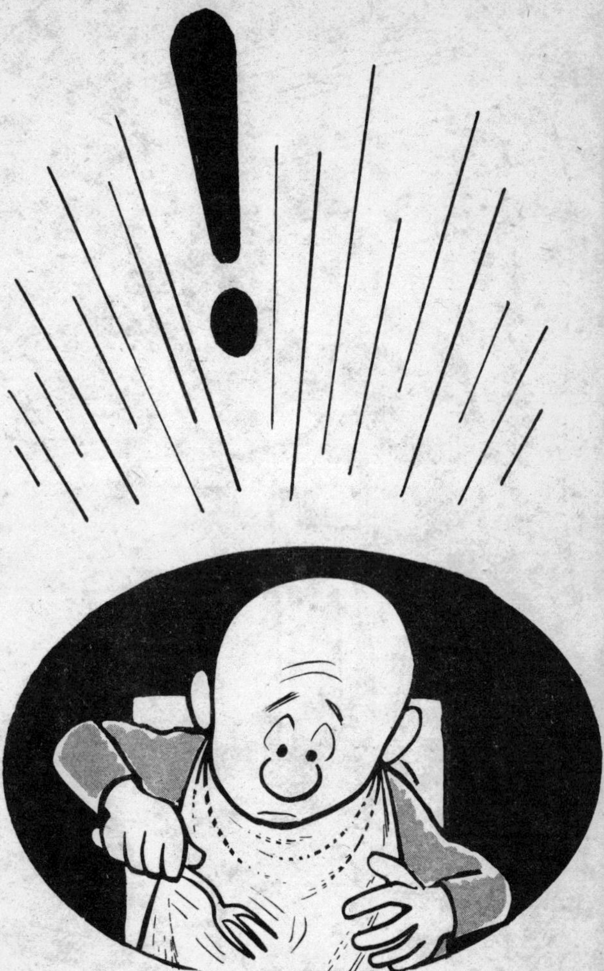

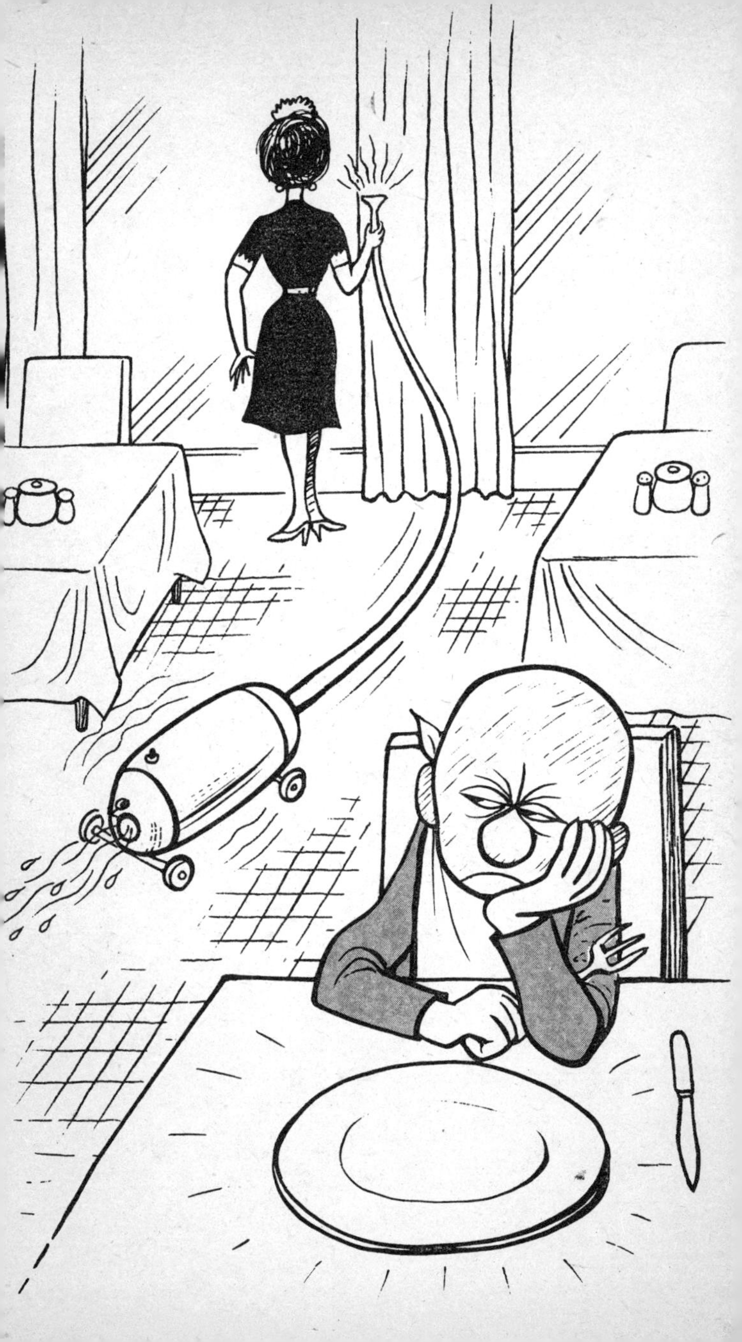

Cartoon Folio Number Eleven

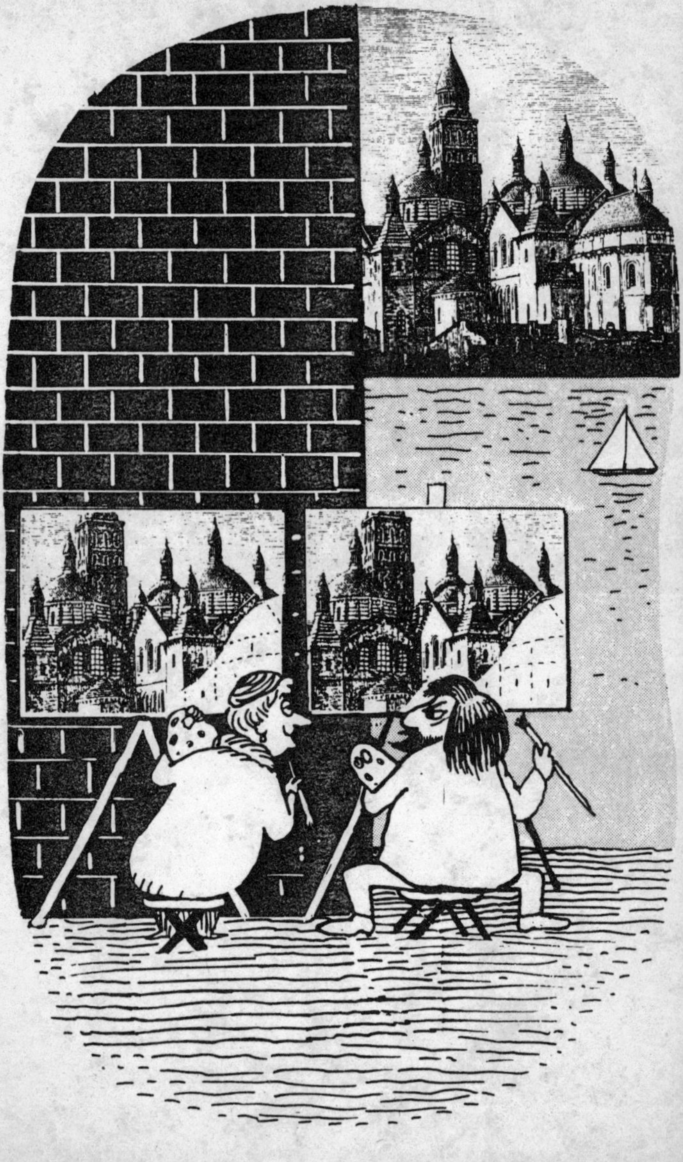

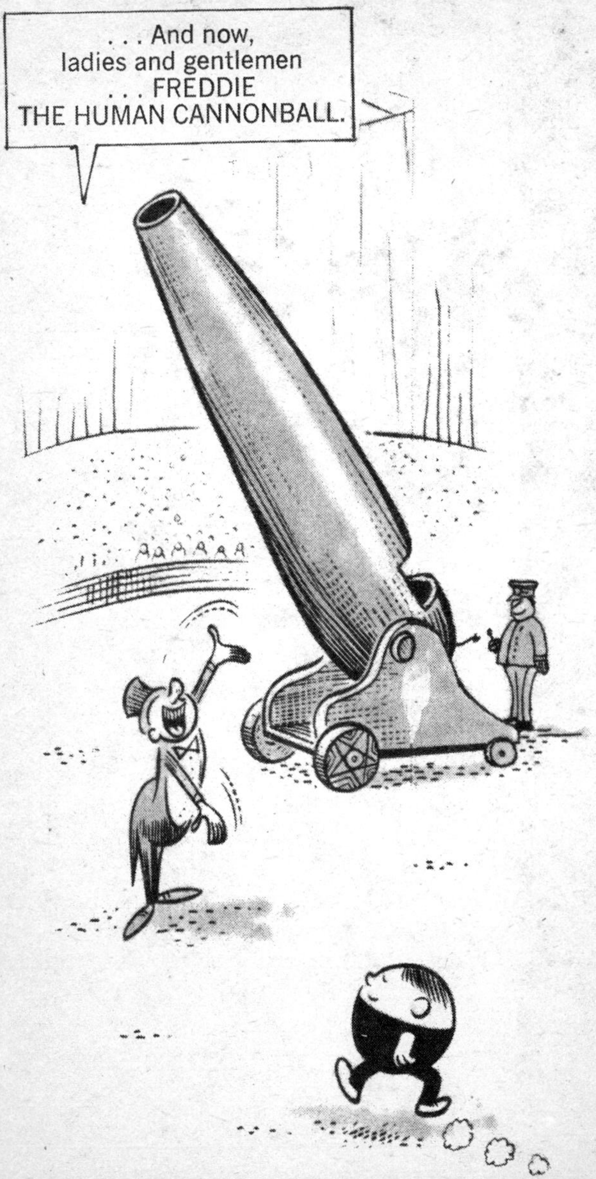
. . . And now, ladies and gentlemen . . . FREDDIE THE HUMAN CANNONBALL.

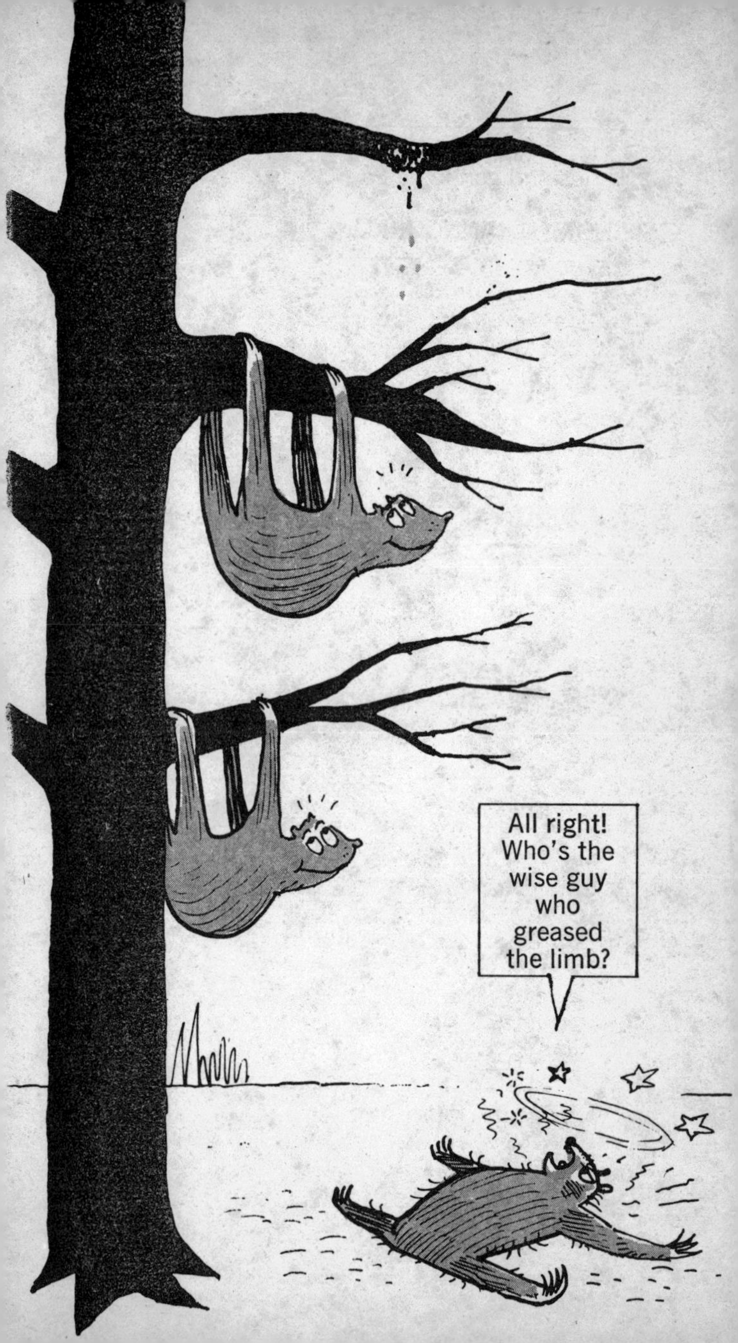
All right! Who's the wise guy who greased the limb?

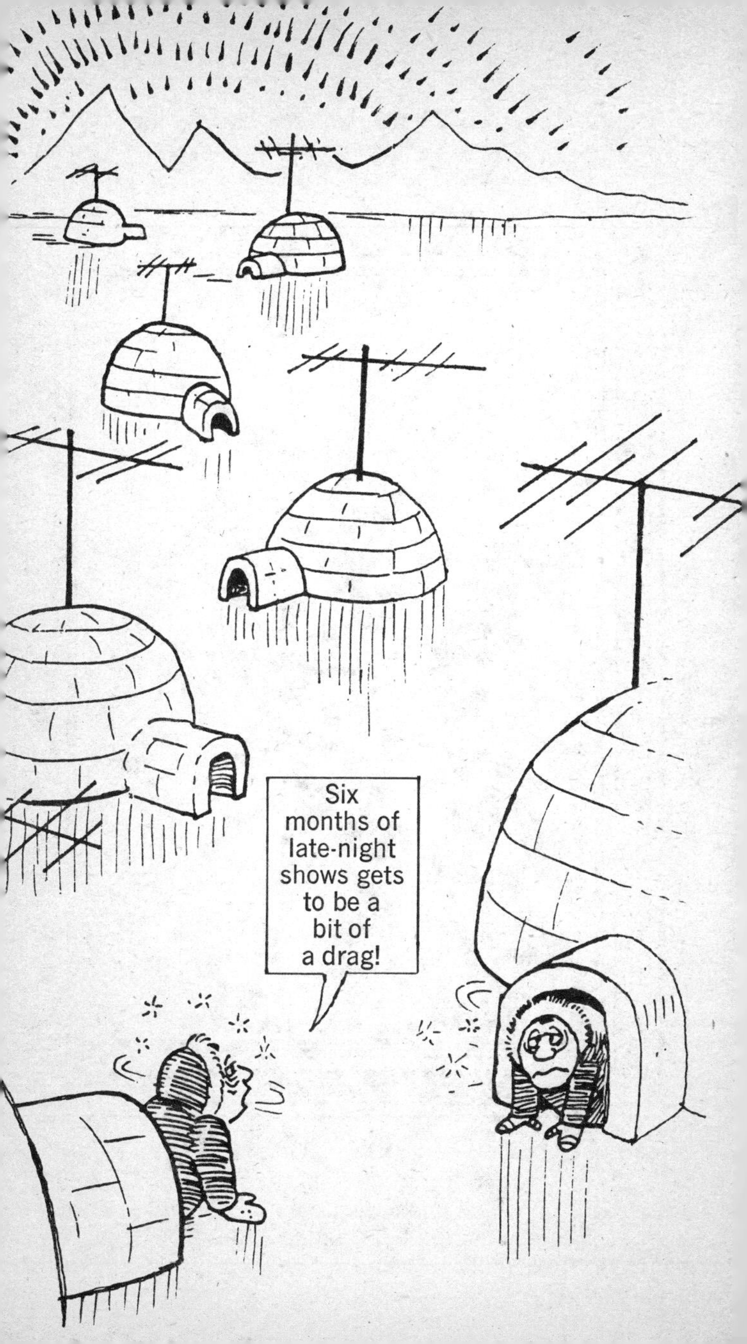
Six months of late-night shows gets to be a bit of a drag!

A GALLERY OF INFAMOUS JAFFEES

BJORN AGAIN JAFFEE
Demonstrated his revolutionary new form of singles tennis in which one individual plays against himself. Died of exhaustion before it caught on.

A FIRING-SQUAD SCENE THAT'S CLEARLY OBSCENE

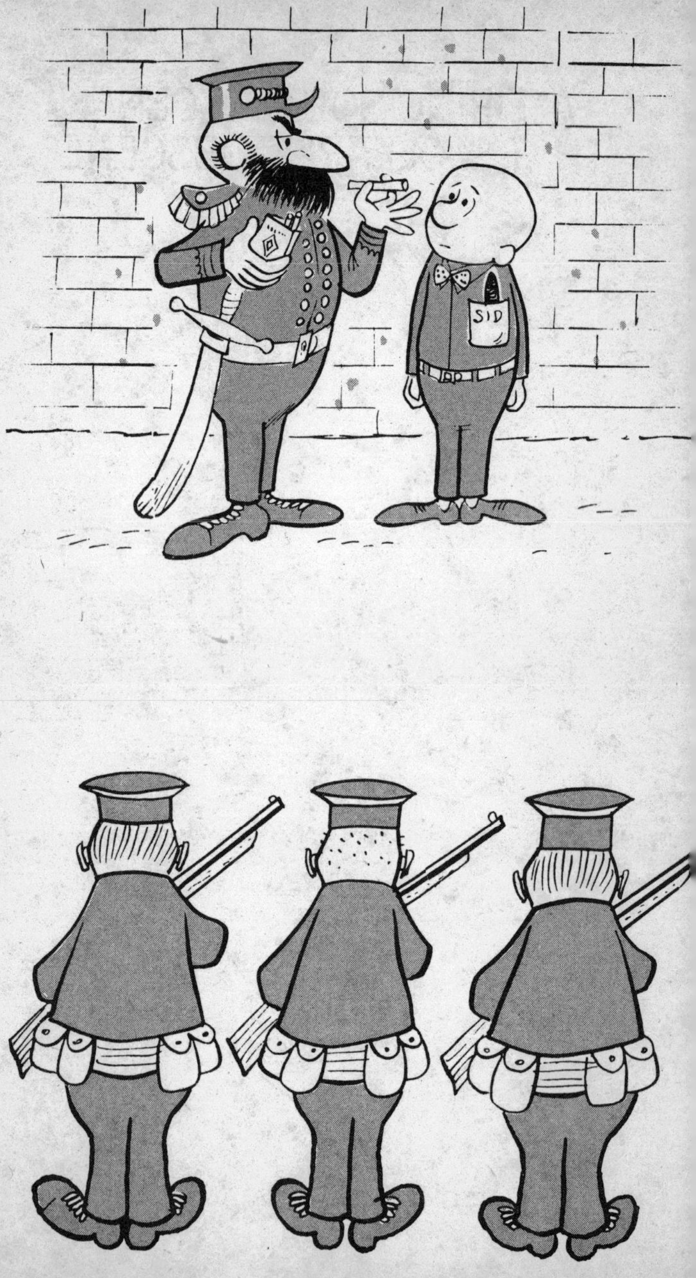
SID

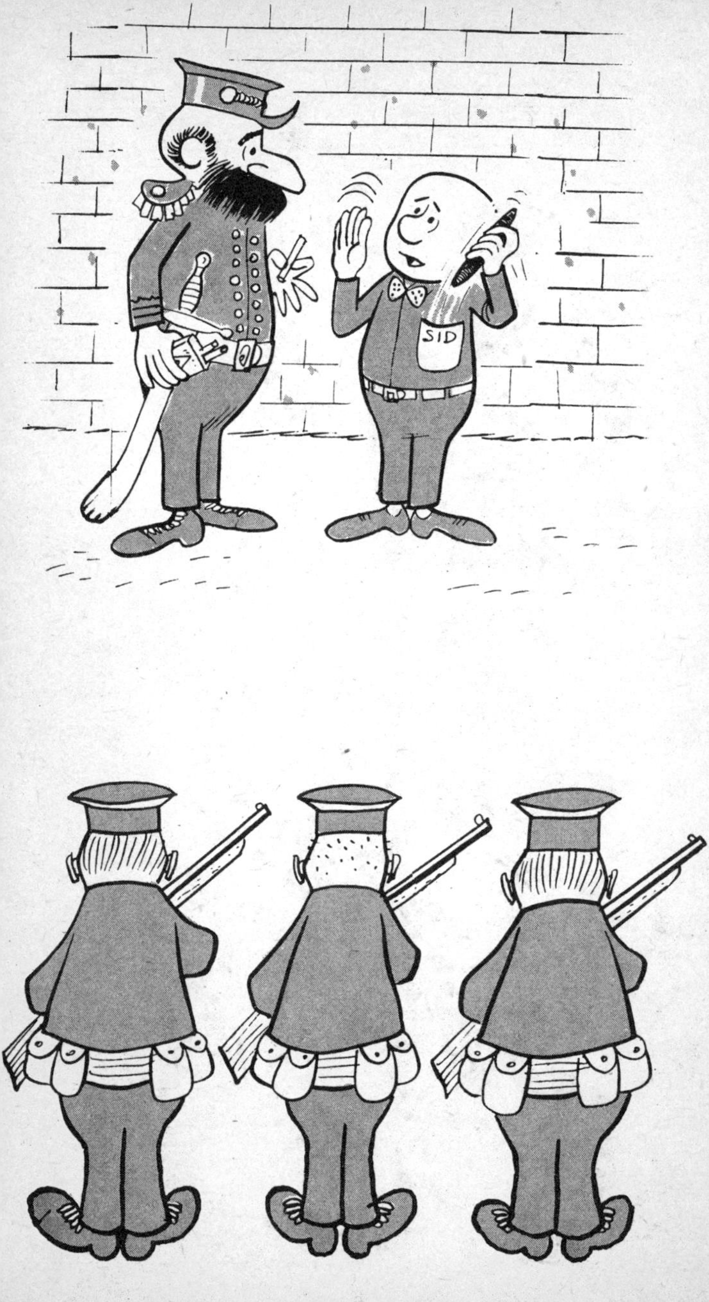
SID

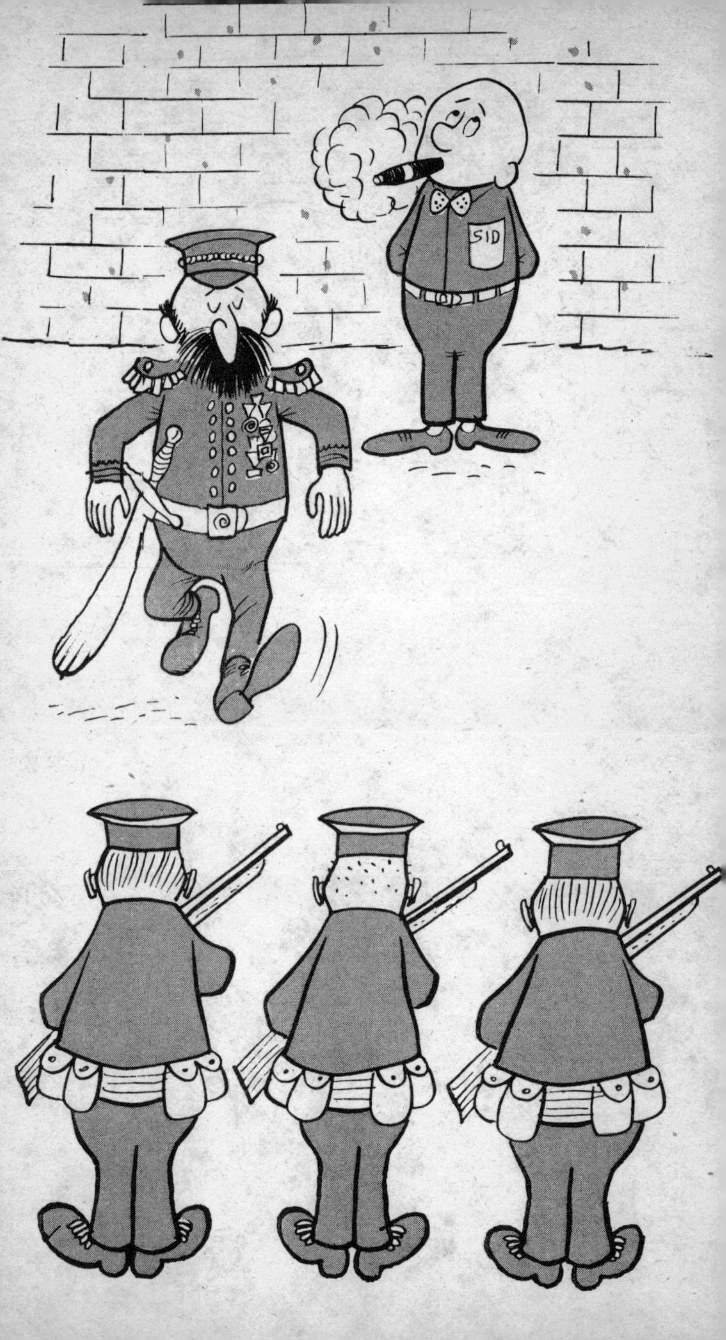
SID

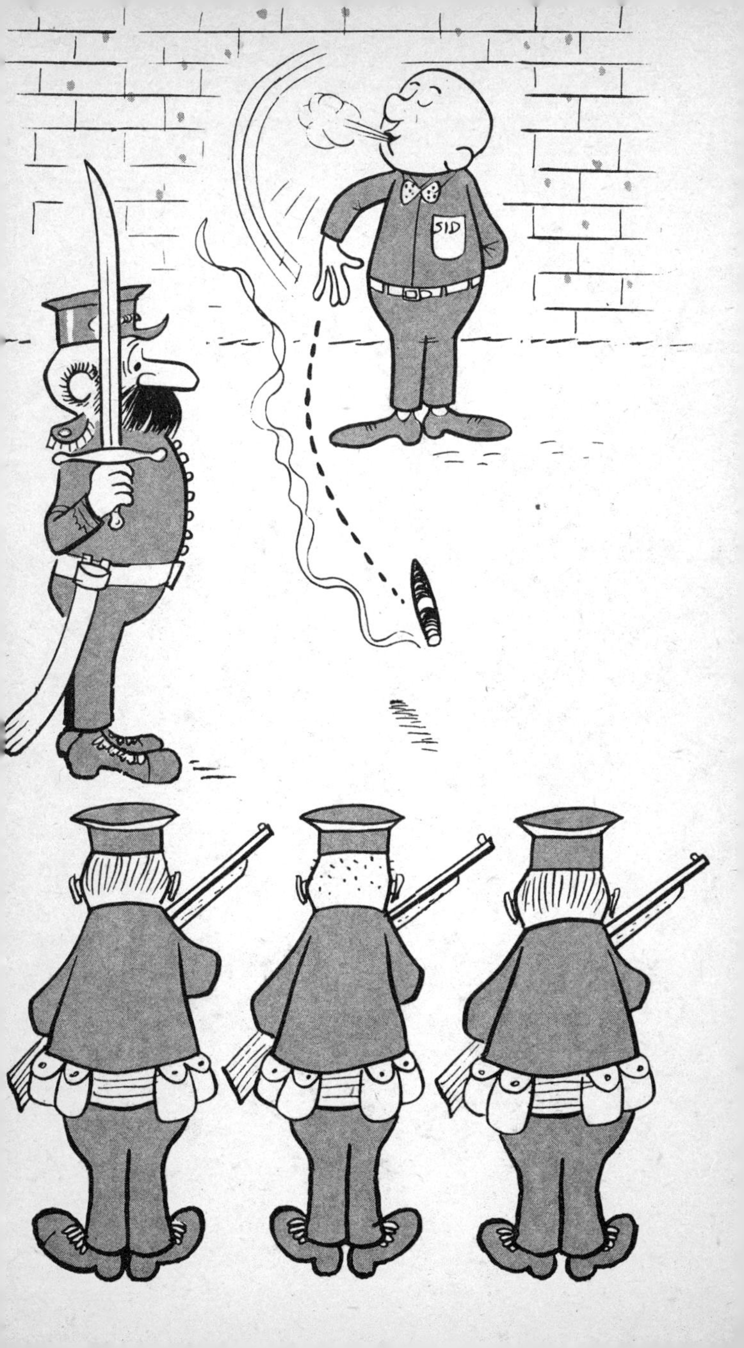
SID

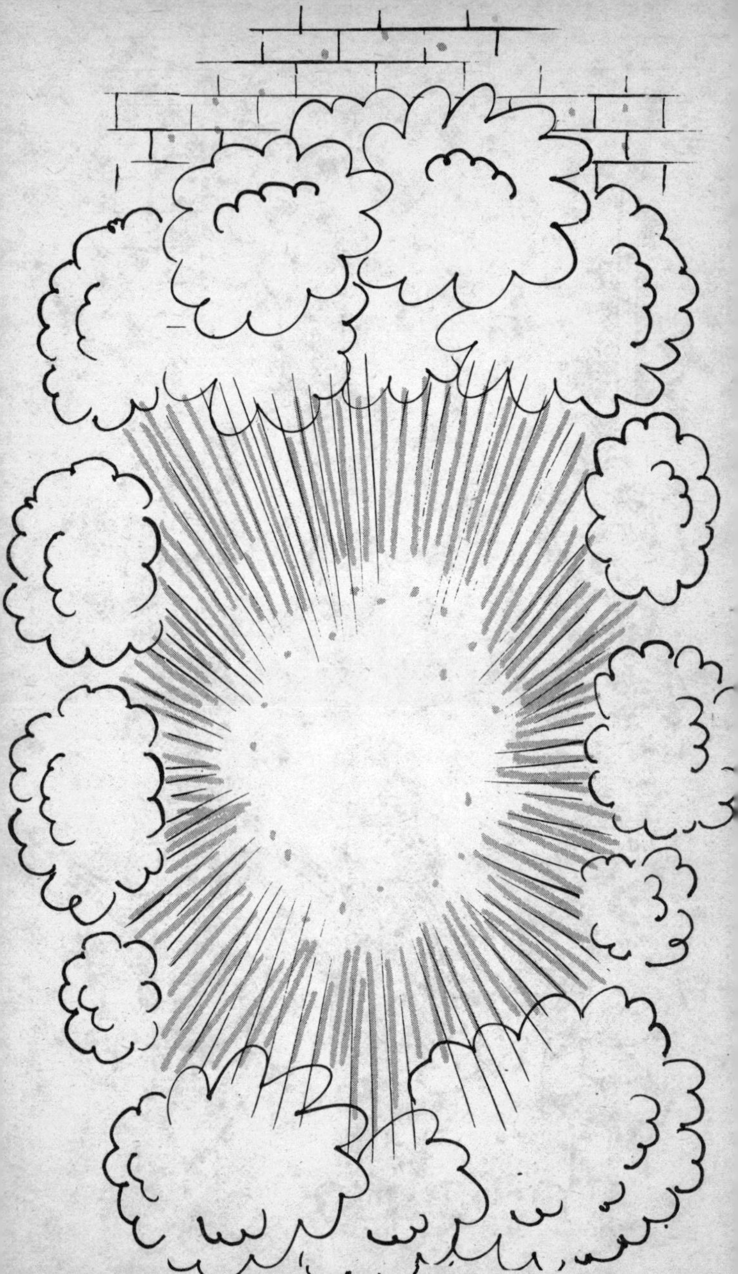

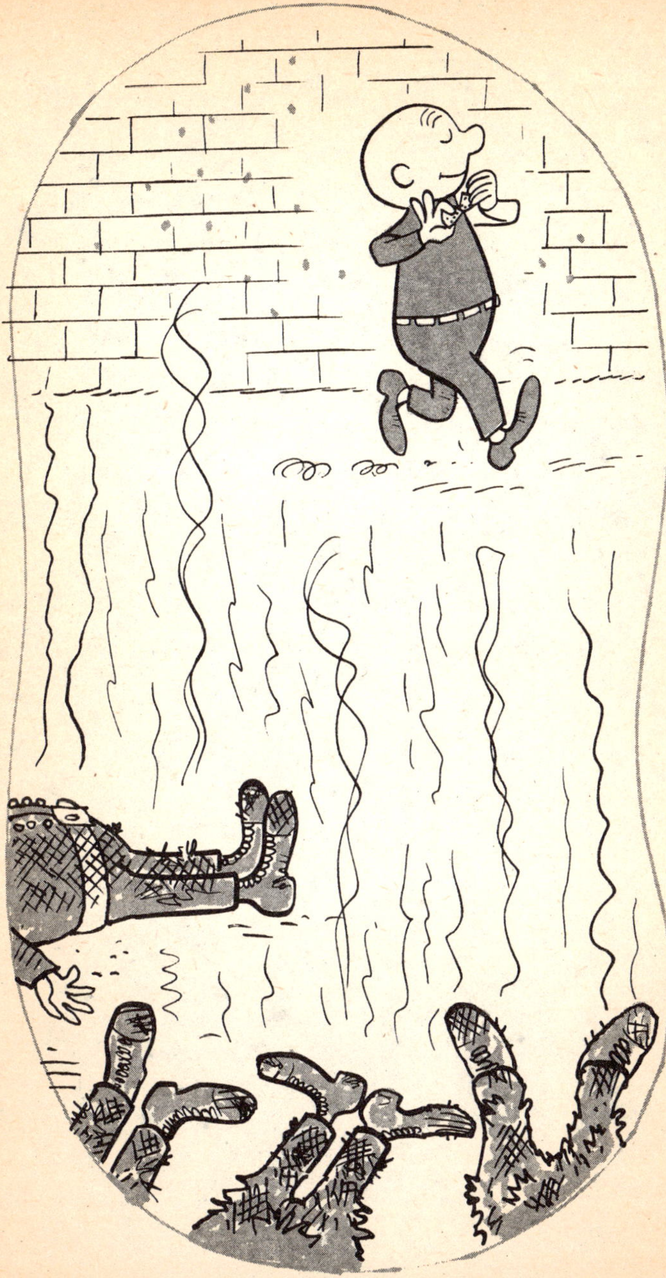

Cartoon Folio Number Twelve

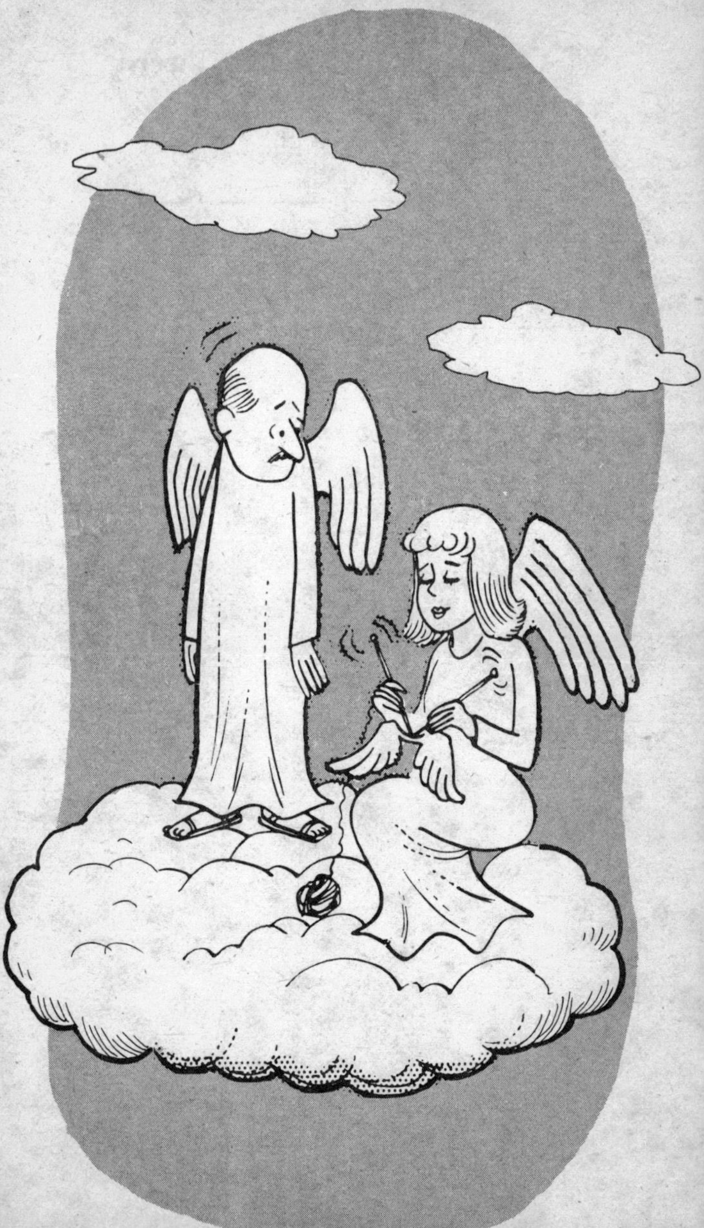

I SHUDDER TO THINK WHAT MY WIFE WOULD DO IF SHE FOUND OUT ABOUT US!

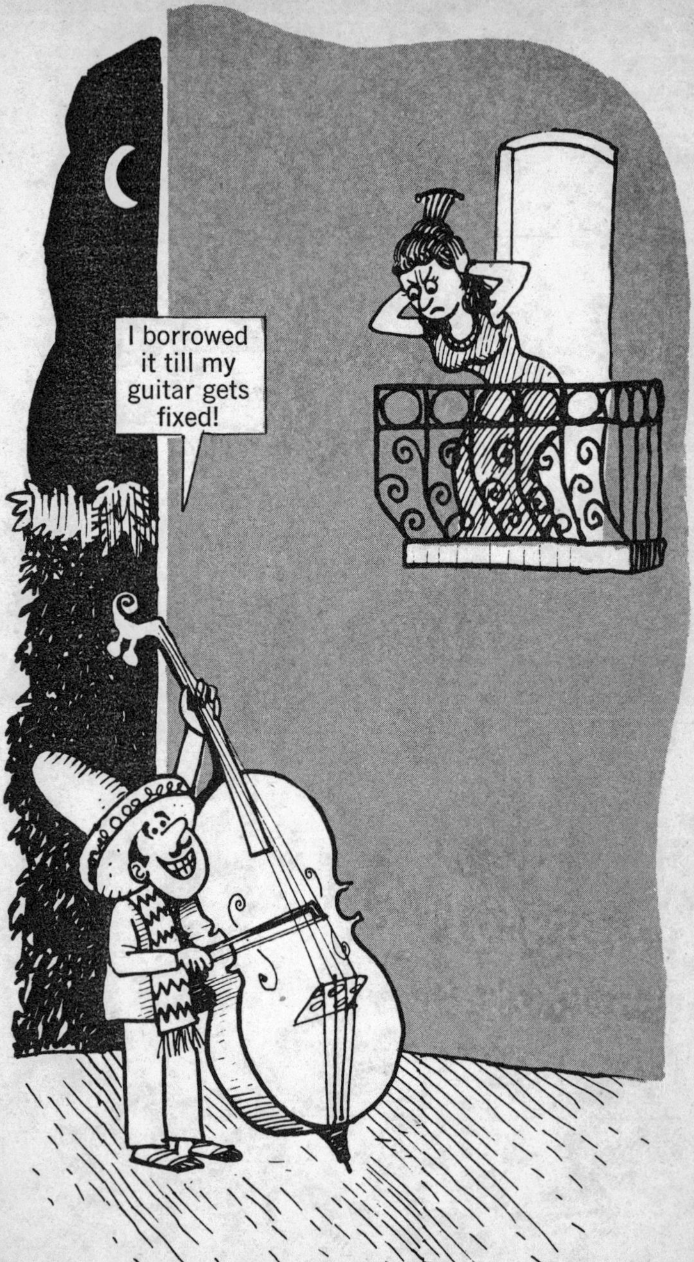
I borrowed it till my guitar gets fixed!

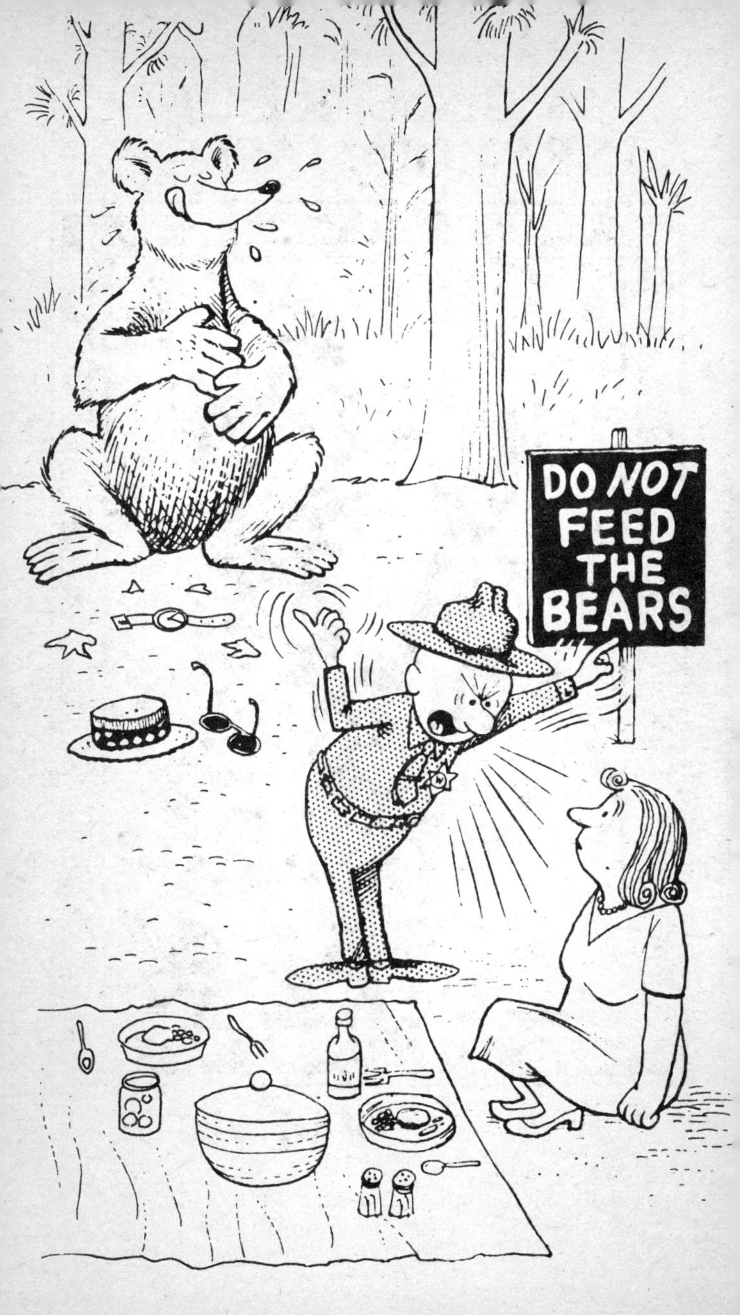
DO NOT
FEED
THE
BEARS

A GALLERY OF INFAMOUS JAFFEES

THURGOOD ODDFELLOW JAFFEE
Society photographer and female impersonator.

A PHONE-BOOTH OCCURRENCE THAT'LL TEST YOUR ENDURANCE

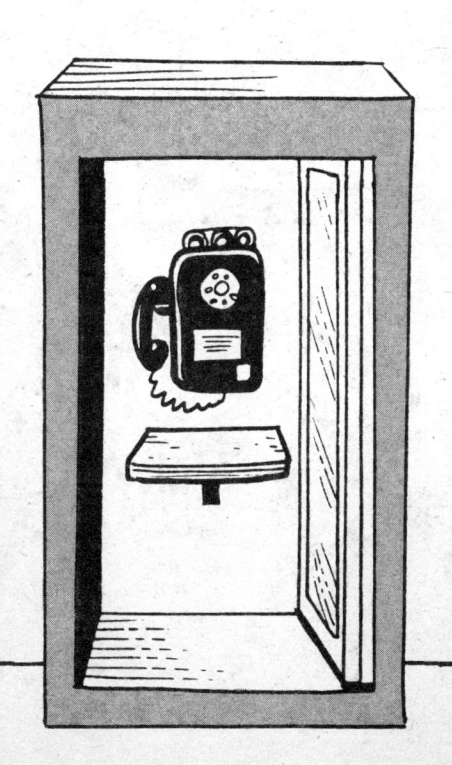

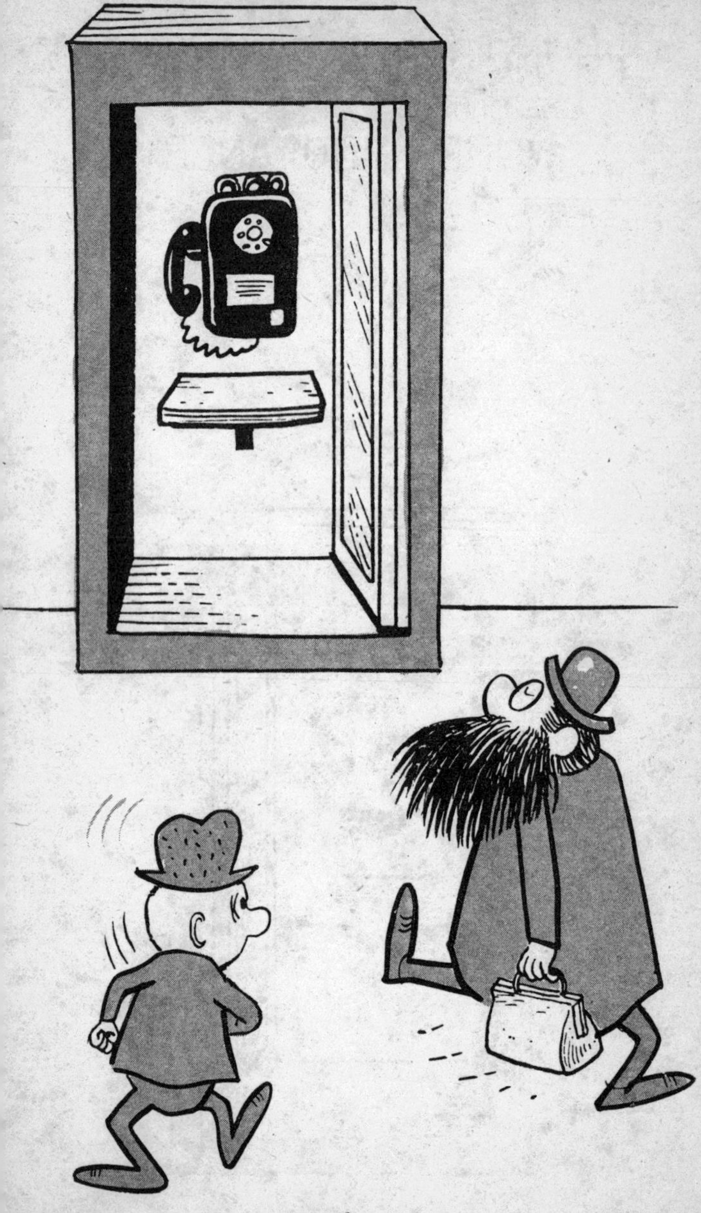

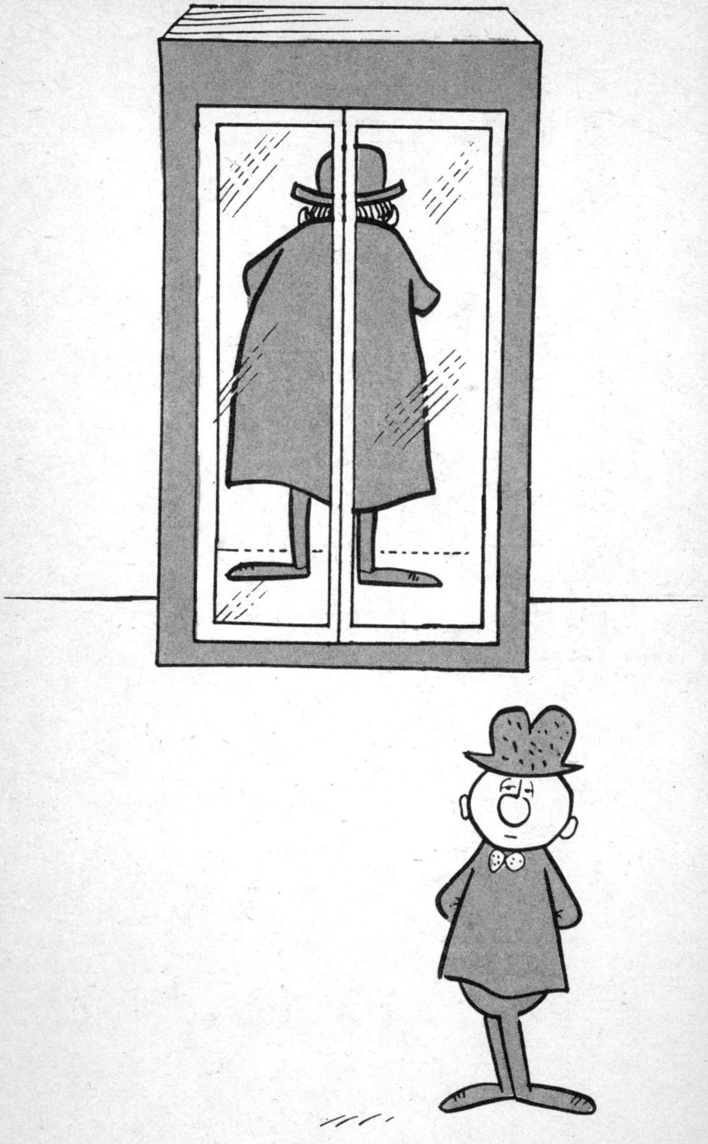

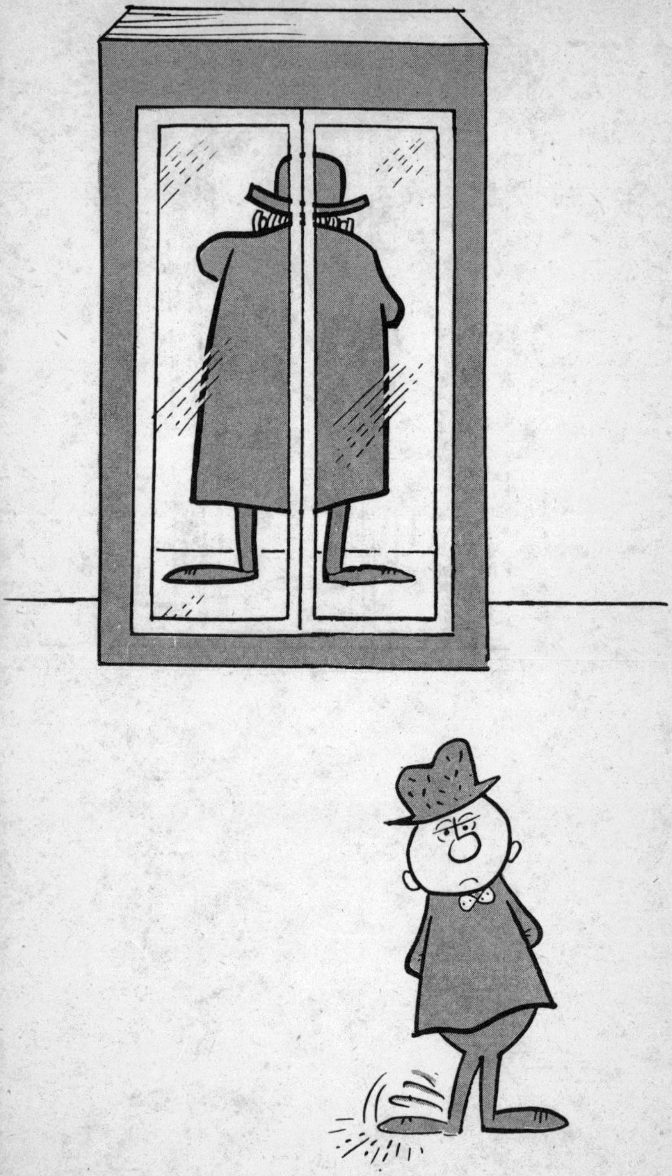

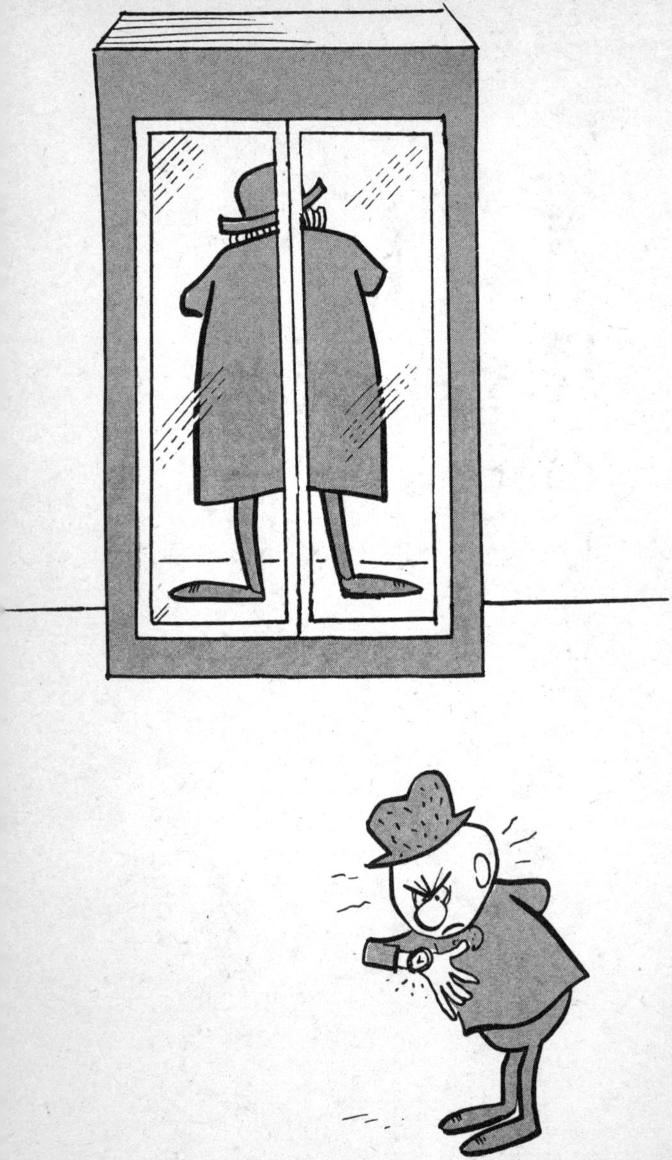

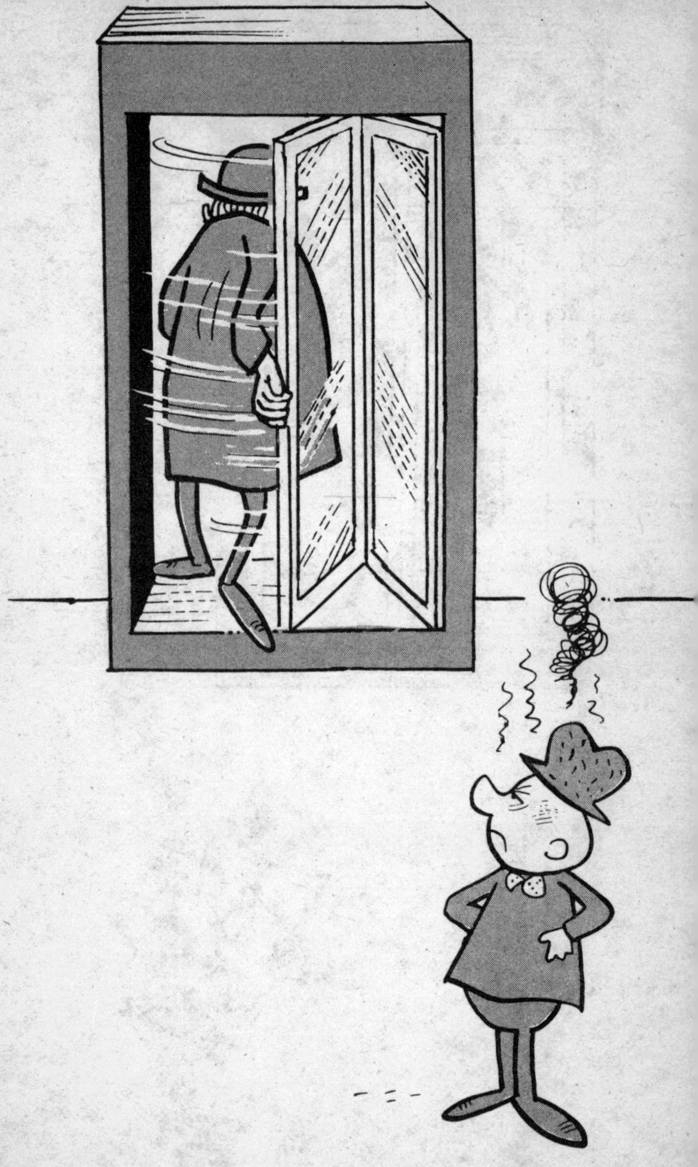

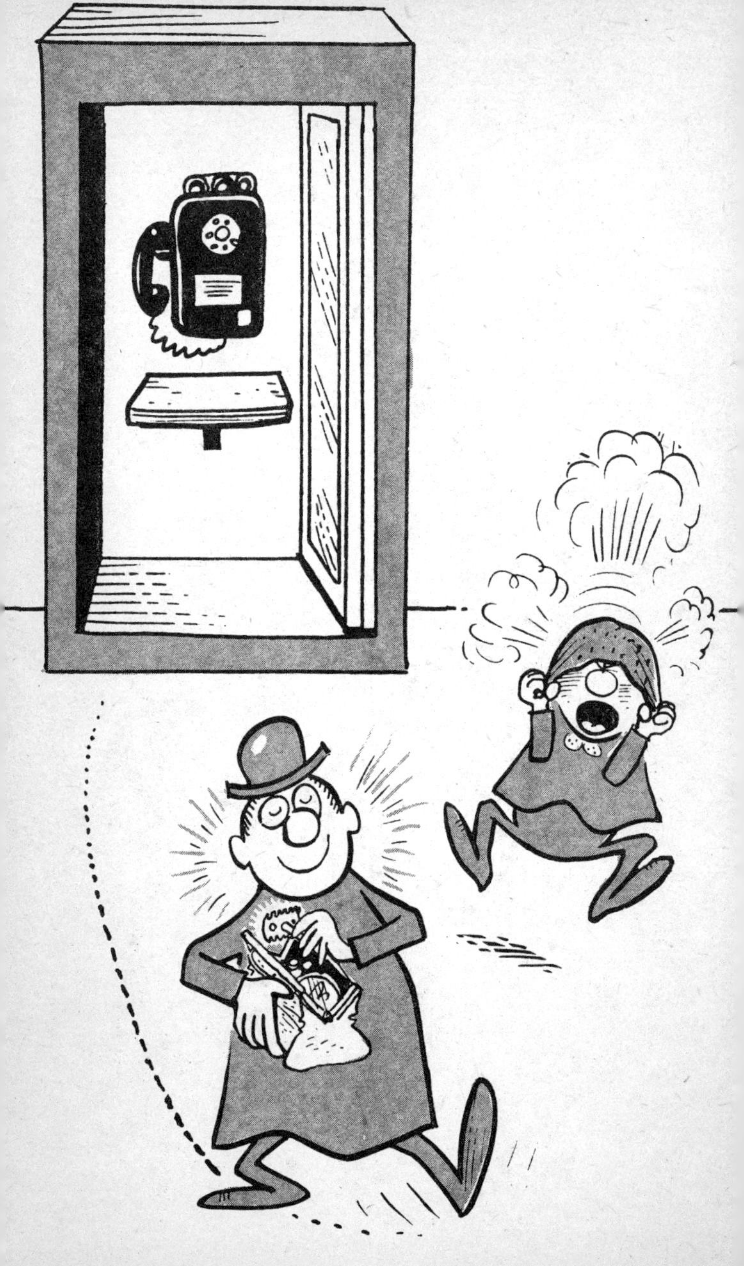

Cartoon Folio Number Thirteen

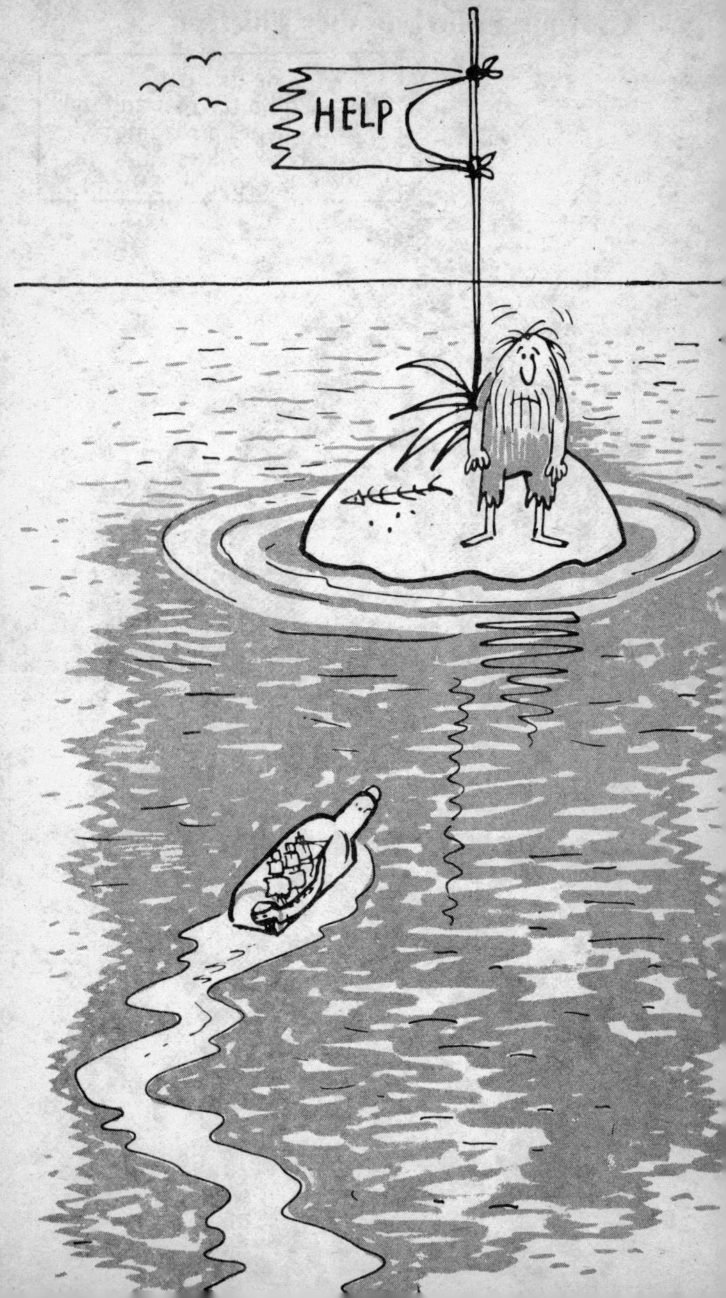
HELP

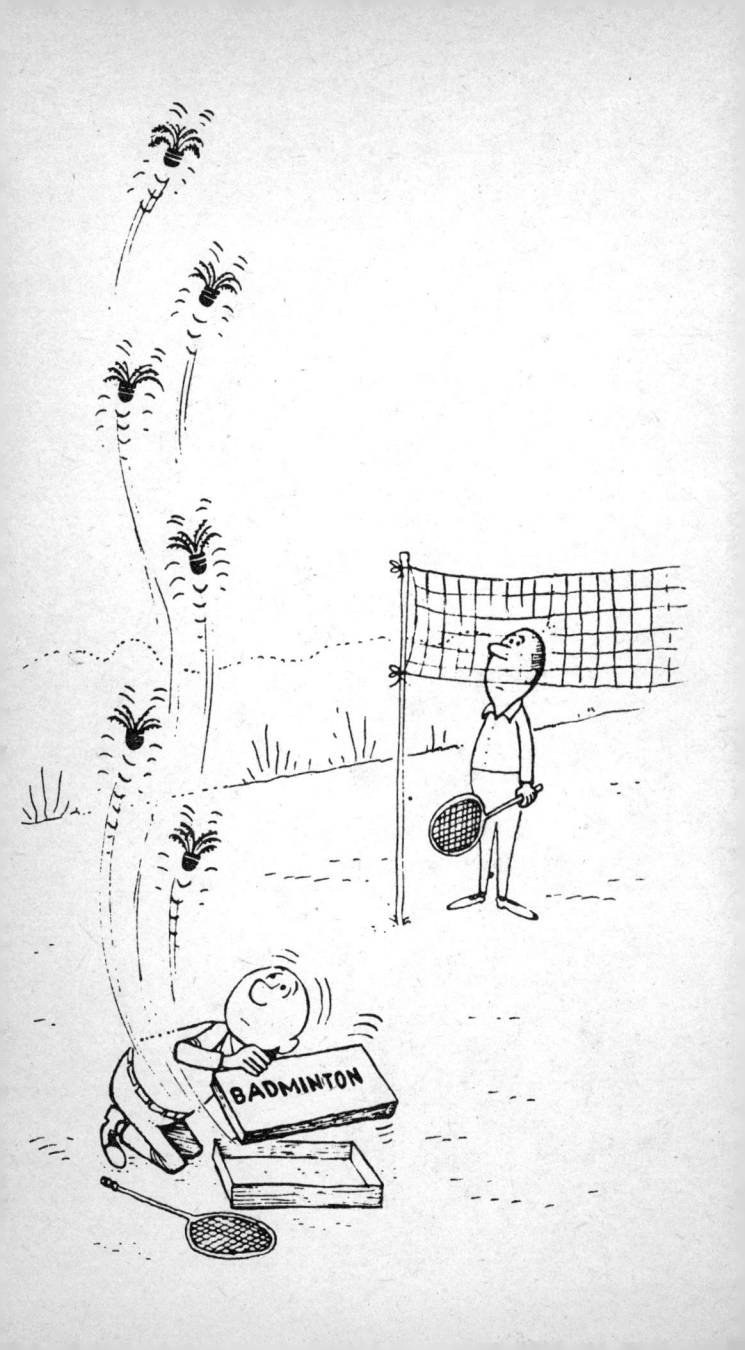
BADMINTON

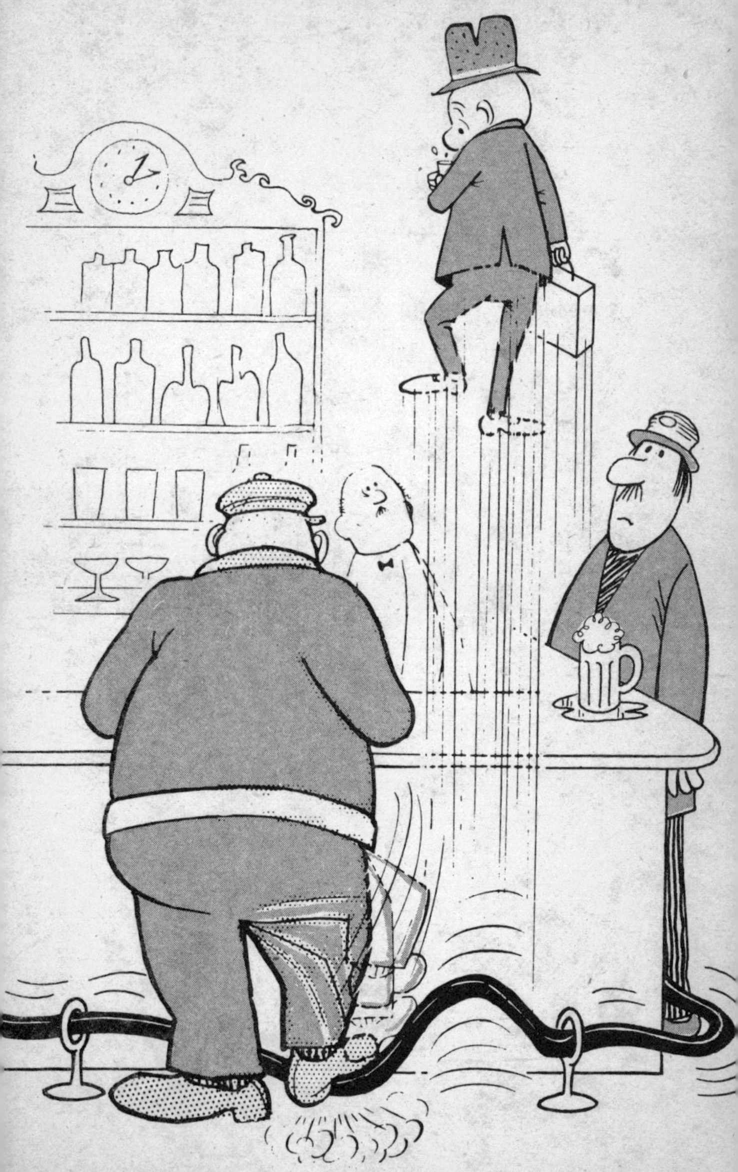

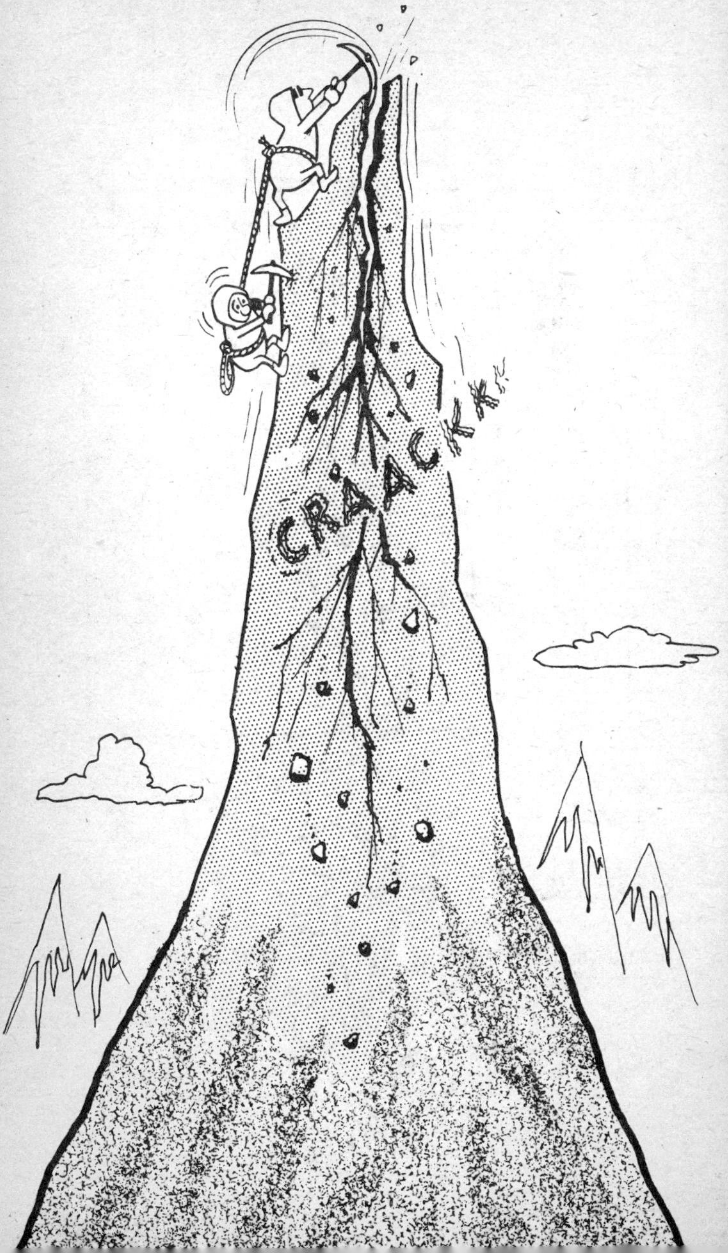
CRACK

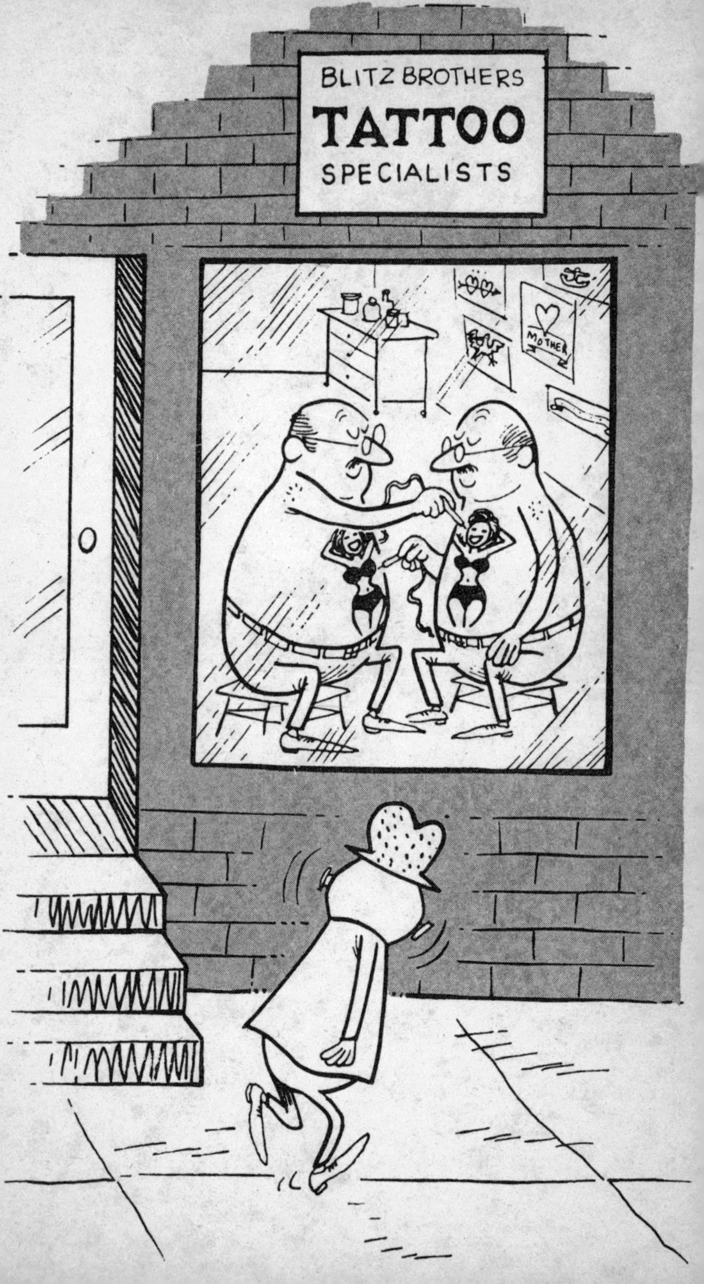
BLITZ BROTHERS
TATTOO
SPECIALISTS
MOTHER

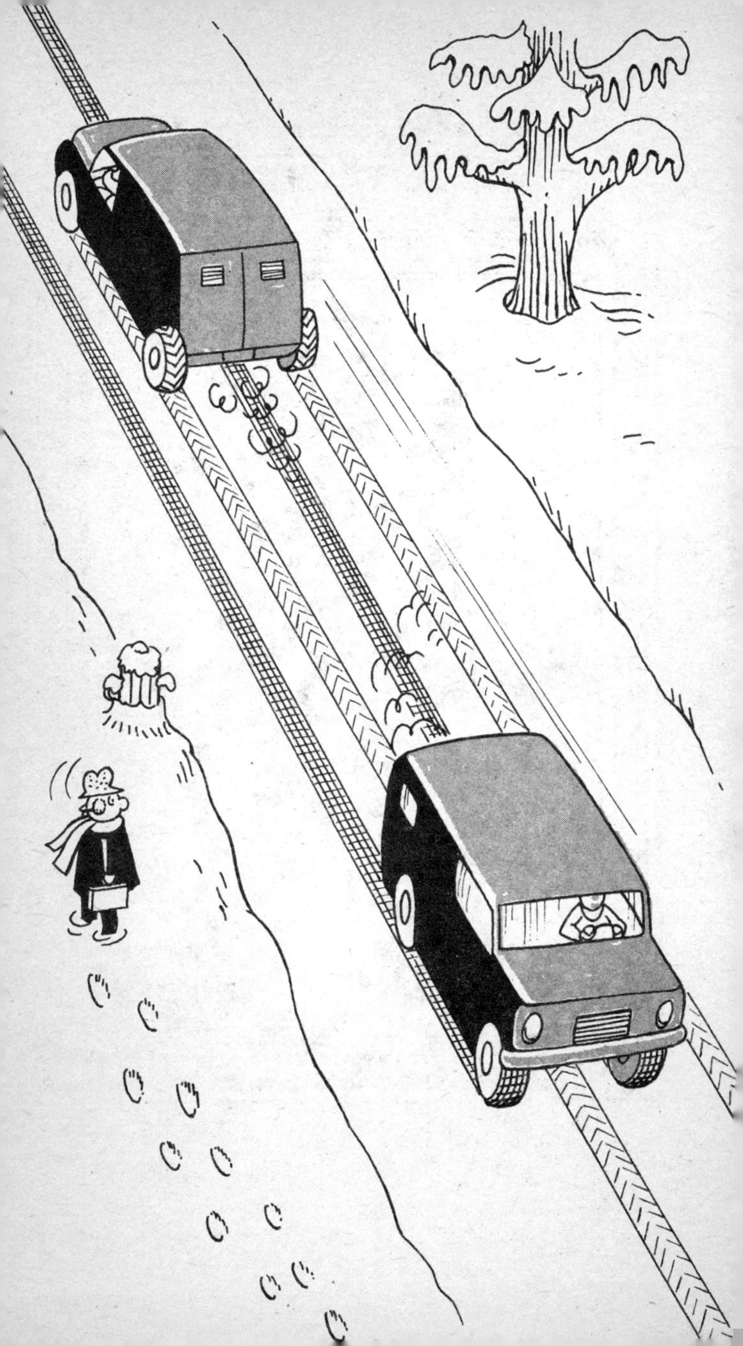

A GALLERY OF INFAMOUS JAFFEES

HAKA CHAINIK JAFFEE
Far Eastern impotentate. Creator of the peekaboo pajama.

YOU ASKED FOR IT
AND NOW YOU'RE STUCK WITH IT

Willie Weirdie #2
On Sale November 1982

That's right. When my first book, *Al Jaffee Meets Willie Weirdie*, came out, you wrote thousands of letters demanding more. So now you're getting what you (yuque!) deserve. My second book, *Willie Weirdie Scares the Pants Off Al Jaffee*, will be in bookstores November 1982. So run and get your copy. If by some revolting chance your book dealer doesn't have it, hound him till he does. Remind him of Willie Weirdie's terrible bookseller curse. It fills every book in his store with (yicchy!) bookworms!

BUY THESE BOOKS JUST FOR LAUGHS...

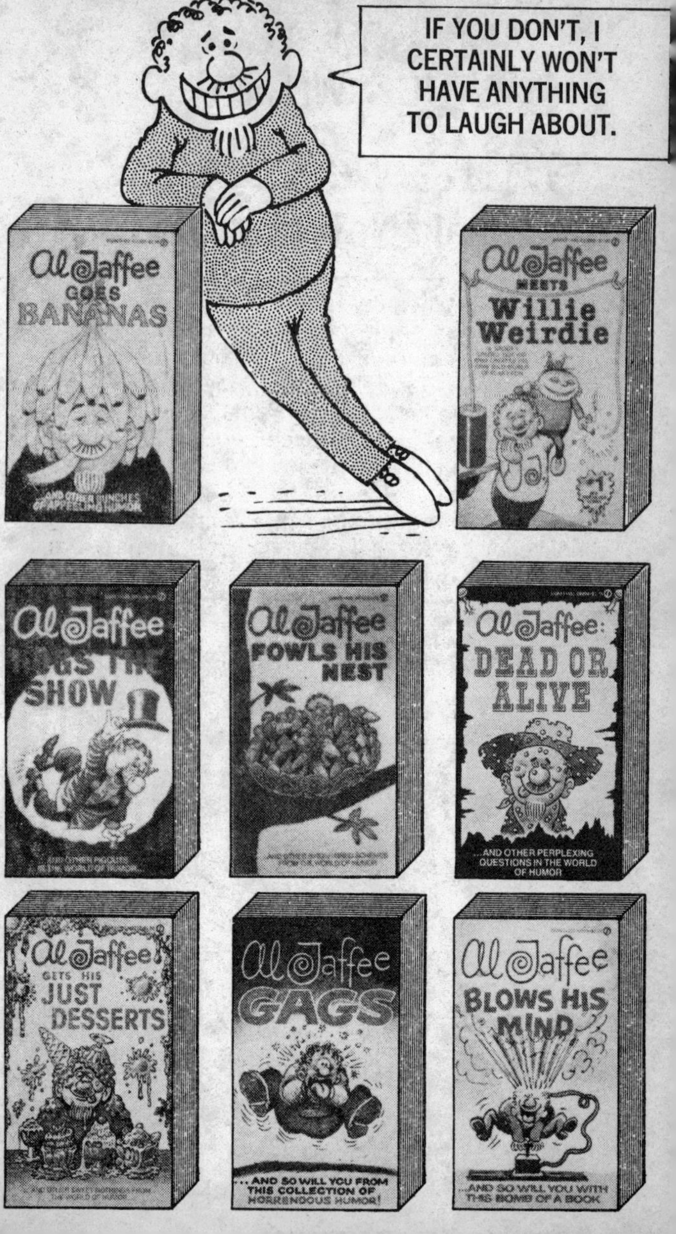

AT YOUR FAVORITE BOOKSTORE OR USE COUPON ON NEXT PAGE.

OUT OF THIS WORLD

That's where this book is now. And that's where it'll stay if you don't get over to your bookstore and ask for it.

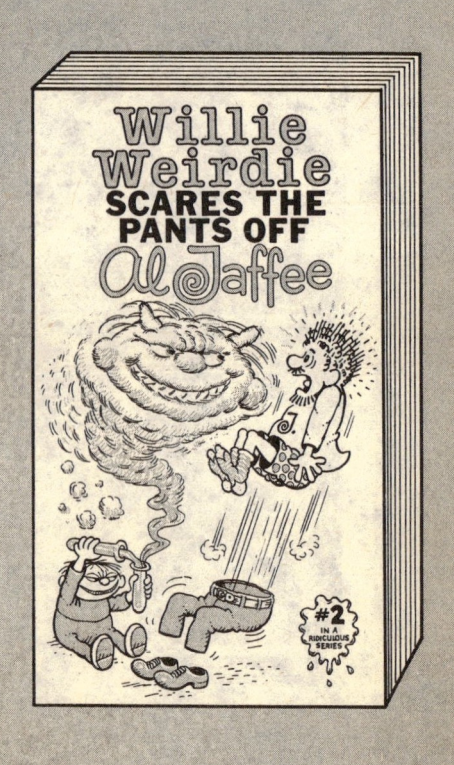